AF427523

THE TALE OF
BLACKBIRD

&

THE DESTINY OF
GUIDO

VOLUMES 3 & 4

PETER BEALE

Copyright © 2023
Peter Beale
A SONG OF METHUSELAH:
THE TALE OF BLACKBIRD
&
THE DESTINY OF GUIDO
VOLUMES 3 & 4
All rights reserved.

No part of this publication may be reproduced, distributed, or transmitted in any form or by any means, including photocopying, recording, or other electronic or mechanical methods, without the prior written permission of the publisher, except in the case of brief quotations embodied in critical reviews and certain other non-commercial uses permitted by copyright law.

Peter Beale
18 Rue de Montpensier
75001 PARIS, France
beale.publishing@gmail.com

Printed Worldwide
First Printing 2023
First Edition 2023

"What now lies in the past once lay in the future."

—F.W. Maitland

THE TALE OF
BLACKBIRD

FORECAST, JULY 4, 2027

Early in July, the hurricane began as a small tropical storm over the warm moist waters of the Pacific, north of the equator, west of Chile and south east of Hawaii, where, for an unknown reason, the El Nino current had diverted. The evaporating moisture rose until enormous amounts of saturated air accumulated and twisted counterclockwise high in the atmosphere. Wind-speeds around the relative calm at the eye of the storm grew to over 100 miles per hour moving on a path which would take it over central Mexico. The storm was being tracked on the radar screens of the National Hurricane Center on the main campus of Florida International University in Miami. One of the scientists working there, Beth Inglewood, said to her colleague, Eddie, "You seen this? Where it will make landfall?"

Eddie grunted. He tapped his screen. "Don't bet on it. Look at these plot lines. One degree north and that thing's coming here, around San Diego. We got a name for it yet?"

Beth checked the list put out by the World Meteorological Organisation who had added men's names to the list of women's in 1978. "We're into the Greek alphabet. This one's 'Zeta'."

"No, that's for the Atlantic. And I think that name's retired anyway."

"You're right. Talk about coincidence, next up is 'Edward'. It's named after you, Eddie."

"Great. Cream your jeans an' watch Eddie grow. You know what they say: women are like hurricanes, when they come they're wet and wild, and when they leave they take your house and car."

"You auditioning for a laugh?" Beth said, rolling her eyes, "Keep at it, get canned, and you can do stand-up with that stale gag in the Comedy Store."

+++

CHAPTER ONE

Omen –
Sleeping arrangements:
beautiful bodies
flying solo.

+++

The drought, now in its fourth year, had forced the Los Angeles Board of Supervisors to issue a county-wide ordinance suspending watering lawns, washing cars, rationing water for showers and other domestic use, and closing play on all the city's 99 golf courses, whether public or private, including the Riviera in Pacific Palisades, where the Starter on the first tee found himself cast in the unusual role of defending the City Fathers for their foresight. A foursome headed by Joey G, given to betting more than he could afford, swearing at every wayward shot and misaligned putt, paying prodigious tips for all the caddies in the group, particularly those astute enough to find his ball on the fringe of the fairway instead of in the trees when last seen, had come to play and were determined to play, and really didn't give a shit about what the ordinance said, after all they paid their taxes, it was a free country, etc. The Starter patiently explained that because of global warming, 866 golf courses in California, each using on average 90 million gallons of water every year to maintain healthy vegetation, the math was real simple: annually 77 billion, 940 million gallons of water was being used to grow grass. Given that an average family used approximately 100 gallons of water per day, 36,500 gallons per year, growing that grass would keep 2,135,342 people dirty and thirsty. No brainer. There were lots of other games people could play.

"Yeah? I mean, what the fuck?" said Joe. "If they can play in Palm Springs why can't we play here?"

+++

In the dark the mules waited stoically, occasional nerves making one of them go off into the bushes to relieve themselves. Their guides, nearly invisible in ghillie suits, crouched some meters away, intent on the hooded TV monitor screen of a drone they were flying in a slow reconnaissance pattern over a narrow bend of the Rio Agua Prieta west of Douglas, Arizona, on the Mexican side of the border. A freakish series of storms from Baja California had dumped sufficient rain to have flooded what was usually a dry river bed, creating an opportunity.

Each of the ten mules, men and women, mostly young, completely naked, carefully coached not to show out as they swam behind individual semi-submerged miniature rafts made of driftwood, beneath which hung a waterproof lightweight backpack containing, sealed in plastic, clothes they would wear on reaching the northern bank of the river, all labelled 'Made in the USA', a throwaway cell phone locked in aeroplane mode onto the GPS, and 10 kilos of cocaine, street value $250,000. They were ignorant that the cost to produce a kilo of llello in Colombia was less than $2000, that, statistically, three of them would be caught within a mile of the border, one would die, lost, trying to cross the Chiricahua Desert, three more would be picked up in LA and add to the enormously overpopulated prison system there, and three would make it to dreamland, America.

A phone vibrated in the pocket of one of the guides. "Si?"

"The cops have left the Railroad Depot and they're in the bar in Gadsden's. Vamos ahora, muchacho! Go, go!"

+++

The usual early morning Zimmer-frame gang from the old people's home across the street watched while Blackbird Crow unloaded his camera gear and lighting equipment from a nearly-new Mercedes SUV and piled it on the sidewalk. He was quick, they had to admit. When the van was empty one of them called out 'You want help with that, Crow?' which fetched a laugh and a grin from Blackbird. 'You guys watch my stuff while I park the truck, okay?' he said. They know Crow; he's made a documentary about their lives or rather what was left for them to live. Not much if you struggle to get to the laundromat and Ah Fong's Chinese Pizza joint a block up the street. In an obscure way they feel their roles have been reversed, that somehow they have been shortchanged and it is they who should be recording the life of a native American who they still think of as the 'Indian'. Crow lives with his ancient mother on Alta Loma off Hightower overlooking the Hollywood Bowl in a small wooden house designed by Lloyd Wright, the famous architect's son. To get to the house you need a key to an elevator built into a campanile going up the side of an otherwise inaccessible hill if you didn't want to climb hundreds of steps, a road so steep no cars have access. Just 30 neighbours have keys and they cannot quite make up their minds about this odd Indian couple living in their midst. Now Crow takes off and for a moment all is quiet, the sun glinting on the aluminium boxes stacked opposite the bench the old men occupy catty-corner from the enormous CBS complex at the junction of Beverly and Fairfax. They watch as a tall man on a skateboard, wearing a sweat-stained topee and djellaba, swerves around the boxes and stops in front of a plain black door marked Studio, under which is stencilled Do Not Enter When Red Light Is On. There being only a broken bulb in the light socket above the door, the man flips the skateboard under his arm with a practised footstab on the tail, bangs on the door, waits a moment and goes in.

Behind the anonymity of the plain black door is an ultra modern conversion of a warehouse, formerly the depot of an Iranian carpet dealer, into a Japanese 12-Jo tatami open-floor plan in polished grey granite, the lines of the 3-metre by 2-metre 'mats' inlaid in onyx, giving a total floor area of 48 square metres. The room was empty other than a black marble desk, also 3 x 2 metres, sited precisely in the middle of the room and, behind the desk, a young receptionist, who said, "Mr. Scroanza? You are early."

"Crollalanza. It's Italian."

"I'm sorry. How do you spell that?"

He spelt it for her, then added, "It means Shakespeare."

"Really." Her disinterest could not have been more obvious.

"How fascinating" said a voice on a TV screen hanging on the far wall. The image on the screen showed the desk, the receptionist and the visitor in high definition, seen from an angle 60° above the horizon, in saturated colour. "Please show Mister Crollalanza into Studio 6."

Down a corridor, Studio 6, laid out to the same Golden Rule, was a 6-tatami room, each mat in original Igusa Omote - woven grass - with Shoji screens for walls which seemed to glow although there was no obvious source for light.

"Please take off your shoes," said the slim, middle-aged man seated cross-legged on the floor behind a low black-lacquered table, "I like the pleasure of walking barefoot on these mats and I find their slight odour calms the mind. I am Blackbird Crow, the owner of these premises. I make documentary films which I sell to the big boys across the street. I heard about you and thought of the story you and your friends could tell to reflect these fragmented times. I think of it like a family tree, where, from a common trunk, each root and branch and every stem, twig and leaf has its own tale to tell. Thank you for coming. We will take it slowly, which is how I work best. But first, do you mind giving me a hand to bring in my gear from outside and then, if you are agreeable, we will make a test?"

"Of what?"

"Of you," the slim man smiled. "Think of it like going to the dentist. I will probe, drill, sometimes hit a nerve . . . tell me, do you always dress like that?"

"When do we start?"

Blackbird smiled. "We've started."

+++

Written in chalk on a clapboard is *#1 Fortunato 'BP' Crollalanza.*

A quiet voice says, "Action." The cameras, there are three of them, on chase cars and mounted on the roof of a truck, track a 1937 Bugatti as it passes the Beverly Hills Hotel, crosses Sunset Boulevard and heads down Beverly Drive. The driver is wearing aviator goggles and a horned Viking helmet. He has been told to be himself and say whatever comes into his head. On the soundtrack:

BP: "The reason I choose to live in Beverly Hills is simple, one is permanently on holiday. The City is like me, always dressed for a party. It does not take itself seriously and neither do I. What's the point? Five years after it ended there is little trace of the pandemic. The New Normal is Make-Believe-It-Never-Happened. They, the very fans who elected him, have forgotten the moron they put in the White House and they've learned to live with the ever-mutating bug. Something's going to kill you, what's the problem? Right. You are filming me to entertain an audience and sell your movie, yes? I live to be entertained for the laughably short time we are here, barely enough time to learn how to breath, then bodily functions, then how to eat, and then what to eat and not to eat, and roll over and crawl and bawl and fall and fall, and never mind language which you don't know yet and so can't say 'What the fuck?' which I have just learned at the Riviera Country Club. This is my philosophy, enjoy."

The Bugatti reaches a red stop sign at the junction with Santa Monica Boulevard but does not stop. Amid squealing tires, brakes slammed on and honking horns, it blithely dodges through the traffic. On the soundtrack one of the trailing cameramen can be heard to mutter, 'What the fuck?'

BP (continues): "I am a Prince of Castile and Aragon, heir to the Bourbon throne of the Kingdom of Two Sicilies, born in jail as my frantic father tried to drive my mother to the hospital before I arrived - alas, too late! The waters had already broken - when he had the inspiration, as we rushed by the local prison, to say to himself 'they must have a doctor in there'. They did, a very sweet axe murderer who had been masquerading as a senior oncologist in the University Hospital of Genoa when he was caught unable to explain the presence of victim No. 9 under his bed. He was sentenced to life in prison with hard labour, but remembered enough of his medical training to deliver me and to commemorate the event my grateful parents gave me my first name, Fortunato, which means blessed in Italian, but chose to honour the prisoner by adding his name next, Bépé, which is the name of a clown. I have made the best of this by adopting the initials BP, but still don't understand what got into my parents to do such a thing. The irony, of course, is now nobody calls me Fortunato, they call me BP;

both my parents do it and even the students at UCLA where I am the Visiting Professor of Adventure (Yes, I know - only in America) sing out 'Hi BP!' when they see me in that annoying egalitarian way, like chewing gum seated on the Presidential dais while he's making his State of the Union address on TV."

The Bugatti is going slower and slower, its driver obviously looking for an address, with traffic piling up behind in a disorderly queue. More angry honking.

BP (continues): "My qualifications for this job are unique given my background. I have never worked a day in my life, but being tall, good looking, charming, funny, well-spoken and well-dressed, with good table manners, a sportsman of some renown in skiing, sailing, motor racing, golf and tennis, generous to the poor, kind to all, modest to a fault and with a willing ear for the multiple misfortunes of my many elderly relatives, I am, or rather, I have become, a serial inheritor. As the old folk fall off the family tree their *stuff* comes to me. Je suis un héritier professionnel.

In fact the Chair I occupy at the University was endowed a couple of years ago by one of these obscure relations who made, or maybe that should be remade, his immense fortune after the fall of the Berlin Wall in 1989 and the collapse of the USSR in 1991 and, probably because he knew Gorbachev and got tipped off in advance, nipped nimbly to the front of the line for restitution of most of the despoiled family estates garnered during the 50-year rule of the Austro-Hungarian Empire, stolen by the Nazis, trashed by the Communists, ruined by neglect, but still a rather stunning portfolio of castles and palaces, manoirs fortifiers, entire hamlets, several villages, various large farms, houses and apartments too numerous to count, thousands of hectares of land in the former Poland, Czechoslovakia, Hungary, Austria, Bulgaria, Armenia, Azerbaijan, Latvia, and a vast estate in Rwanda, to which he had title. I was advised by a great aunt to give the old man a hand in preparing an inventory of all the missing content, which to do properly would have needed an army of specialists in every field from furniture to jewellery. Realising he could not remotely afford this - at the time he was eking out a living as a painter - I suggested co-opting the help of major Universities in Europe and America which he thought a brilliant idea, and the two of us cobbled together a business plan where, in exchange for providing the manpower and legal expertise needed, the Universities would have first rights to the sale of any property or artefacts in situ or recovered by their efforts, a share of profits from any such sales, an obligation to finance the renovation of those properties he wanted to keep and a share in the rents generated from these and any other source, including the intellectual rights for any books, documentaries, TV shows or movies. Excluded were the rich copper mines on his Polish estates. As a result he became wealthy. Obscenely so, much, much more than some crooked oligarch. And his life went to hell with all the hands held out for charity. In today's woke-blinkered mind nobody believes me when I tell them this. Mais c'est comme ça.

It was another suggestion of mine, in hindsight stupid from the personal point of view, that he create a foundation into which he should put all his wealth and thus insulate himself from the greed with which he was surrounded. He did this to such good effect that it allowed him to go back to painting, which is all he really wanted to do anyway, leaving his Foundation, and the miserly bunch of flinty-eyed accountants who ran it, to hand out the vast sums it earned to endow assorted Chairs, in the fields of Biology, History, AI, Physics, Mathematics, of the various Universities who had helped him make his fortune. Knowing I had no skills in any of these fields, out of his affection for me and a touch of whimsy, he persuaded UCLA to especially create a Chair of Adventure, amply endowed it and named me Professor Emeritus - with no salary! My darling mother having told him I must not be spoiled! So I have tenure, no money and nowhere to live."

The Bugatti turns into a parking lot behind the Beverly Wilshire Hotel.

BP (continues): "I go three times a week to Westwood, to the campus of UCLA, to tell tall tales to pretty coeds, but for me this is not work. It's a chance for them to dream and be curious, and me a chance to be curious and dream. I tell them stories the old man told me of going to India in 1903 for the Durbar to crown Edward V11 and Queen Alexandra, Emperor and Empress of India. 'What's a Durbar?' they ask. How did Edward meet Alexandra? Who decides who can be an Emperor? Or an Empress? Every name has to be explained, every action questioned, every motive examined. They are very naive.

The old man's mother somehow knew Mary, the American wife of the Viceroy, Lord Curzon, and got herself invited. They stayed at Maiden's, a new hotel built for the occasion, just north of the walls of Old Delhi, near the railway terminus where the King's brother, the Duke of Connaught, came by train from Bombay exactly on time to meet Curzon and his entourage coming in from Calcutta, plus an enormous assembly of Indian Princes and Maharajas and their retinues, most of them on caparisoned elephants. It took weeks for them to come from all over the sub-continent smothered in their most precious jewels whose collected value was reported to be the greatest concentration of wealth gathered in one place that the world had ever seen. An entire tented city built of some 15,000 embroidered shamianas covered a vast dusty plain to offer the multitude shelter from the elements, food and rest, electric lights, the convenience of sanitation not to be found in Delhi itself, with a post and telegraph office, hospital, private police force and magistrate's court. There were fireworks, banquets, sporting events, polo matches, exhibitions of art and crafts, displays of every kind including General Kitchener himself. The Right Honourable Earl, Commander-in-Chief of the Indian Armies, in full dress uniform, with an alphabet list of medals and awards parading endlessly across his left breast to the tunes of the massed regimental bands of Pathans, Sikhs, Bengalis, Gurkhas, Rajputans and Punjabis all decked out in their colourful military uniforms, marching bravely under the burning sun, followed by a squadron of handsome young troopers, a beautifully mounted cavalry, could be justifiably proud as the crowds cheered themselves hoarse. In the Royal Enclosure, the old man's outspoken mother shocked Lady Curzon by saying, 'Mary, I'm surprised you invited the old bugger and his bumboys.'

'Ilse! Mind what you say in public.'

'Why? Everyone knows and nobody cares.'

'You should be more discreet.'

'I should be? You mean he should be. Surely he should keep in the bedroom what should not be paraded in public? The man's a peacock.'

'The man's a hero.'

'Because he machine-gunned natives armed with spears and then executed the wounded? A hero to whom?'

'Ilse! At least keep your voice down.'

'In this din?'

Next to his wife Lord Curzon was seen to smile.

I left out what he said about the clamour and the smell, the flies and the dust. There were minute particles of dust hanging in the air and hundreds of men in dhotis with leather water-bags hired to sprinkle perfumed water on the ground to keep the dust down but when the elephants went by each step they made sent up a puff of dust which got in the eyes of little children."

The Bugatti noses astride two parking lots.

"Of course they hadn't a clue who Kitchener was or that he ended badly, going down with his long-time aide-de-camp when their ship hit a mine at the end of the war. If you think about it there's probably not another soul still alive who was at that Durbar. I sometimes find myself wondering, if it wasn't for someone like the old man, did any of this really happen? What remains if nothing is remembered? Who cares?" Pause, while BP got out of the car. "Guess what the coeds wanted to know?"

"What?"

"What's a bumboy?"

+++

"Cut. Excellent." Blackbird Crow took off his cap. "You'll get a ticket for parking like that. And try not to get us killed, okay? Here we usually obey traffic signals. Let's go for lunch and you can tell me how you met Mimi."

+++

Another day.

Written in chalk on the clapboard *#2 Fortunato/Mimi S.*

"Action."

She is photographed in silhouette driving her open antique-white, Rolls Royce Corniche down Rodeo Drive, elbow on the window ledge, an ultra-thin Patek Phillipe watch on her wrist, while smoking a cigarette in a long white holder. On the soundtrack:

Mimi: "The first thing I thought when he came into the office was 'Eurotrash'. He had these buggy blue eyes standing out in a thin tanned face, long, unwashed yellow-grey hair, multiple bead necklaces around his skinny neck, half a dozen rings on surprisingly beautiful hands, wearing, of all things, a faded burnoose with the hood up over a turban wrapped around his head. No shoes, sandals. Carrying a spear. Oh yes, and he got out of a 1937 Type 57S Bugatti Atalante Coupe painted yellow and black, inherited he said, which he parked in front of the fire hydrant in the no parking zone far away from all the hybrids and electric cars which is all you see in BH these days since the last gas station closed on Crescent Drive. My secretary was squeaking in anxiety that he'd get towed and he just grinned at her with this carnivorous knowing look like he could see her wetting her pants. The feminists would have lynched him. So, I said, you want to buy a house? Where? How big? How much down? Financing. No financing. Cash. No cash? No, not no cash. 'No money.' No money?

'Madame', he said, 'I am told by my friend Joe G. that you are the most important broker in Beverly Hills, that you know every house for sale and even the houses that are not for sale but that can be bought, si? So I am sure you know that in every community, no matter how rich and expensive, there is always a house nobody wants, e vero, it's true, no? I am the buyer of such a house.'

Immediately I thought of the old Modine place above Summitridge, empty now for sixty years, maybe more, completely overgrown to the point you could hardly see the house for the vegetation. And rats. 'Do you mind rats?' I said.

So, one day, we go up there, eight acres, gated access, great views all over the City and even the Valley. We have some Mexicanos in tow armed with machetes that he hired from where they stand every morning on the corner of Melrose and La Brea looking for work, and he gets them going chopping down the vines, poison oak, poison ivy, thorn bushes, what have you, without the permission of the owner which I warn him is against the law, and he does his shit-eating grin, takes off his shirt and joins the gang like he's done demo jobs all his life and by evening what we have in front of us, once all the crap has been stripped off, is an early mid-century, steel-post-and-concrete moderne masterpiece, ransacked, vandalised, graffiti covering every surface and even the ceilings, busted windows, no water, no electricity, with the accumulated filth of generations of squatters and that stench of old weed permeating the rain damaged walls and the even worse smell of rising damp and mould.

'Stupendo!' said BP. He looked as if Santa had just landed. 'Meraviglioso!' he said to his new mates, a fairly wonderful bunch of castoffs and misfits with tats looking like central casting's idea of a family gathering in the hood. 'Bien, manana empezamos.' Because of course he spoke Spanish and when I said the obvious that he'd be trespassing and if he had no money his crew would probably kill him when they turned up for work, he patted me on the shoulder, winked, not to worry, you contact the owner, the boys and I will get stuck in and a week later, when I brought the owner's attorney for a meeting on site, she, the owner, an incredibly old silent-movie star hanging on for dear life in the desert in Arizona where she had moved to treat her arthritis, hearing him report back to her that a new hand-lettered sign hung over her cleared and transformed house, 'Estados Unidos Mexicanos', with a Padrone and his campesinos, their wives, children and pets, living in a lively compound, where music, laughter and the smell of cooking, tortilla de patatas, frittatas, enchiladas, tacos, filled the air, she was delighted, and even more delighted when he gave her the details of the deal he had struck.

CLOSE ON the Attorney:

"Action."

Attorney: "The guy's an Italian Prince, or so he says. There must be thirty people living there with him. The neighbours called the building department to complain about the noise and on your behalf, after I received a registered letter for you from Building and Safety - here, listen to this: 'Effective immediately - A Professional of Record shall provide the City of Beverly Hills as-built digital-format plans of the existing structure BEFORE ANY RENOVATION WORK IS UNDERTAKEN, in caps, etc', - and were sending an inspector to the site, who was already there having lunch with this Prince and some of the workmen seated at a long trestle table when we got there, it was delicious actually, because they made Mimi and me sit down and join in, and it turns out the Inspector was from Michoacan, an original, one of the Purépecha, and so were a couple of the workers, unemployment down there was over 50%, wasn't it great to be in the US so they could send money home, and 'what about those fish on Lake Patzcuaro when you got up before dawn to go fishing with your Dad, yo recuerdo? Who could forget, and come back anytime, bring the wife and kids.'

After the Inspector had gone I said to the Prince, okay, you conned him, now let's get down to it, how much are we talking about? Eight acres, in the heart of the City, with this view? The house is probably a tear-down but the land alone is worth something north of $10Mill, right? He grinned, spoke to one of the men about ratas and the guy goes and brings back a garbage can full of dead rats. "El pasatiempo preferido de mi gato es matar ratas." As the killer black cat in question purrs around with a family of siblings.

"I'm going to make you an offer that Onassis himself could not make." the Prince said. " I'm going to offer you all the money I have." And he puts three grand down on the table. I couldn't help laughing. "Three thousand dollars? You must be joking?" I said. "You see any of these guys laughing?" said the Prince. "You've been trying to sell this place for more than sixty years. My guys clean it up, connect the utilities - don't ask - kill the rats, the rattlers, the tarantulas and all the other protected vermin at no expense to the City, you think that's a joke? And five families are taken off the housing list, how's that for a punchline?"

The old actress clapped her hands. 'What fun,' she said, 'I wish I'd been there.'"

CUT TO:

Mimi: So BP makes a deal. Or, to be accurate, he agrees to the deal I make for him. The three grand is the monthly mortgage payment on a purchase price of $500,000, with nothing down and a first mortgage carried back by the old lady, giving her a yield of 7.2%, but more importantly for her, paying the monthly charges for the retirement home where she lives. She has no children, no ex- anything to worry about, no heirs and prefers

BP and the Mexicanos to inherit the house than the State of California grabbing it when she dies. Who cares if it's worth millions, it would all go in taxes. The attorney handles the paperwork pro bono, I make diddly squat, we fly out to Scottsdale for the closing since she can't travel and wants to meet BP. He reserves a table at Monarchs and I get stuck with the bill. End of story. 'Mimi', he says, 'you truly are the greatest broker in the City.' Ta da!"

+++

"Cut. Brilliant. You're a gem, Mimi," Blackbird kissed her. "This is going to work. Let's go get lunch."

+++

CHAPTER TWO

Aesthetic Theory:
A lover's discourse,
"Nobody's perfect."

+++

The letter arrived in a nondescript envelope. What made it distinctive was the fact of its existence in an era where all orders arrived by email. It also had no stamp on it but was marked 'By hand'. The gunmaker found the envelope when he pushed open the door to his atelier on Via Vincenzo Bellini, which had been his father's and before him his grandfather's and before him his great-grandfather's, who set up as a specialist gunsmith at the end of the 18th century after Beretta bought out the arms manufacturer for whom he had worked half his life.

For fifteen generations under the same family control, Fabbrica d'Armi Pietro Beretta SpA, the world's oldest firearms company, having received its first recorded order from the Arsenal of Venice, in 1526: "Today, October the 3rd to Master Bartholomew Beretta from Gardone, in Brescia region, for 185 barrels for harquebus, to our House of the Arsenal, 296 ducats have been given." owned every major gun manufacturer in the small village of Gardone Val Trompia, ten miles north of Brescia, including Benelli, Franchi, Uberti, Sako, and Stoeger. Together they manufactured 1500 firearms per day, 60% destined for export to the USA. But they did not make plastic one-off specials for unknown clients.

The gunmaker read the letter. The specification was exacting. He re-read it, his mind already grappling with how such a weapon could be made, and it took him a moment to focus on the last paragraph: 'Wired today to your account with Banca Monte dei Paschi di Siena -' the amount took his breath away. He put the letter down to gaze out of the window at the imposing bulk of Casa Beretta across the street, then picked it up, re-read it again, then called his bank to make an appointment. He then called his lawyer and arranged to meet him after his siesta, at 5pm, across the river in Falconiere, by which time the lunchtime crowd would be back at work.

That afternoon, a glass of Montepulciano within reach on a bare dining table, having taken a sip while reading the letter, the lawyer said, "You checked with the bank?"

"Yes. It arrived in two payments. Both are just under ten thousand dollars."

"You know what that means?"

"Yes. The banks have an obligation to report sending or receiving amounts of ten thousand or more."

"Provenance?"

"One from the Bahamas, one from Liechtenstein. My guy just winked, it's business. I'll buy him a drink."

"You know these people?"

"No."

"You want my advice? Send it back."

"How can I? I can't. I need the money."

"How'd they get your account number? IBAN? The lot?"

"I don't know."

"Listen to me. Send it back."

"Can't."

The lawyer looked at the letter again. "What do you usually get?"

"Normally? Six hundred. For a standard gun."

"So? What's special about this? I don't understand the specs, but it says here when it's ready you have to send it in four pieces to four separate addresses in Mexico. Make sense to you?"

+++

A hand can be seen writing on the clapboard *#3 BP/UCLA Campus.*
"Action."

Two cameras track the Professor as he crosses Westwood Plaza on the University campus, weaving through pockets of students, headed for the staff canteen. On the soundtrack:

BP:" It does have a ring to it: Avventura! Il Professore d'Avventura. The students rag me because I wear a tie which they regard as an elitist affectation, much like my rich American acquaintances who make it a point of honour to do the dishes together rather than hire a maid who may or may not be an illegal alien - the fact that 61% of Californians are now Hispanic and that without the work of these mostly humble people the State would cease to function is not their concern - but then the rich in America are absolutely hopeless, particularly in BH. Their only ambition, dream, aim, goal is to possess, the corollary to which is cost. Everything of value comes at a cost; the greater the cost the more valuable. You any idea how much that cost? She was a cheap date. I stole it at auction. Did I ever get a great prenup! Don't ask, it was a bargain. There's always something heroic in the phrasing, the implication clear, no matter how many millions the picture, the car, the boat, the house, the wife, the plane, the watch, might have cost, it was a deal, man! And the way the game is played, how you score, stack up points, is to have more than the next guy, more is better, more is much more, the possessive endgame of accumulation, with the not-so-subtle subtitle: aren't I great? Apart from money - M.O.N.E.Y - what do these people contribute? Nada. They would not be welcome in the compound, it is agreed. Because in the evening, after dinner and putting the kids to bed, smoking a little of the State's largest cash crop in the hammocks that have been strung up between the posts supporting the roof over the broad verandah that runs around three sides of the house, the stars competing with the distant glow of the city lights, someone softly strumming a guitar, we talk. Lying back in the arms of their women, the men are tired, their muscles ache, weary in spirit, worn down by the daily grind of looking for work knowing they will make much less than minimum wage.

'Todos son bastardos,' is the central groove of our conversation, with improvised riffs on the stinginess of this bastard contractor in Van Nuys, don't believe a word he says, all he wants is cheap labour to get the asbestos out and fuck the hazmat suits, do it at night, and that washed up singer in his zillion dollar McMansion on Roxbury, won't pay a plumber to fix the leak in his gold-plated bathroom tap, cruises Melrose in his Tesla roadster, you guys know how to do this shit, right, take a couple of hours, you get paid when it's done and, surprise, the maid tells you he's in rehearsal, can't be disturbed, come back tomorrow and tomorrow and tomorrow, he stiffs you for fixing a tap? 'Lo que es un bastardo', the maid agrees with you at the back door. Why stay and work for him? Shrugs. It's a job and I steal food for my family, he doesn't notice, never looks in the fridge. She's cute, I tell her she should come here. My son needs a girlfriend.

Screw the son, I recognise her immediately when she turns up, Maria-Celestina, with the knockout figure, mass of curly, jet black hair, flirty knowing eyes and perpetual grin in the corner of her mouth, all things I am not meant to notice because I am her teacher, as the ground rules at UCLA make explicitly clear: no fraternizing between staff and students, even one moonlighting as a maid."

+++

"Cut!" Blackbird Crow got out of the director's chair. "You fancy Madeo's today? We've a few things to discuss after lunch."

" No sir. I have a date."

"Not when you work for me. Call her. Tell her you're making a movie, take a rain check. In this town she'll understand."

+++

Libya was already just a smudge over the horizon as the light grew. With the dawn came a freshening breeze strong enough to blow tendrils of drift from waves that smacked into the bow of the battered scow making its way north towards the island of Lampedusa. Huddled in the boat, with a maximum carrying capacity of 30 passengers, were 168 refugees, men, women and children, fleeing from every corner of Africa and the Middle East for the

20

promised safety of a new life in the European Union. Frightened, silently staring overboard, drenched each time the boat dug into a wave, unsure of their fate despite having paid dearly for their passage, they earned the contempt of the man on the bridge, woollen skull cap pulled down to his eyebrows, dark glasses, scarf knotted at the throat, effectively camouflaged, who had organised and guaranteed their escape along the deadliest migrant route in the world. He glanced at the compass and told the helmsman to modify the course he was steering, then said, "Can you believe their Pope once came here to bless trash like this?"

The man beside him, who would make the bomb, said, "Good cover though. I'm going below to rest. Call me when we're near. I'll need time to dress. Allahu Akbar."

"A moment, Hassan. You are being given a great opportunity. Everything is in place for you but you are impetuous. You think too highly of yourself. The skills you have been taught will be worthless if you are caught. Keep in mind that they are very efficient, their cameras are everywhere and so are their informants. You may be sure they know of you even if they don't know who you are. I will tell you something you have not been taught. Be humble. Are you listening to me? Humble."

"Who are you to say these things to me?"

"I am the man who is bringing you to his target. But I am also the man who has stood where you now stand and I have survived ten years on their most wanted list, Inshallah. Think on it."

+ + +

"Everything is a fraction of the whole."

They had finished lunch and Alfio had poured each of them a digestive thimble of limoncello made by his grandmother in Puglia. Blackbird Crow was staring down into the tiny glass, now empty. "Everything," he repeated. "There are no linear stories left in a society that values sound bites, Twitter tweets, cell photo selfies and the endless navel gazing of social media. I teach an epistemological class at Pepperdine for their film studies degree and the stuff the kids shoot is juiced up YouTube. Forget notions of moral, aesthetic or ideological importance to a modern humanities program. All they really care about now is race and gender."

"Sex?" said BP.

"Less than you imagine. You think they give a shit what's going on outside their world? They're scared, man, insecure, and they blame us, our generation, for the mess they're going to inherit. Can't say they're wrong. But they're the audience, seven out of ten of those going to the movies, half the eyeballs watching TV, changing channels as fast as they can click. So I have to hook them, trick them into taking a trip, grab what I can shoot and tell a story. I want to hear you thinking and film your thoughts. Then it's all in the editing. I am telling you this so—"

He was interrupted by raised voices at the entrance to the restaurant, a woman saying "I don't care if it's closed, I know he's in there!" and the simultaneous arrival of Alfio's son, Lorenzo, trying to hold back a curly-haired bombshell aimed at BP.

"She says you stood her up?"

+++

Clapboard *#4 Maria-C. A./BP*

"Action."

Maria-Celestina A: She is in her bedroom in her parents' house in Inglewood in her underwear. The camera closes on her painting her toenails. On the soundtrack:

"Ay, caramba! as soon as I saw him I knew. Qué hacer, es su destino. The girls tease me in class and my friend Lucinda she warns me, pinche cabron, don't do it, don't even think of it, chica. Mi destino. Only my abuelita, my loving little grandmother, understands and defends me over the anger of my father and the piercing shrieks of my mother which drowns out the thunder of the jets flying over our house to land at LAX when I tell them he has asked me to go with him to Europe on a reconnaissance for a planned class field trip later in the year. 'Eres tonto?' Are you crazy was certainly the mildest comment, followed by every negative thought from, they'll throw you out of the university after all our sacrifices to get you in, to, you'll come back pregnant as if there aren't enough single mothers in this family already, a reference to my second cousin, Gabriela, knocked up on a one-night stand by a DJ in Compton, and to Jimena, my aunt, who has two kids by two different guys and can't remember which one made which child although one of them is a pale tan and the other black-as-in-beautiful black. We are 8, 9, 10, 11 kids in and out of the house at any time, depending. The principal participle of our lives, depending on the money we have as a family, hinging on who has work, contingent on DUIs, restraining orders, jail time for assorted misdemeanours, weather patterns, market fluctuations, that time of the month, all of which could turn on the proverbial dime if we didn't watch out for each other. 11 kids, 5 to 19. I'm the oldest. 'No one ever asked me to go on a journey to Europe,' my lovely abuelita whispered to me in our bedroom when the other four kids in there with us had finally fallen asleep. 'What an adventure.'"

CUT TO - the exterior of an Aids clinic. The Professor pushes open the front door. The camera tracks him and his students through the lobby, onto an elevator, down a corridor, into a ward. On the soundtrack: "Action."

BP: "Not having a set curriculum, which drives the Dean insane, I design my own course which is always to do what entertains me. I set the kids various tasks that I dream up to incite curiosity, encourage imagination, take chances, weigh odds, defy logic and the righteous protestant ethic behind teaching in America. Since it's an elective course, for some reason I only have girls, praise the Lord. On a visit to an AIDS clinic in West Hollywood, my English hairdresser friend, Art, thin as a shadow, who used to play the piano in a gay pub off the Fulham Road, now patiently waiting out his time, was more than happy to instruct my collective of students on the realities of a shared life or a shared needle. As he struggled to sit up, even dying, Art was funny.

'Well ladies, unaccustomed as I am to entertaining your sex, and this may sound elementary, but if somebody is going to stick something into you, be it a needle, a penis, a fag or a joint, try to make sure it's clean.'

His glazed eyes told you how much he hurt lying there so flat and horizontal he scarcely made a bump in the perfection of his white-and-beige hospital bed, but he chuckled.

'You know the acronym for Aids? No? All I Do Sucks. Heh. Heh. Now I'll gross you out, because il Professore here wants you to hear the unvarnished truth about the last great adventure - there is no easy way for the body to die. Got that? No easy way. If you want to know if you're infected, learn the language. The human immunodeficiency virus, popularly known around the block as HIV, is a lentivirus which, over time, mutates into it's pal, AIDS, which is a condition in us humans in which progressive failure of the immune system allows life-threatening opportunistic infections and cancers to exist, live, thrive and mutate. Without treatment, after infection with HIV, you may, stress may, survive 9 or 10 years, depending on the HIV subtype. In most cases, HIV is a sexually transmitted infection and occurs by contact with or transfer of blood, pre-ejaculate, yeah, that clear stuff before he actually comes, semen and vaginal fluids. Whatever he says, this includes blowjobs. Non-sexual transmission can occur from an infected mother to her infant through milk from those lovely breasts you have. And, get this, an HIV-positive mother can transmit HIV to her baby both during pregnancy and childbirth due to exposure to her blood or vaginal fluid. Within these bodily fluids, HIV is present as both free virus particles and virus within infected immune cells. The initial period following the contraction of HIV is called acute HIV, no kidding, primary HIV or acute retroviral syndrome. It feels like the worst flu you've ever had or mononucleosis, 10 on a scale of 10, and it usually kicks in a couple of weeks after your last orgasm. Symptoms you get include fever, enlarged tender lymph nodes, throat inflammation, headaches, and/or sores in your mouth and genitals. You get a rash half the time on your torso and some unlucky sods also develop opportunistic infections at this stage. You vomit and shit, and vomit and shit, ad nauseum. No fun, but after a while things settle down.'

It was so quiet in the room the sounds from the street five floors below could be heard through the double-glazed windows. The girls were transfixed by Art's calm authority and total lack of self-pity. He took them through every stage of the disease, no polemics, the empathy shared of someone who could see the finish line and those just starting the race. At the end he was tired, his face pale, head on the pillow, and, eyes closed, gave them his benediction.

'It has been divine to have you darlings brighten this ward. Off you go now. Remember what the great man said: 'Dyin' comes easy, it's livin' that's hard'.' Then, before we got to the door, his eyes popped open. *'I have it -*

homework for you: commemorate your field trip to a dying land. Elaborate.'
And fell asleep.

A week later he was still alive and sent me an SMS: *Hey, Pretty Boy, you got a mo, nip over. Something to show you.*

'He's sleeping,' the nurse said.

'No problem. If it's okay, can I sit by his bed and wait?'

'They sleep a lot,' she said, then shrugged, 'but go ahead.'

Watching Art asleep, his breathing so slow, a small pulse rhythmically beating in his temple, it took a moment for me to register that through half closed eyes he had been watching me.

He smiled when I cottoned on and very quietly said, 'Ciao, Fortunato. I was thinking about us with the old man in the Picasso on King's Road. Remember how we lusted after that girl, Ingrid?'

'You?'

'Of course. I've always been a switch-hitter, you know that. Funny what your memory brings back. We couldn't think of a good line to pick her up. That dodgy chap who had Antiquarius, Dougy something, said you should always have coins ready in your pocket and if you walk towards a pretty girl as you pass her you drop the coins and when she looks back you say I think you dropped these and bend down to help her pick them up. Bingo; bit of chat; in like Flint. Worked every time he said.'

'And that's why you've had me over?'

'Don't be daft. See that -' he pointed at an envelope on his nightstand, 'your kids send me stuff, well some of them do and I'm grateful. Most of its juvenile mumbo jumbo, but not that. That's different. Go on, open it. Read what's inside:'

<u>*The Daisy Chain*</u>

The sun was shining when the telephone rang.

- Hello?

- H-hello . . . Alan?

- Yeah, hi . . . just a second . . . got to turn down the TV . . . hi, who is this?

- It's me, Laurie.

- Laurie?

- Yes, Laurie . . . remember, Sunset Plaza?

- Oh, yeah. Yeah, what's that — three-four years ago? Kit's place, right? Sure, I remember you. How you doing?

- Well . . .

- Good. That's great — by the way, how'd you get my number? I must've moved a couple of times at least.

- No, listen. I don't mean well like that. I mean well, look . . . I don't know how to say this . . . but, I've got to see you!'

- Hey, no shit, just like that, after three-four years: I gotta see you!

- It's important.

- Speak up. I can't hear you if you whisper.

- It's IMPORTANT!

- Really? An' what do I tell my old lady? Cause I'm married now. Two kids. And they're all by the pool waiting for their Sunday barbecue.

- God! Oh, God, don't you see that's why it's important?

- No, I don't see — no, what's so important? What're you talking about?

- Dear God. I don't want to tell you on the phone. But I must see you, because — listen, please listen . . .

- I'm listening.

- This is terrible . . . but . . . Oh God . . . listen, this guy I used to know, used to date before I met you back then, he called me . . . he called to tell . . . to tell me . . . he had . . . AIDS!'

‘ . . . ‘

- Hello?

‘ . . . ‘

- Hello, Alan? Please . . . please, Alan, talk to me. Listen, I'm scared . . . no, worse than that, terrified, but the doctor told me I must contact anybody I'd been with since that time —

CLICK.

Silence.

When the phone rang again, it rang and rang, until Betty called from where she was playing with the kids:

- Alan . . . ? Are you going to pick that up?

+++

'Know who wrote it?' said Art. 'Your little Mexicana hottie. The one with the curly hair you couldn't keep your eyes off. She gets it. She's special, but that piece is no school essay, that's up-close and personal. Beware. You have been warned. By the way, what are you doing on Friday?'

'Friday?'

'Yes. Want to come to my funeral? Last gig. It will be a blast. Bring the girls.'

Friday was three days away. How did he know?"

+++

"Action."

Maria-Celestina A: "The traffic is always bad; on Fridays worse. The radio was playing the new hit 'I'm a virgin, a 21st Century girl' being pushed by those ageing bitches of #MeToo to the top of the charts. What planet do they live on? I'm a 21st Century girl and so are all my friends and there's not one who is still a virgin, in fact there's probably not one in Uni. We're in my younger brother's car, an Olds 442, all pimped out the way he likes, having been stripped to the metal, primed, sanded and hand-polished 14 coats of insect-green metallic paint, lowered shocks, louvred hood, chrome pipes, fat lot of good it does him in Club Fed, Lompoc, where he's doing a stretch for receiving and we're only allowed to visit him once a month. Anyway he'd freak if he saw the girls in the car with me. Sitting next to me is Amy, from Columbus, Ohio, spectacles, fat, mother and father architects, now divorced, but in counselling to see if they can make it back together despite repeated infidelity on both sides, she with the woman they hired to walk the dogs, he with the proverbial temp, there in the office like bait, recruited by her mom, if you can believe Amy, deliberately to ensnare her dad and make her mom feel justified. Behind are twins from Salt Lake City, Mormon, blonde, stacked, with incredible IQs and a focus on math, string theory and blockchains, but so dumb you almost have to say not just Paris, France, which is a geographical cue most freshman get, but Paris,

France, Europe, Continent of. Between the twins, like the Continental Divide, is 6-foot tall Lorraine of the copper-red hair, from the Upper East Side, New York City, father on Wall Street when he's not on his fourth wife. Lorraine is a superstar athlete, who has already played Wimbledon but prefers to hangout with the surfing dudes at the Pier in Huntington Beach where she is a bigger prize than winning Vans Triple Crown since she will one day be a billionaire when her dad croaks. Nobody from the barrio, you'll notice. The only thing we have in common, apart from going to the same school, is the fact that all of us are descendants of immigrants. We're following our Prof, BP, in his Bugatti on the way to this funeral and trying not to cry, complicated for me because BP's passenger is this svelte, honey-skinned Indian girl, with fabulous long straight ink-black hair down to her butt, on a Fulbright scholarship from Delhi and I am jealous looking at the back of the two of them in that streamlined two-seater chatting intimately as if they were on their way to a dirty weekend at the San Ysidro Ranch in Montecito, because, of course, we're already shacked up, BP and I. Not an item - yet - because we have to keep it secret or both risk getting thrown out of the university. Hence riding in separate cars. All this going through my mind in dense traffic when Amy said, 'I'm never going to be skinny like you guys.'

Sniff.

'The social sites are useless, and even if I get a date, one look at me and they're out the door, so, guess what, I've decided to become a donor mother. I'll get sperm from one of those sperm banks, maybe that guy's in Copenhagen who's already fathered thousands of kids, and, with my genetic background, make super babies.' Amy spent hours a day researching her ancestors on the net, building a complicated family tree stretching back centuries, contacting complete strangers all over the world to compare degrees of ethnic affinity. She not only had her DNA tested, but also those of her parents, A - to make sure they both really were her parents, and B - to dig out any hereditary diseases. She had been banging on about her 5-star heritage for months, but 'donor mother'?

'I don't think that's a great idea,' said Lorraine from the back seat.

'Yeah? Why not?' said Amy.

'You haven't finished school. Without a degree you won't get a job. Without a job you won't have anywhere to live. With nowhere to live you'll end up back with your parents - do I have to go on?'

'And if you took a mitochondrial DNA test you only learn about your mom's ancestry, nothing about your dad,' said one twin.

'Plus, if you go back as little as 10 generations,' said the other twin, 'that test is telling you something about only one ancestor out of more than a thousand hanging around in the branches of your family tree. Same goes for the guy in Copenhagen. It's all bullshit. If you want to do it, pick ten guys at random, check their sperm for bugs, deep freeze if good to go, get impregnated once a year for ten years, stop when you're 30 and mathematically one kid will become a millionaire, two will do drugs, one will be a murderer and the rest will be your run of the mill butcher, baker, candlestick maker and you can have a choice of colour if you pick different ethnic groups, better marketing too.'

So maybe not so dumb. When finally we reached the cemetery out in the Valley it was easy to spot Art's gig by all the LGBT flags flapping in the breeze and 'You don't have to say you love me' in Dusty Springfield's throaty voice on the speakers, Art's way of reminding us he was a child of the '60s. None of my passengers had been to a funeral before, in fact never seen a dead body before, a comment I shared with the Indian girl when I found myself standing next to her in the scrum around the grave.

'I think I was 3 when I went to my first one,' she said.

'Oh? Like me. In the barrio we go so often it keeps the laundries busy cleaning the clothes because you must always wear freshly washed and pressed suits and dresses to honour the dead.'

'We make a puja,' she said, 'and wash the body with scented oils before it is wrapped in clean white cotton by the husband or wife - or parents if they are burying their child - and cremated on the funeral pyre which is always lit by a relative. Death is not an end for us, but a way to say goodbye to the body that clothed the soul until it is reincarnated again in another body. Kirat Karō, we say. Pray. Work. Give. It is simple really.'

'We bury them in their best clothes,' I said, 'surrounded with some precious possessions to enjoy in the afterlife. Since most have very little it can be a favourite hat or belt or handbag, then we eat and sing and drink and remember good things we did together. We are like the cockroaches whose motto is limpier, soporter, sobrevivir. Scavenge. Endure. Survive.'

Procol Harum had taken over from Dusty and we were in the smoky swirl of 'A Whiter Shade of Pale', Gary Brooker singing the line 'I wandered through my playing cards' with those emphatic licks of Ray Royer on guitar, when she said, 'How long have you been dating BP?'

Like that. Ba-da-boom. So much for secrets.

'Don't worry,' she said, just as the music stopped. Somebody tapped a microphone to get our attention and into the attendant hush, BP's voice said, 'Our friend Art has recorded a poem to say goodbye to us,' and with a now muted 'Whiter Shade' accompanying him in the background, Art's voice, right on key, softly murmured:

<u>Ode to the son I never had.</u>
The pistol fires - though the shots are blank
In the country of the young - stories of men
Men without women - keepers of the truth
Pages for you - wildwood boys
Both Father and Son - both Father and Son.
The day after tomorrow - a night to remember
All that remains - the debt to surrender
Out of the flames - a paradise lost
We are the miracle - where two worlds touch.
Father and Son, Father and Son
We are the miracle
Where two worlds touch
Where two worlds touch

Art's voice died as they lowered the coffin into the grave. We stood in silence, the hum of our great city a distant canopy over us. I suddenly felt hollowed out by the loss of someone I only met twice and, as tears rolled down my face, felt a hand take mine and the Indian girl whispered, 'We are the miracle where two worlds touch.'

Karma."

+++

CUT TO:

BP: "Talk about bloody karma. God knows why I brought her with me; she's not even in my class. She's doing astrophysics with a focus on climatology on which she is said to be an expert. Hard to believe she's the granddaughter of a rickshaw-wallah. I got a message, more an order, from the witch who runs the old man's foundation in Genoa to keep an eye on her, and since that's where my bread is buttered, I had diligently shown her around since she got to LA. Her name is Savera, which in Punjabi means dawn, but it never dawned (Ha!) on me that she was gay. The truth is I fancied her, e vero. Only an idiot takes a girl he fancies to a funeral while the girl he's fucking sits in the car behind. Cretino! And then for this to happen? They're a happy couple and I am the schlemiel on the sidelines playing with myself. Che palle! Plus they have nowhere to live so they move into the compound, where else?, which dented my authority with the campesinos. C'est la vie aujourd'hui, but I have the distinct impression of things out of control with me on my bum on a waterslide.

On campus nobody batted an eye seeing Savera and Maria-Celestina wandering about hand-in-hand in that love lost haze peculiar to amore stupido, but if it had been me in Savera's place they would have rolled out the guillotine. The hypocrisy in this country! Abroad in their bikinis they do what they like - make that what I like - topless, even bottomless, on every beach from Pampelonne to Spiaggia della Marchesa, come home tanned and happy, and then crucify some fellow in the elevator at work who compliments them on their good looks. For the life of me I cannot fathom the gutless response of men here, doormats for these megera, shrews supposedly seeking to redress the unfairness of life between men and women by the sudden recollection of an incident from fifteen, twenty even forty years ago, of a misplaced finger or word, unverified and unverifiable. When did un po 'di schiaffo e solletico - slap and tickle - hurt anyone? Just saying this exposes me as a social terrorist with a bomb in my soul if not in the sole of my shoe. Professor M, (I'm not allowed to say her name or risk a lawsuit), a senior alumni of Management and Policy, refuses to speak to me, and her colleague, Professor T, School of Intuitive Artificial Intelligence, une salope mal baisée if ever there was one, has started a campaign to oust me. It infuriates her that my most ardent supporters are the coeds I teach and in the open forum where, in the interests of supposed 'transparency', all critique, whether of students, teachers or policy, must now take place, they howl her down when she sets off on her well-polished, made-for-TV, diatribe of the much molested, maligned, mis-managed, underpaid, man-made modus vivendi of modern women. Bizarrely, they chant the school motto, 'fiat lux' - let there be light - which drives T to an excess of purple rage such as to suggest something nascondere sotto il materasso - hidden under the mattress. I smile at her, with a polka dot, pale blue silk kerchief peeking jauntily in the breast pocket of my vintage lemon yellow Yohji Yamamoto linen jacket, over still-fashionably torn faded blue jeans and my favourite Docksiders, no socks. I may be a Neanderthal but I am also a peacock and I will not be cowed.

I digress, because of course you want to know what I teach. This week it is garbage, disposal thereof. We are off to the City Dump to see what can be scavenged. Did you know you could build a 12- foot high wall annually from LA to NYC just from tossed office paper?"

+++

"Cut! Wow! Great stuff." Blackbird Crow was smiling. "You're a natural, BP, fucking beautiful. My mother wants to meet you."

"Your mother?"

"Yeah. I tell her what I'm shooting and show her outtakes. She's a seer. Now she would like you to come over for a picnic and a concert."

+++

CHAPTER THREE

Invisible Man -
A mythic life, a knot of time,
A time for Astrology, the secret powers of Numerology,
Fortune telling, Palmistry,
The written hand (and) Phrenology.
All the strange hours in review.
Don't look back,
Balthazar.

+++

"Morning, Chief."

"Senator."

"I hear you caught a couple?"

"Yeah, on 191 near Elfrida. Junior league stuff compared to the tunnels, but they keep trying. They're clever, ducked our telephone app delivers topography, personnel locations, distances and mapping from all those multiple sensors we activated, but they still got under the wall and the wire in that flood, swam across west of Douglas. Teenagers, both of them. More in their backpacks than I make in a year."

"Is that an official complaint?"

"You can laugh over there in DC, Senator, but it ain't a joke down here. My guys risk their lives for a lousy six grand a month."

"Don't go there, Chief. You make as much as the Vice President."

"Who does sweet fuck all as we both know, while I work fourteen hour days. But I'm not talking about me, I'm talking about the dumb schmuck with a badge who has to go climb into the shit for us and all you guys do is talk about corruption in the force."

"Booking fake overtime is corrupt."

"Not that old chestnut. Christ, we been through this bullshit ten years ago. You don't seem to get it."

"What? The bullshit act sitting on your ass parked up in an SUV with the aircon on listening to KABC and knocking back a Bud while your partner lights the joint he made out of the MaryJo he confiscated and forgot to hand in? I get that."

"Let's cut to the chase, Senator, I may be your snitch down here, but you're my snitch at those hearings. You go to bat for my boys or -"

"What?"

"Your seat comes up for re-election in November, if memory serves. You any idea how many votes I control?"

+++

Clapboard #5 - *The Compound/Alejandro X, a handyman.*

The camera pans up slowly from his shoes but stops before his face is shown. On the soundtrack:

"Action."

Alejandro X: "You forgive, okay, I do not give you my last name. I do not want you have problemas with those perros locos - mad dogs - in Homeland Security. If they see your movie, ask you how you know me, what is my name, you don't know, you cannot give. Better, si?

I work at the landfill and live with my wife in Senor Fortunato's compound - nuestro compuesto, how he insists we should call it. Our compound. It is hard for us to believe. We, Mexican peasants, living in Beverly Hills, no es possible. We have painted the place in colours to remind us of home. I come from Perula, a village in Jalisco near Careyes, and helped repaint the houses there after that hurricane in 2015. Pink. Turquoise. Oxblood red. Lemon Yellow. Magenta. So these are now the colours in our compound. The amigos, friends of BP - this is how they call him - are shocked when they first see the house, then they are encantado - enchanted, and want us to come and make their place the same. We can all do many thing, painting, electric, gardening, plumbing, build anything, wall, roof, bathroom, fix car, road, fence. Everything the gringos cannot do or do not want to do. Not a single white man works with us. They drive tractors, oversee, never dirty hands or kneel in dirt. I have been deported three times. Each time, like vacation, go home, help family, see friends, la vida mexicana.

I met my wife here. She is legal, the daughter of immigrants whose ancestors came to work with the descendants of the Chinese coolies who built the first railroads and the aqueduct from the Colorado River to Los Angeles. 1933. She will tell you this history because she is proud of it and it should be known and even if she works sorting trash, which is what she does and how she got me my job, in the barrio, over there by MacArthur Park where her people live and where I first saw her, they admire her. She is outspoken, a leader.

She is more intelligent than me, I admit, but maybe I am more cunning. You have to be to survive. It is our hope our two boys, Esteban and Jesus, inherit estos rasgos - 'these traits' I think you say. She is pregnant and we hope for a girl this time. Where we are all lucky is that Senor Fortunato loves children and they flock around him like pigeons waiting to be fed. They love the disfraces locos - crazy costumes - he wears and he dresses them up like the little courtiers they are on his estate. He treats them as his own, remembers every birthday and gives them presents he cannot afford. We all contribute to the monthly mortgage payment whatever we can and it is my wife, Esmé, who is the book-keeper who makes sure the $3000 is taken in cash to the lawyer and that he gives us a receipt for the money. She makes the tortillera - the lesbians - pay their share even though they are students. We are wary of these two girls but they are like beautiful wild animals you cannot take your eyes off when you see them and the one called Maria-Celestina has a habit of walking around completely naked which is going to start a revolution one of these days."

CUT TO:

Esmeralda X: "My husband, he calls me Esmé, which means beloved, but in our group, at work, on the street in the barrio, I am Esmeralda, which means the emerald. My parents gave me this name because they believe your given name is sacred and defines who you are and what you will become. For them - they are still alive - this name means the gem stone that is both precious and strong, with a divine colour hidden inside. God decides if you are worthy of your name. I believe this.

We are poor, which is like saying water is wet. But we are blessed with having two sons in good health despite la plaga. Now I am carrying another, which is not yet a problem at work but will become one because, of course, there is no maternal leave. One of my cousins will substitute for me and they will never know, nor care, who the woman is in overalls, wearing a yellow hardhat, with the goggles and particulate respirator mask and ear mufflers standing 10 hours every day at the conveyor belt sorting garbage for $11.15 per hour before tax. If she looks up she will see stencilled on the wall, in faded black letters two feet high, 'The average American tosses 4.4 pounds of trash every single day. 323.7 million people live in the United States, which equates to 728,000 tons of daily garbage – enough to fill 63,000 garbage trucks. BE PROUD. YOU ARE PART OF THE SOLUTION.'

Through the mufflers the noise of the machinery and trucks is damped down to the sound of distant thunder, but the whole giant plant, the size of three football fields, vibrates through the soles of their zip-sided, steel-cap boots. In the sorting room on the first floor in the Material and Recovery Station, two massive parallel conveyors bring up the garbage which has been dumped on the tipping floor below by an endless column of garbage trucks coming in from the four surrounding districts. The operating principle is simple: sort out what can be recycled to reduce what goes into the landfill. Everything that can be sorted mechanically is done by machine, the rest by hand. Standing belly-up to the conveyors, are women. Cheap labour.. Mexicans, Guatemalans, Nicaraguans, Puerto Ricans, Hondurans, a few blacks, no whites, wearing leather aprons, special long yellow protective gloves up to their elbows, pulling out stuff as it goes by at 5mph, faster than you think, so all gestures are automatic as they toss without looking paper, plastic, metal, glass, toiletries, diapers, hypodermic needles, batteries, you name it, into large bins waiting behind. What is not sorted ends up in the compactor which compresses 65 tons of trash per hour into 37 feet long, 7 feet wide slabs, each weighing 24 tons, 48,000 lbs., the maximum load the trucks can take to the landfill 60 miles away.

'It is what the Professor wanted his kids to see. From the expression on their faces I do not think they regard sorting trash as a long-term career opportunity.

I am the obligatory Latino/Latina face on the Beverly Hills City Council. I have no official position but, since I represent Garbage Disposal - make that Refuse Collection - speak the language and have a head for figures, I am 'co-opted' to various projects, just as they co-opt our obligatory black, Sammy. Sammy Sunshine, Poolman to the Stars, 'does' our pool and those of most of the Councillors. He's not really black because his Dad's Japanese and his Mother comes from Trinidad. He also has, inexplicably, blue eyes and a physique that acrobats in the Cirque du Soleil envy, and he knows my secret - I am crazy about him. But so is every woman who sees him out there in the sunshine by their pool, stripped to the waist, singing to himself, a quiet smile on his face. "Life's good, dahlin!", is how he greets you. We make a good team, Sammy and I, co-conspirators in a white man's world. We are paid peanuts - but need the money.

Give or take, 35,000 people are residents of the City, 55% female, the rest men or others. I didn't make that up, it's a category here as you can see in the latest census: Caucasian 88.2%, Asian 6%, African-American 2%, Other 4%

That's what Sammy calls me: Otherwise, what you doin? (How 'bout a date?) Other than that, you free? (Ref. Husband) N'otherwords, yo no different than me. (Black-n-beautiful!) I love him. He makes me laugh in a world where laughs are rare as steak. He also never lets on he knows Alejandro has sneaked back into the country.

The median age of men in the City is 45, less if you include the 200,000 'moving' population of 'dailies' coming to work. Not on the Council, where it's more like 145, an ancient rearguard determined to protect the status quo, their god-given right to a pension, free medical, and their initialed parking spot. They've put 44 items on this month's list of City Council Priorities which Sammy and I text back and forth to decide if we want to volunteer for an appointment before they stick us with something like maintaining the 83 Eucalyptus trees on Civic Center Drive.

The choices range from Seismic Retrofit, Water Conservation, Traffic Mitigation on the delayed metro station at Rodeo Drive, Anti-Voter Fraud, CCTV expansion, Autonomous Vehicles, and, Sammy's favourite, Marijuana, use of, pros and cons. "Finally, somethin' right. Buy from the Pros, sell to the cons. Let's volunteer yo pretty ass for that - I'll ride shotgun," he says.

Each of the 44 items is headed with an instructional verb from a lexicon: support, expand, coordinate, oversee, implement, explore, complete, require, attract, continue, update, evaluate, expand, prepare, develop, utilise, examine, create, conduct, pursue, assess, acquire, to name just half, and, despite our wishes, we're stuck with:

E&S: REMINDER: The city of **Beverly Hills, California, 90210** is one of the most iconic affluent communities in the nation. **And its mayor is probably the most beautiful, intelligent and dynamic city official in the country** . . . . a blonde bombshell of a woman known to all by her initials, **LB,** who is serving her third term as mayor of the wonderful little city set right in the heart of Los Angeles, surrounded by the much larger Los Angeles County and West Hollywood. (Huff. Post)

E&S: Public Safety. Continue to strengthen the ability of Police, Fire and Emergency Management to prevent and respond to incidents and emergencies. **Work** plans to include: Police facility upgrades, design and purchase of a new Command Center; **train** all Fire personnel in Tactical Emergency Medical Services, participate in the California Department of Health Care Services-sponsored Ground Emergency Medical Transportation reimbursement program; **work** with School District on updating disaster and safety plans, stockpiling of resources; Homeland Security Strategic Plan implementation

Develop Masterplan for facility upgrades to the existing PD Facility including potential expansion. **Implement** a new Crime Impact Team to address crime trends. **Develop** a succession plan. **Update** the PD's policy manual and implement an automated system. PD to evaluate body camera program. PD to implement strategic plan. **Enhance and expand** current PD social media presence with a planned strategy. **Explore** feasibility of the Nurse Practitioner Program. **Complete** purchases of fire engine and fire truck and explore donating retired fire engines. **Transfer** the CERT

Program. **Complete** Point of Dispensing (POD) Plan. **Conduct** monthly emergency management training, drills, and exercises. **Continue** stockpiling resources **Increase and coordinate** disaster planning for people with disabilities and others with access and functional needs. **Update** Inundation Map. Complete Debris Management Plan. **Interface** with medical centres to assist with CMS Compliance. **Report** results.'

'Right,' said Sammy, 'No problemo.'"

+++

"Cut."

The weather had changed with sullen clouds rolling in from the Pacific to mar the habitual postcard-pretty image of California.

"Can't shoot in this. Let's take a break," said Blackbird Crow. "You feel like riding out to Pepperdine with me? I've got a surprise for you."

"I don't like surprises," said Fortunato.

"You'll like this one. Louisa, my assistant, dug up one of your old man's films on videocassette, a black and white film, of the first World War?"

"'Alias!' Christ, how's that possible? Where'd she find it?"

"Well, let's say she had some help. The Motion Picture Academy identified Monogram Pictures who bought several of his screenplays in the '30s. They made 'Alias' and a western and sold his script of 'Queen Christina' to Rouben Mamoulian."

"The old man told me he didn't get a dime for that. Bastard Mamoulian was clever. The talkies had just started. Once he had Garbo on board he shot it like an old silent film because he knew the public wanted nothing more than the chance to watch her. I've seen it. Something like a third of the footage is of her, full face, left profile, right profile, in those tight close-ups blurred at the edges. He didn't give a shit about Christina, her story, historical accuracy, or anything that came between the audience and Garbo. One of the studio hacks, an English fellow, got the credit for writing, but Rouben had a laundry list of writers he used on it, 7 or 8 all told.

Sam Behrman did the dialogue; even Ben Hecht had a shot, but got no credit. Mamoulian used some of the old man's stuff, also uncredited, cheeky sod. I've seen clips from 'Alias' but never the whole movie. Is that what we're going to see?"

+++

CHAPTER FOUR

Socrates' Café:
One world,
The examined life,
A long day's journey into night.

+++

The distant church bells for Matins reminded the gunmaker that he had worked through the night and it was now Sunday. He stood up from his bench as a throb of memory pricked his conscious, bringing back the image of an ancient aunt whose sole task was to see the orphaned boy got to church on time. He rubbed the pain from his aching back. The traced outline of the weapon he was going to print lay on the bench. He knew what it represented. A killer's gun. What he could not fathom was why go to the trouble when for a few dollars at any gun fair you could buy an entire arsenal, no questions asked. He knew the statistics by heart, the mad penchant people had for deadly acts of violence. In the United States alone this insanity killed one person every fifteen minutes, 35,000 per year, over 2 million since the start of the Second World War, four times more than all the military casualties suffered by the Americans, even adding in the Korean War, Vietnam, Iraq, and Afghanistan. With 5% of the world's population Americans owned 42% of privately held firearms, 88 guns for every 100 Yankee. His bread and butter. Because of his expertise in advanced composite materials, specifically in ceramic matrix composites, he had been contracted to build extremely lightweight handguns and ever since the release online of 3D printable files for a gun ten

41

years before, he had adapted his knowledge to this new method of fabrication. But, and it was a worrisome qualification, very, very few people knew of his skill. How did they know? And who were 'they'?

+++

CBS, San Diego. 6.30am PDT
'The National Hurricane Centre in Miami issued the following advisory: In the Pacific, tropical storm Edward has moved slowly north north-east with sustained winds increasing to 120 miles per hour, gusting to 150 miles per hour, and is now categorised as a Category 4 Hurricane. The expected landfall is south of Camp Pendleton, near San Diego.'

+++

With the lights out, in the darkness of the movie theatre in Pepperdine, the picture had the quality of an old black-and-white newsreel with fuzzy definition, low contrast, marred by dirt and scratches. Students sat thrust forward in anticipation. Glancing across to Fortunato, Blackbird Crow, dressed in a fringed buckskin shirt the colour of old wheat, his long black hair plaited down his back, raised his eyebrows. "Here we go, "he said.

+++

*On a dark night, distant searchlights crisscross as a title scrolls across the screen – '**The Western Front, Verdun, World War** I, **1917**' - A field of deep snow stretches to the horizon; moonlight sifts through high clouds, sending shadows across the snow as a few snowflakes drift down. Close on undulations in the snow, trenches, lines of trenches. In the trenches are lumps covered in snow. One lump moves.*

"What's that?" A girl's voice in the auditorium.

Soldiers, hundreds of exhausted soldiers, fast asleep and on the soundtrack, in German, softly, as if heard in a dream, 'Punkt, Punkt, Komma, Strich - Fertig ist das Mondgesicht.' The voice is young, almost boyish.

Close tight on a gloved hand in a German field-grey uniform as the forefinger finishes drawing the moon's face in snow fallen on a window-ledge.

The audience shivers, then jumps, as *BAM!* -

Suddenly a star light climbs into the sky, its magnesium flare explodes and abruptly, machine-gun and rifle fire open up and by the muzzle flash of the guns reflecting on snow the British soldiers come awake grabbing for weapons.

Close tight on the barrel of a machine-pistol firing down through the snow rim of a trench, massacring the soldiers below in great gouts of blood and flesh. "Hans?" A voice says "Hans" as the machine-pistol swings back on a wounded soldier trying to get up while in German, as softly as before . . . "Punkt, punkt, komma, strich . . ."

BAM! Another star light climbs into the night sky, its magnesium flare explodes. Machine gun and rifle fire intensify. In chiaroscuro, between flashing vignettes of battle, the soundtrack pounding, warily, amid the ghastly carnage in the trench, two German soldiers covered in mud advance, putting a bullet in the head of those few British soldiers still alive. "They're finished," one says, exhausted, leaning against a bloodied snowbank as up and down the line the guns fall silent.

A girl squeezes her neighbour's hand, her eyes staring, hating what she is watching, unable to look away.

"Who's left?" the other German asks.

"No one, just us two." With his boot he rolls a body onto its back. "Christ, they're just kids!"

"So are we -" A moan stops him. At his feet the wounded soldier opens his eyes, looks steadily up at him, says, "It is you. Fancy that, Hans. Never thought of you on Jerry's side . . . "BLAM! He is shot between the eyes.

A girl screams . . .

"Cut!" Blackbird Crow said, standing at the rostrum in front of the packed auditorium.

As the house lights came on, he added, "I am sure you are all familiar with Johann Gottlieb Fichte, who in 1880 famously said that 'you could not remove a single grain of sand from its place without thereby changing something throughout all parts of the immeasurable whole.' Shakespeare," here he smiled, nodding to BP sitting in the front row of his audience, "called it 'the concatenation of phenomena'. We know it, in Ray Bradbury's original coinage, as the 'butterfly effect', the idea that one butterfly flexing its wings in Asia could, weeks later, predicate a tornado in Kansas. The thrust of my lecture today is to posit a formulation starting with you, each individual here, as the butterfly and to imagine what effect you will have on the world five years from now and even fifty years from now and how this may be shown on film as we have just seen. I propose a collegial experiment where each of you butterflies will imagine an event in the past, where, perched on a twig, you flexed your wings and caused something to happen in the unimaginable future. Let us begin with our visitor from a rival campus, UCLA, the Professor Emeritus of Adventure. I give you, Professor Fortunato Crollalanza."

Chaos theory and the sensitive dependence on initial conditions fundamental to the butterfly having any effect was not in the forefront of Fortunato's mind at the moment he was singled out, and he was miffed the movie had been cut, but he loved the spotlight. As the audience clapped, he stood up.

"Ants," said BP. "I am fascinated by ants. Did you know they have been here for 120 million years? And we've been here for, what, 200,000? Who knows better how to survive? In our garden in Genoa, when I was a child, I spent hours crouching or lying on my stomach, my chin on my fist, watching them go in and out of their little hole in the ground to which all their trailways led. Imagine the journeys back and forth by thousands and thousands of ants to make those trails. Do they know what they are doing, that looking down on them I could see a map of all their activities and wonder why the trail for no apparent reason suddenly made a wide detour only to return within inches of where it left and then continue straight over hills two inches high and rocks that were pebbles? I would try to help them by making a shortcut to eliminate the oxbow detours with tiny walls of sand and dirt only to find the next morning they had breached my walls and resumed the long march around the detour. I once saw one walk across a mirror and I could see its back and its belly simultaneously and in bed at night I would wonder if I lived in their world or they lived in mine and tried to imagine what went on through the little hole down into their nest and whether the straggler I had seen carrying a leaf three times his own size made it safely home."

+++

Clapboard #6 - *An anthill.* The camera tracks ants coming and going. Voiceover:

Weime: *We can't see him because we can only distinguish black and white, night from day. But we know he's there, a mass giving off heat and smell, both reported in detail back to me by the antennae loaded with pheromones of my selfless workers. We, I and Me are the same in an ant colony, one and at the same time separate, hence my name. We are eusocial. I am the only Queen in our colony and all I do is lay eggs. I carry enough sperm in a sac from the males, now all dead, with whom I mated and can make up to 1000 babies a day if needed for many years. Most are non-reproductive females who live one year, do most of our work, cleaning the nest, tending the larvae until they become pupae and eventually adults, fetching food down from the surface, acting as workers, guards and foragers; the rest have short lives, 90 days to 6 months.*

The complex architecture of our nest has a main vertical tunnel, numerous secondary shafts and nearly two hundred horizontal chambers giving off them. They all have drainage and can be individually sealed. The ambient temperature is normally a comfortable 80° Fahrenheit, optimum for peak activity. Completely in the dark with no plans, no rules, no group or individual giving instructions, we instinctively build these elaborate structures as we have done for millennia. I live in an oval chamber 7 feet under the ground and never go out. Since our lifecycle is seasonal, once a year I give birth to thousands of winged sexual males and females tasked on a certain day to fly away to establish new colonies. Most of them will die but a few females will become me in another place, gathering to themselves their own colony in an endlessly repetitive biological clockwork whose minutes and hours are measured in millions of generations of ants. There are more than 20,000 different species of us, inhabiting every continent except Antarctica, in colonies of a few hundred living in a mango seed to super-colonies where, over vast areas, many ant colonies unite. Ours is amongst the biggest with 30 ant mega-populations along a 3700-mile stretch of Southern Europe's coast estimated to have millions of nests and queens and trillions upon trillions of workers. We recognize genetic differences in order to mate, cooperate, and try to avoid aggression.

Our colony is still young, we've been here less than two years, with a population of just under 240,000 which I regulate depending on the seasons, and the availability of food and water in this small corner of earth. We will survive 10 or 20 years or until I die. Ant nests are socially complex, with no one ant in charge giving orders, not even me, the Queen. We, collectively, 'know'. Within our hierarchy the young stay close to me to protect me and the babies, but as they grow older they move out to other jobs further away based on their personal preference, always attuned to the proportional balance of tasks we need for the colony to survive. Collectively we work as an empathic uber-mind sharing all the information gleaned by each of us as we go about our different chores to constantly update weather reports, where to find food, beware of enemies, set traps, and find the best sites in case we have to move. At any one time as many as a quarter of all the ants are resting, but even resting they know and share all we know as it happens. We are interconnected by underground passages to surrounding nests, meet and exchange information with the ants from neighbouring colonies, but carry in our DNA the survivors' instinct - you're on your own.

At the front door of our colony is the midden, an ever-growing composite pile of dirt, sand, twigs and other stuff being excavated and carried up to the surface in the mandibles of myriads of workers, each of them able to carry twenty times their own weight. What is carried up must be carefully put down so that it doesn't roll back into the nest and we have special workers on the surface who monitor and help to make sure our exit is safe. They also guard against parasitic-ants who try to sneak in and steal our larvae, and right now they are signaling an alert: the mass has moved.

+++

BP: "But one day I was bored and, I don't know why, I saw the gardener had left the hose with which he watered the plants to go and do something else, and I stuck the end of it into the ant hole, turned the water on to see what would happen, and heard my mother call me in to lunch. I didn't want to go but she yelled at me so I ran into the house and left the hose with the water running which ended up causing a flood at the bottom of the garden and I got spanked and sent to my room without dessert because I was bad and the gardener got scolded for leaving the hose unattended."

+++

Weime: *Of course it was a disaster - not the water in itself, we deal with that every time it rains and normally have ample warning through our ability to sense changes in temperature and humidity - no, the disaster was that we had no warning and the waterfall cascading into the nest caused significant damage as it flooded multiple chambers with mud and clay before they could be sealed. Most ants can survive about 24 hours under water since we don't have lungs but breathe through spiracles, small holes in our bodies, and we are so light we can walk across the surface of puddles. The torrent never got near me at my level but the reported damage had to be dealt with quickly, the dead carried off to be dumped in the midden, the injured gathered, a triage organised to determine those ants too badly hurt who would be left to curl up and die and those that could be saved, cleaning their wounds, applying appropriate antibiotics to fend off infections, our manic mantra for cleanliness and fear of contaminating the nest dictating all our actions. After two hours the flood stopped and in a flickering of pheromones and antennae we calculated I had to replace 232 casualties and, when that was done, life went on . . .*

Abruptly Fortunato said "Thank you," and sat down. "Thank you, Professor," said Blackbird Crow.

+++

In the car driving home, he looked across at Fortunato. "Ants, eh? Why did you stop? You had the kids in the hollow of your hand. You were going to say something else and changed your mind, right?"

"Yes," said Fortunato, "it's odd, and I didn't feel like telling them, but even now, after all these years, I have a guilty twinge when I'm on the terrace in that corner of the garden. Standing there is an amazing Femminello Ovale lemon tree, under the fragrant leaves of which, Serafina, the resident witch, who must be nearly 80 now, takes her siesta every afternoon in a chaise-longue with her two Persians lying on her lap, the same two that are at her feet in the full-length portrait the old man made of her which hangs in the library like something by Boldini or Sargent. I resent her living in what I think of as my mansion although I know my parents never owned it and only lived there as glorified caretakers until the day, unannounced, the old man turned up with his new bride and a couple of children to turf us out. I was four or five at the time and didn't grasp why my parents had to bow and scrape to these newcomers and do as they were told. Now I know."

"Sorry?" said Blackburn Crow. "I didn't get all that. Serafina who?"

"My ancestor's wife. The old man I mentioned who got restitution from the Commies. She runs the show now. Can't stand the bitch."

+++

I had been summoned to her presence when she heard I was back in Europe scouting locations for the field-trip I was planning for my students. As if she could read my mind from where she lay, Serafina said, 'Why the hangdog expression, Fortunato?'

'I once drowned some ants under where you're sitting,' I said.

'And you feel sorry?'

'As a matter of fact, yes, I do.'

'Very noble. Don't worry, there are millions more.'

'You wouldn't understand.'

'Ants? Or you?'

I always felt breathless talking to Serafina, as if she used up all the available oxygen. She was famously well-read and annoyingly well informed as she proved with her next remark.

'What is it that so fascinates you about young girls?'

'Firm flesh.' No point in not telling the truth.

'Haven't you grown out of that? All this hopping around for a man your age. How old are you anyway?'

'Fifty-seven.'

'Liar. You're over sixty. Christ, where do you find the energy? Isn't it a case of plus ça change, plus c'est la même chose?'

'Not when they reach their sell-by date.'

'Incorrigible. I'm surprised you haven't been hung and quartered. Tu n'aura jamais de paix dans le caleçon, tu sais. Your college has already informed me they insist a chaperone must accompany the girls on your erstwhile field trip and we will be charged for her expenses. Don't look so incredulous. They believe you are living in a ménage-à-trois with Savera and one of your students, a Mexican girl.'

'Arrant nonsense. Not that I would mind, mark you. They're a couple, worse luck. Did you know about Savera?'

She ignored my question and just looked at the view from the terrace over Genoa, out over the bay to the grey-blue blush of the Mediterranean in the distance, then, to my surprise, said, 'What do you make of this?' - and gave me a dusty manilla envelope. Two round washers riveted to the seal flap and the body of the envelope were joined by string twisted in a figure eight. On the flap someone had written *Se trovato, si prega di tornare a . . .* 'with her address in Genoa to which the envelope should be sent. 'Recognise the handwriting?' she said.

'No.'

'It's the old man's,' she said. And then added, 'Don't just look at it, open it.'

Inside there was a notebook, a heavily annotated copy of a screenplay and a covering letter from a retired schoolteacher:

Salutamu Signora,

I write to explain to you how this envelope came into my possession. I am the schoolteacher, now retired. I regret to inform you that with the disappearance of the owner, and no heir or other claimant stepping forward, uninhabited, over the years the Roman watchtower so laboriously restored by the old man has sadly decayed. There have been rumours of expropriation by the State but they have fizzled out since a Genoan Fondazione pays the annual property tax. (You may already know of this?) Only our ageing shepherd on his eleemosynary rounds to find sustenance for his flock goes there. Each time he gathers a bunch of wildflowers and from the parapet wall drops them 50 metres down the face of the cliff onto the ledge, where, carved into the stone itself, lies the statue of a young woman, eternally asleep, her hair fanned out to cover her face. It is signed anonymously, A.Friend.

This winter snow fell on Mount Etna and the surrounding countryside, an event that delighted schoolchildren when La Stampa reported schools would be closed and warned of icy roads with temperatures below zero. Seeking shelter, the shepherd, more used to the sun and drought, thought of the tower and was dismayed to find the front door torn off its hinges, the interior vandalised, obscene graffiti on the walls, the furniture trashed and bits of it used to build a fire in the middle of the floor, blackening the ceiling and blistering the paint. Broken books and papers were strewn everywhere, some used as toilet paper embedded in frozen lumps of faeces. It was as if a church had been sacked. He did his best to clean up the mess he told us in Rizzo's, but there was only so much a man could do and without tools he couldn't even rehang the front door.

'But I found this,' he said, 'right at the back of a shelf on the first floor. They're written in a language I cannot read but maybe you can.'

+++

"With the kind of mail service we have nowadays I suppose I'm lucky it got here," Serafina said. Have you ever read a screenplay?"

"Yes," Fortunato said.

"Well, I had not. I didn't expect to see the pictures in my head when I read the words. It's about the war. His war. Listen -"
OPEN: *SCROLL TITLE –*

"VERDUN, THE WESTERN FRONT, WORLD WAR I, 1917 " on a black night.

FADE TO:

EXTERIOR. A field of deep snow to the horizon ; moonlight, sifted through high clouds, sends shadows across the snow as a few snowflakes drift down. Close on undulations in the snow, trenches, endless trenches stretching into the distance. In the trenches are lumps covered in snow. One lump moves, soldiers, exhausted soldiers, fast asleep.

VOICE OFF

(in German, softly, as if heard in a dream)

Punkt, Punkt, Komma, Strich -

Fertig ist das Mondgesicht.

Close tight on a gloved hand in a German field-grey uniform as the forefinger finishes drawing the moon's face in the snow:

HOLD . . .

"Can you see that? It took me a couple of hours to read and it was dark when I finished but it made me understand what he once told me about how he enjoyed the war. He said 'it's why I reenlisted. I found actual combat exhilarating - life lived in the most intense way imaginable. I suppose I was reckless when I was young. Yes, fairly reckless, and I've stayed that way. So you could say I was too stupid to be frightened.'" Serafina nodded. "E verro." she said, then flipped to the last page. "You'll have to read the whole thing but this is how it ends -"

And read the last lines out loud:

'CUT TO:

KATE SANBOURNE stands, pulls out of her purse a beautiful dark-red leather presentation case, gives it to him.

KATE (continues)

. . . and I want you to have it.

(and kisses him again)

Suddenly, all thumbs, Inspecteur NABON fumbles open the latch, opens the case, looks down at the crushed Victoria Cross nestled awkwardly in its outlined velvet space. CLOSE TIGHT. Even battered, the words 'FOR VALOUR' can still be made out.

KATE (continues, V.O.)

Whoever the original owner was I'm sure he would be proud to know you have his medal now.

FADE OUT..'

"I was sitting here just as I am sitting now," Serafina said, "and I made a decision. I want to show you what I found. Come."

Nodding to herself, Serafina stood and, followed by Fortunato, slowly walked indoors, up the three flights of stairs to the attic room used for storage. Switching on the lights in the dusty space, she wove her way past furniture, filing cabinets, rolled carpets, boxes of books, shelves of pottery and kitchen implements, a life-size portrait of a girl wearing a blue kaftan with a turquoise-green and coral necklace standing on a rock in a field surrounded by a herd of goats and sheep, until she finally found a Victorian roll-top desk crammed with papers and a locked central drawer, a small brass key in the lock.

"I hesitated to open it," she said, "because I knew what lay inside and wondered for my own sake if it were not best forgotten. I saw it briefly years ago and thought nothing of it at the time amongst so much junk." Abruptly she twisted the key and pulled open the drawer. "Look," she said, and Fortunato looked down on a beautiful dark-red leather presentation case inside which was a crushed medal lying on purple velvet. He didn't know what to say.

"The original owner? Could it be him?" said Serafina. And remembered what she had thought - If it was the old man, who was he? She had had a premonition about the notebook before she opened it. Why, she thought, wasn't he here to share the moment instead of leaving her to go gallivanting off to the ends of the earth? What had he said? 'Turn the page.'

They had just come home from meeting with lawyers in Zurich, the Isle of Man, Grand Bahama and Curaçao where she had been given powers of attorney to effectively run the foundation set up by her husband. She had acquiesced, signed the hundreds of documents put in front of her and in so doing became one of the richest, most powerful women in the world.

'Why? 'she had said, when at last they were alone at home. 'It's what we have to do now,' the old man said. 'What's the point of repeating what we've already done? We have to turn the page before we get bored with each other, forever reliving the lives we've already lived.'

She was, she knew, both saved and absolved by the old man who told her children that wonderful story and mysteriously appeared in the night to spirit them out of Sicily after destroying Lividiani's fortress, both the saddest and the most beautiful moment of her life.

"Now he's gone." she said. "And fate has put these papers of his in my hands, something he could not have foreseen." Then she added, "Are you hungry?"

Before Fortunato could answer she led the way back downstairs to the kitchen to instruct the cook what to prepare for dinner and then remembered it was her day off.

"Never mind, " Serafina said, "it will only take a few minutes to prepare a salad with some cheese, bread and a glass of wine. You open the wine."

Then, seated at the kitchen table, she opened the notebook, its pages yellowed with age smelling faintly of dust. On the first page, in large fine capital letters, a childish hand had written 'TO MY FRIEND' and on the next page 'The Bookshelf Poems', with a date, 1968, and crammed on each of the following pages were poems, astonishing in their maturity, the first being titled 'Boarding Pass'. It was short, like a haiku.

"Read to me," Serafina said to Fortunato:

"Omen.

'Sleeping arrangements:

beautiful bodies

flying solo."

followed by

"Aesthetic Theory:

A lover's discourse,

'Nobody's perfect.'"

On and on - Serafina would not let him stop reading even when he said "I feel we're eavesdropping. This is private. A communion. An intercourse of words to unrequited love."

Dozens of pages. Tens of dozens of poems.

And on the last page:

Will you miss me when I'm gone?

Between the sheets, the promise, the captive flesh

Game for anything? Tempting fate.

A Man, with

A Maid.

All the trimmings behind closed doors.

Great expectations, the last of the wine

Will you miss me when I'm gone?

Will you miss me when I'm gone?'

with a signature at the bottom of that last page in the same childish hand,

Sophia, today I am 14

Thank you for being my friend.

Finis.

Serafina found herself breathless, her mind scarcely comprehending she was listening to the words of a child for the old man. Words of love and longing - 'Sleeping arrangements, beautiful bodies, going solo' . . . she wept. "It is so incredibly sad," she said, tears running down her face as she raised her hand to wipe her cheek where the distant memory of a blow is imprinted, the memory of her shame from 30 years ago, and she is not sure if she is crying for herself or for Sofia or, in relief, for the miracle of her union with the old man. 'Turn the page,' he'd said.

"Are you alright?" Fortunato asked.

'Sorry," she said. "Sorry. Years ago I was a victim, part of something despicable. I got carried away. Forgive me." And regaining her composure, she said, "Anyway, it's important it be remembered. The old man was preoccupied by memory, you know. Unforgettable years forgotten, if you don't remember them, he said. In a way, specific memories haunted him, like the boy with whom he shared a desk at his boarding school. That's in the screenplay. It was personal and unique to him, which in many ways identified him, and then there was what he referred to as the 'collective memory', the shared memory, that came about in conversation or that was recalled over a photograph or re-read letter, or like this, these poems. He was deeply concerned lest he forget something and by forgetting make the thing no longer exist, vanish without a trace, robbing it of its being or having been. Maybe that's why things that are strange in a junk shop also have something familiar about them?"

"Déjà vu?"

"No, that's not what I mean, more déjà vécue. Like a forgotten memory forever lost, out there in some dusty limbo, an old piece of furniture that looks familiar just as you look familiar to that piece of furniture. But, enough of the past, that's not why I've asked you here. I need your help. The US Department of the Treasury has been making enquiries about the provenance of our funds."

"Surely . . ?"

She shook her head. "He's been gone for years. With his other family."

"What other family?"

"The one in Africa . . . or what's left of it. I'm not the only wife, you know."

"Good heavens!"

"He had a medical degree. From Heidelberg. Became a doctor or something on the family estates in Africa between the wars. Now he's out of reach in a Zen Buddhist retreat in Japan, supposedly to learn calligraphy . . . if he's still alive."

"It's unbelievable . . . what do you mean, if?"

"He'd be 127. What are the odds?"

Fortunato stared at her.

"Do close your mouth," she said, just as a nun, slim to the point of anorexia, came out of the mansion onto the terrace. "Ah, my daughter, Sister Allegra. I believe you met once?"

+++

Allegra B.: "1984, the Olympics in LA, I was 18 and the golden haired boy in front of me would not let go of my hand. He rowed for Italy in the coxless fours and we were introduced between heats at Lake Casitas in the hills near Ojai and the chemistry between us caused his crew to make signs of the devil and I ended up deflowered by him in the Marquis' house above the Roxy where the French pole vault team was staying because they did not want to live in the Olympic Village. L'Equipe had a picture of all of us naked in the jacuzzi under a sarcastic headline accompanying a critical article about the team's lack of 'serieux' in training and who should win the only gold and bronze medals? - Right! We celebrated at Le Dôme, where Eddy, the owner, laid on a feast, everybody got drunk toasting our two heroes, standing on the tables singing the Marseillaise wearing nothing but their medals and that English kid with the red Cadillac convertible then drove them, still naked, waving the Tricolor down Sunset with motorcycle cops as flanking outriders, sirens blaring. My mother hadn't a clue. And now I'm a nun.

God's ways are mysterious. I hadn't seen BP since that time, and now here he was, 42 years later, dressed up in a faded Lothar-blue caftan, red-and-white chequered turban on his head, his blue eyes still full of mischief

- our chemistry intact. I touched the white rope around my waist with the three knots to remind myself of my vows: poverty, chastity and obedience.

'No stripy black and white silk trousers, eh?' He remembered all right, probably remembered how difficult they were to get off.

'Ciao, BP,' I said. How is a nun supposed to greet her long lost lover? I could feel the intense scrutiny of my mother. She was reticent about discussing the past and so was I, yet, to myself, the thud of lust long forgotten would be an interesting diversion in my usually boring confessions. In my coif and simple and black veil, framing my face and covering my shorn head, dressed in the brown habit of the Carmelites, an ivory crucifix on a chain around my neck, my faith was plain and to be seen. But we are human, too. Even in the enclosed cloistered Order that is a convent, the Mother Superior always encouraged us to acknowledge our frailty, confess, and pray for forgiveness. When I was ready, it took over twenty years, with the blessings of our monastery, I became an urban hermit doing work and ministry out in the community, her lessons stood as a firm template for how a Sister should conduct herself. Though no longer a monastic, when I'm on the island I still do the Liturgy of the Hours every day in my little chapel. This was one of the most difficult things to commit to during my postulancy, but just repeating the invitatory 'Lord, open my lips. And my mouth will proclaim your praise' which gave me goosebumps when I first said it, now opens the page on each new day, and to hourly recite the versicle 'God, come to my assistance. Lord, make haste to help me', even if I don't follow through and recite all the obligations, reaffirms my vocation. Lauds, first thing in the morning when I wake up, and Compline, in the evening, are the prayers that bookend each day and buttress my faith. Thus armoured, I said 'Would you excuse us, Mother, I would like to have a private word with BP.'

Mothers, it must be a built-in reflex, instinctively protect their young and mine went to say something negative, forgetting I was no longer her kid but a 62-year old woman. She must have read my thought because she revised what she had in mind and with a domestic flourish of 'I'll make us some tea,' left me to the languid contemplation of my old Lothario, unscrupulous and impertinent.

'Have you tried to imagine, BP, how different my life would have been if I'd never met you?' I said.

'No,' he said. 'I am much too selfish.'

'At least you recognize that. I am not ungrateful about what happened, only that it had hardly begun before it ceased to exist and I felt stranded. Hurt. Abandoned.'

'But alive to what might have been? The old rock and roll. Instead of pointing fingers ask yourself what you were doing there? By the way what were you doing there? You never told me.'

'My stepfather was exhibiting some of his paintings in the Olympic Art Competition downtown. As a family it was our first trip to America and for it to coincide with the Olympic Games made it that much more exciting. I remember we could only get tickets to secondary events like rowing and archery since the main stadium for athletics was sold out. I was with some Italian friends who knew one of the crew in your boat and -'

'The rest is history. I didn't mean the anecdotes, I meant the doing. That wasn't just chance, you wanted that to happen just as much as me.'

'I don't deny it. But three days later it was over, you were gone.'

'We lost in the quarter-finals and had to go home.'

'Without a thought for me.'

'On the contrary, short of a gold medal it was the best thing I could imagine winning. Everybody was jealous, even our coach. 'Che premio! Bastardo, Fortunato! Sei ben nominato.' he said. 'What a prize! Lucky bastard.'

A prize? That's what I was to the only man I have ever known. I was one of those who prayed at night and didn't believe in the day. Also superstitious, so who would want me now, is what I thought back then. And doubts. With my eyes wide open, how could I be so blind?

'Yes, a prize. Don't you remember what you looked like? You weren't skinny like you are now - sei una bomba.'

Not a description you would share on your CV trying to gain admittance to a convent and an ascetic life of prayer and contemplation."

+++

The British movie critic of The Guardian, reviewing the documentaries made by Blackbird Crow in the weekend edition of the newspaper, wrote:

'The singular style of Mr. Crow is akin to that involved in being on a crowded underground train headed for a distant terminus, with passengers, jostled by the motion of the train, getting on and off, occasionally making eye-contact, sometimes life changing, mostly not, their random thoughts filmed on handheld extremely expensive Red Weapon 8K cameras giving unlimited configurations in shooting and editing on the fly. L'effet Métro, as Cahiers du Cinéma has christened it. The most obvious reason to use this camera is the sensor. In the Weapon body or brain as RED likes to call it, is their HELIUM sensor which shoots 8192 x 4320 video at up to 60 frames per second, but the benefit of this is not something of which the average person would be aware. It's not about publishing at 8k, it's about flexibility in post. Being able to edit the footage with very minimal loss in image quality. Filmmakers can zoom into the footage, reframe, crop, all without any noticeable loss of sharpness. Crow uses this advantage to get perfect symmetrical compositions in post-production and gets better motion tracking, because more resolution means more detail to track. Intuitively he gets the most out of the camera's native ISO where its dynamic range capabilities are ideal and everything needs to be balanced to get the right amount of light on the sensor. Ambient sounds, dialogue, voiceover and music are intrinsic elements in the incredible mosaic of life, real or imagined, as seen through the eyes of an iconoclastic director following his instincts and his subjects into perils that would even daunt Pauline.'

CHAPTER FIVE

The Autograph Man,
He names all the names,
The untouchable, the crazed,
The woman most likely to . . .
Cut to the heart.

++++

Clapboard *#7 - BP/bedroom/BHPO*

BP: "Deep in the night, after getting back to the States jetlagged, I was recalling in a dream details of the moist, firm plumpness of young Allegra, when a gloved hand over my mouth woke me up and I looked into the eyes of a masked man with a gun. 'Give me your money or I'll kill you,' he said, the clichéd instruction delivered Hollywood Gangsta-style right on cue. And on cue I went into an Oscar-winning performance of an old invalid, struggling awake, sitting up in bed, trying to understand what was happening. 'Don't yell,' he said, removing his hand from my mouth, 'get up.'

'You shouldn't be here, I'm sick.' I said. 'You'll catch what I've got.'

'Shut the fuck up! Come on. Out.'

And he actually helped me out of bed, my hand on his shoulder, his on my elbow heaving me up. Close to, under his balaclava helmet he smelled of stale sweat and under his camouflaged tunic a pungent body odour made me gag. I pretended to stagger as we went into my dressing room. He had produced a pencil torch in the beam of which he nailed my wallet where I had left it on a shelf under my tie collection. 'Open it,' he said, 'show me the money,' but when he saw the few euros I'd brought back from Europe, hissed 'What's this shit?' and with a swipe of his hand swept all of it to the floor. That's when my brain started trying to tell me something, only to get sidetracked by the torch smacking me on the cheek as he said, 'You want me to kill you? Where do you keep the fucking money?'

'I just got back from Italy. I don't have any dollars.'

'Fuck that! Where's your gold Rolex?'

Another cliché. Since I didn't own a watch, leave alone a gold one, which it was hard to tell him, I reverted to my usual tactic to buy time, I lied. 'In the den,' I said, heading for the door to my bedroom. He hesitated.

'You going to walk out there with no pants on?' he said. I only slept in a T-shirt and walking bare-assed at home never bothered me; he obviously came from a different culture.

'What if somebody sees you?' A fine ethical point to bring up waving a gun about. 'Asshole.'

Anyway, we ended up in the den where I made a song and dance of trying to find the mythical watch, and, - the Lord loves his little tricks, - would you believe one of the kids had left his broken Swatch in a drawer? 'Here,' I said.

He took it from me in one hand while with the other he shone his pencil torch on it to identify the loot, just as my brain cleared and a window opened: where was the gun? Given the opportunity, I grabbed him by the balls.

I may look tatty and frail, but in fact I'm quite strong and crushing his scrotum and testicles was no great feat. Hanging on was a different matter. The man went berserk, howling in pain, out of control, lashing at me in a frenzied action to free himself, crashing into furniture, smashing a chair. I hung on and yelled for help.

The floor plan of our house was based on that of a two-dimensional drawing of a snail's shell, the common mathematical ratio found in nature that creates designs of surpassing simplicity. All the bedrooms faced out over Beverly Hills in a broad curve, the back of the 'shell' so to speak, such that each had a private terrace and could not be overlooked from the next room. The guest room next to my bedroom was occupied that night by a visiting French healer in Oriental Medicines, an elegant, middle-aged French woman given to meditation when she was not conversing with the Tibetan monks who came to consult her, and it was no small surprise to now see her leap to my rescue at 3 o'clock in the morning."

+++

Marie-Thérèse F.: "Men always think women are weak and fearful. I am a light sleeper and the noise that woke me was unnatural. Going into the corridor outside my room I could hear the sounds of a struggle and when I opened the door to the study, the den they call it here, in the semi-darkness I could make out the aura of the two men fighting, good and evil. I am laughed at by people when I tell them I can perceive their aura, but it is so. I am trained in many forms of the martial arts and taking up kiba-dachi, the horse stance - to observe before joining the fight - I began the ginga, the rhythmic dance I use before delivering an attack. I am an adept of this triangular footwork of capoeira, providing confusion while allowing me to maintain the torque I need to strike. Sensing an opening, I crouched in a paralelo, then launched an aù, changing my cartwheel at the last moment to land on the back of evil, my legs locked around his waist, my forearm in an armlock around his throat. This should have been the end but in a surprising move the man threw himself backwards shattering a glass table with me under him and BP on top - when the lights came on."

+++

Santiago G.: "I am called Santiago. My wife, Luciana, woke me up. There is a noise, go and see, she said. She is expecting so she is nervous. Our bedroom is at the far end of the house and when I went out into the corridor I saw Alejandro come out of his room with a machete. 'Get yours,' he said, which I did, and silently, on bare feet, the two of us went to investigate. We heard a great noise and then the crash of glass in the guardia and when we put on the lights, such a spectacle! There was blood everywhere. The French lady was badly hurt but would only let go of the bandito when I offered to cut off his head. Senor Fortunato - I cannot permit myself to call him BP - let go of the cojones of this man after Alejandro had tied him up with a clothes line from the laundry room. We found the gun where it had fallen. It was a child's toy pistol. And it was in this moment that the swat team arrived.

+++

SWAT (Special Weapons and Tactics) Team Commander Jennifer B.: "The call, police request assistance, was clocked in at 03.03am. A silent alarm from an address in the BHPO indicating a gunman with one or more hostages was relayed to us in Burbank. We put up a helo with two armed officers and ordered two vehicles to be deployed, each with a negotiator, rifleman and entry officer, all armed with submachine guns, sniper rifles, stun grenades and other assault weapons. First reports from the helo in a stationary position over the target house after firing magnesium flares to illuminate the scene showed a large compound with numerous people, including children, in night clothes, running away from the main structure. After disabling the locks on the steel gates leading to a 500-metre long driveway, the officers in the vehicles cautiously approached the house, bathing the front in headlights and searchlights, calling, by loudhailer, for the occupants to come out with their hands up. There ensued a shouting match, recorded, where one or more of the occupants called out 'Don't be frightened!' 'He's tied up!' 'It is safe.' 'Don't shoot! You can come in.' Not knowing who was calling or if the gunman had cohorts, following correct operational procedure, the assault teams fanned out, the riflemen deploying to sniping positions in pairs, while the entry teams contained the area and one of the negotiators again urged the occupants to come out unarmed and with their hands in the air. Someone, it has not been ascertained who at this stage in the investigation, then fired a short burst into the stucco above the oversized front door. A voice, recorded, said 'What the fuck!' and the door was violently thrown open. A semi-naked man, wearing only a T-shirt covered in blood, came out and said, 'Che cazzo! Are you mad? Shooting my house?' Through the loudhailer, recorded, the negotiator said, 'Put your fucking hands up.' 'Va fan culo!' the man said, putting up his hands, then walking down three steps onto the forecourt, turning to look up at the damage the bullets had made, 'You will pay for this.'

+++

BP: "Can you believe those morons shot up the house after we had the guy roped on the floor? Plus the interrogations we had to go through you'd think we were the crooks. And documenting all the Mexicans to prove they were not illegals, that they really were co-owners of the property which inevitably pissed off the cops. What's that? Alejandro? Alejandro who? Never heard of him. Anyway, all three of us end up in emergency at Cedars-Sinai on adjacent gurneys, with Slim Jim, our robber - no kidding, that's his name - in manacles, bitching about California's three strikes, how it wasn't armed robbery because it was only a toy pistol, and how much his balls were aching. I told him to shut the fuck up, look how much trouble he had made, and he said, yeah, wait till you do a stretch of hard time, you ever even been in jail? and I said, no, just born in one. Poor Marie-Thérèse had to have forty stitches put in her forearm where it had been slashed by glass from the broken table, whereas I thought I was lucky in only having a few small cuts and bruises until the medic attending me said, 'You looked at your left hand?'

'What about it?' All I could see was a few puncture marks and scrapes covered in red mercurochrome.

'Those are bite marks. He bit you.'

'What the fuck?' - such a versatile phrase in the vernacular I was beginning to feel at home with it - 'Put on some more antiseptic.'

'No. Bites over the knuckles where the skin is broken is taken very seriously and we may have to keep you overnight to check for swollen glands. You may get that near those bites as the lymph glands react to protect your body. Worse, I have to caution you about any sexual relationship, male or female, as you may carry HIV, or the human immunodeficiency virus, and if you should be in an intimate relationship, and your partner contracted Aids as a result, you could be liable for manslaughter.'

'What the fuck?'

'Slim Jim here, has been in detention for half his miserable life and, though he denies it, his record shows multiple homosexual encounters while incarcerated. There is a high incidence of HIV amongst inmates and the odds are he may be a carrier.'

'So? Test the fucker.'

'Not allowed. Invasion of a person's privacy.'

Only in America. So every month for six months I am tested and though I feel perfectly well and I am sure I do not carry any bugs my stress level spikes as each month rolls over and the next Aids test looms on the horizon. Slim Jim, whom I see in court as his case progresses, in which I am just one of dozens of witnesses against him for multiple holdups and armed robberies, always solicitously inquires 'how's it going, man?' One of the Sheriff's deputies came up to me to ask if I was sure I wanted to testify as the defendant would get a good look at me and, you know, one day he'd be free and . . . he left the threat hanging there. Or maybe it was a warning. I laughed. 'Slim and I are intimate friends, Officer,' I said, 'go ask him about his coglioni.'

+++

Slim Jim: "Course it's not my real name. I've had so many I can't remember the first one. My bastard Dad called me Bonce, and when smoked an' mad, Big Bonce, while he smacked the back of my head or pounded my shoulder or kicked me in the ass, didn't matter I was six years old, five years old, whatever, an' when he done with me he beat up on Sis when he wasn't tryin' to get in her jeans. She run away, can't say I blame her. Some trucker picked her up at the gas station she worked out on I-95, Mom said. When she can talk, 'cause she's drunk most times. They put me in Juvee when I was eleven. I had this newspaper round and you could tell which places were empty, folks gone on vacation or out of town, forgot to cancel their paper, most of their locks a joke I could jimmy open in five seconds - 'swhere I got my nickname. Nobody suspected me, the newsboy, and I only got caught when Lil Ali, fence I used back of Wilcox, on 37th near the IHOP, ratted me out. He's wearing the black-n-white in Maricopa County on a six year stretch for carjacking, livin' in those tents 120 in the shade, gets two 15-cent meals a day. Fucker. Here, they got me in TT - the Twin Towers Correctional Facility - that's downtown, built to hold five thousand prisoners, now got seventeen, thousand, triple tier bunks, macho gang bullshit, fuck you never no mind the monster, HIV baby, an' no condoms no way. HepC? 2000% higher than outside. Scary bad. Lots of clavo goin' round, deps in on it, cons, all them. Beat the shit outta you for nothin'. I've asked for transfer to the ding wing on the 7th floor, better in with the nuts than out on the floor. My guy, Court appointed kid lawyer can hardly find the john, is tryin' to plea bargain down to receivin' stolen goods. Fat chance. Three strikes, know what that means, Buck Rogers time, here to eternity. An' all because that fuckin' Granny jumped me. The worst thing? They confiscated my cell phone. My life's in there. They got it now."

+++

"Holy shit!", said Blackbird Crow. "CUT!"

+++

CHAPTER SIX

Pilgrim,
Now Sheba sings the song
Of mice and men, children of the rainbow.
Voices on the wind in the Dalai Lama's Secret Temple
(the Sacred Landscape, where wildflowers grow.)
Where the rivers flow
North

+++

After two days at sea and within sight of the island they were first spotted by a helicopter and then caught by the Italian Coast Guard cutter patrolling off Rabbit Beach, Lampedusa's hangout for Euro VIPs. Even arrested, for all of them it was a relief to get off the scow, away from people screaming and dying because they could not breath below deck, with others vomiting bile into the ceaseless waves amid the mob crammed above. Taken to the refugee centre in the middle of the island for documentation, medical inspection and interrogation they all told a similar tale of hardship, loss, stoicism and hope. The whole process was tiresome, a bureaucratic nightmare insisted on by worried wonks in Brussels who had nothing better to do than create endless multi-coloured files to justify their outrageous salaries, benefits and pensions with no regard for the realities in the field with temperature in the shade at 108°, perspiration staining your shirt, noting mundane details - 'We threw the bodies in the sea.' 'Two women gave birth on the boat, one baby lived.' 'My husband was washed overboard, my son tried to save him but did not know how to swim.' 'I was raped in the night.' 'I was robbed.' 'Nothing. I have nothing left.' - on and on. Elisabetta D'Angelo put her pen down. She had volunteered for work in the Red Cross to justify a long-held belief in doing good. Now she yawned. A widow, past 50, from Syracuse, the thought nudged her that this horror story was not what she had imagined and certainly not what she had signed up to do. She felt herself being watched. It was the same boy. She had already interviewed him, a scarecrow from Ethiopia, just turned 15, already three years on the road, who had camped on the beach in Libya for six months doing odd jobs to get together the money, 250 dollars, for the people smugglers who promised him a new life in Europe. Abébé. No second name. He had shown her his knife as if telling her a secret. And he had said something strange. Just before they disembarked, a man he had not seen on the boat before stood at the rail next to him smelling of soap. And patchouli. In that fly-filled filthy stench of oil, petrol fumes, vomit and blood, it was remarkable. This small detail worried her and she knew she should report it, and, as if he could intuit her thought, she saw Abébé nod at her, yes.

+++

"Mommmmy!" the alarm in her little girl's voice made Betty look up the stairs to the first floor where her daughter had her bedroom. "Mommy, come quick , Daisy's sick!" Daisy was her pet rabbit which lived in a cage next to her bed.

Down in the kitchen where she was making breakfast, Betty exchanged an exasperated look with the maid, Maria-Celestina. "Go see what she wants, please." Maria-Celestina stopped unloading the dishwasher, wiped her hands on her apron, and went up the stairs, conscious of how guilty she felt. Because the bedroom had an uninterrupted view down the driveway, this is where it happened every time the wife went shopping or took the kids to school and left them alone, both standing, Alan, the writer, the stay-at-home husband, behind her, holding her firmly by the waist while he pumped into her in a slow, syncopated rhythm that accelerated into a head-spinning climax which she loved, her palms pressed into the window ledge hoping it would be finished before they saw the car coming back. What had started as a lark, a flirtatious what-the-hell fling, had become an obsession. Once or twice they nearly got caught, comically separating, scrambling back

67

into their clothes, he theatrically back at his desk pretending to write, she switching on a conveniently placed vacuum cleaner, its domestic noise their best ally. Knowing she was promiscuous, a magnet to either sex, was a heady aphrodisiac. Until that overheard phone call. Momentarily her heart fluttered in panic. She should do something, say something. But what? Going into the bedroom now, she said, "Que pasa nina?"

"Look!" The little girl pointed at her rabbit, crouched in a ball of shivering fur pressed into a corner of the cage.

"She does not look sick," said Maria-Celestina. "She looks frightened."

+++

For a forensic accountant, J.J. Nicholson's appearance was deceptive. Nearly 60, barrel chested, an avid kite-surfer, father of five - four girls and a boy - he came into the squad room carrying an old-fashioned leather briefcase wearing a smile on his ruddy face. The Chief, from where he sat in his glass-fronted office in the U.S. Customs and Border Patrol's headquarters on Swan Road in Tucson, Arizona, watching the man, thought - is this guy tough enough? Little did he know.

After the usual introductions, two Alpha males smelling each other out, the Chief said, "I've read your CV. Impressive. You've put a lot of white-collars inside. But what we've got down here's a little bit different than cooking the books in a startup."

J.J. laughed. "Those guys in Silicon Valley think they're smart because they know how to fire up a computer. They wouldn't last a day with the bean-counters in Detroit."

"Detroit?"

"Yeah. You any idea how complicated just-in-time supplies have become. Build a car with no inventory. All the bits and pieces on the road in a critical supply chain going all over the world, depending on contracts in multiple currencies, hedging their value against the dollar, pay a bit of baksheesh here, a little forward trade there, big bets on the price of commodities, tax shelters in countries you've never heard of, profits held abroad and re-invested in derivatives not even the guys who wrote them understand . . . you want me to go on? Some of the bigger manufacturers own literally hundreds of subsidiaries,

some huge in their own right, with crossover financing and collateral arrangements going back decades. Get a worm in there good at covering his tracks, he's got room to wiggle and bloody hard to detect. So what's your problem?"

"No problem. I just don't want to get you killed."

J.J. smiled. "That a warning?"

"No, Mr. Nicholson, that's the way the game's played down here. The cartels don't take kindly to anyone snooping around their affairs. Homeland and CBP together employ over 280,000 people and, inevitably, there are a few bad apples in such a large workforce. I understand, heck, I even sympathise when guys complain they can't save anything for retirement. They book a little extra overtime? I don't care. But out and out corruption bugs me. I don't like it and I will not tolerate it."

J.J. nodded, took out a pad and pen from his briefcase, made a note, turned the pad around so that the Chief did not have to read upside-down to see: 'This room clean?'

For a moment taken aback, the Chief took the pen from J.J.'s hand and wrote: 'Think so.'

In turn J.J. wrote: 'Not good enough. Meet me in the Wooden Nickel.' And aloud he said, "Not sure we write the kind of insurance you guys need. But good of you to see me," put the pad in his briefcase, stood up, shook hands with the Chief and left.

An hour later, in the cool bedlam of the pub on Country Club Road, tucked into a booth, beer in hand, J.J. said: "Can't be too careful. How often do you check for bugs?"

"With our budget? Every six months - maybe."

"Six months! Shit, the technology changes every six weeks. I bet they even read your mail. Give you a tip. Move around, no two meetings in the same office. Same for phones, change 'em all the time and never, never keep the same number."

"Yeah?" The Chief scratched his grey hair. "Guess I'm getting too old for this. When I called you -" he hesitated.

"You hinted at graft and said you might have a suspect."

"More'n one, can't say exactly, maybe a team. One guy goes to a conference in Vegas, ends up in a bordello outside Reno, no big deal, except he's comped all the way. Begs the question: how does a border patrol officer get comped? Next, one con bitches to another in the holding pen about the heat, the shitty food and it's too fucking crowded and he got screwed 'cause he delivered and that CBP asshole in Douglas is goin' to get what he deserves. Then the officer's wife who puts down 20% in cash on a home loan she's negotiated with a young banker from Wells Fargo she's banging, buys a small condo out on that new golf course near Desert Canyon in Fountain Hills. Median household income in that part of Phoenix is north of $135 grand; they file a joint tax return of half that. Stuff. Noise. More'n there should be. You see it in the statistics. You know how everything returns to the mean over time? Even drugs. There's more on the streets than there should be, hard stuff. It's getting through and in my gut I have a bad feeling the cartels have infiltrated our force and are being fed info from the inside."

"Rules of engagement?"

"Not sure what you mean? You have carte blanche to audit payroll, accounts payable, receivables, inventory, whatever it takes."

"Personal bank statements? Dark funds used to pay snitches? Physical audit of drugs seized, stored, supposedly destroyed? Access to all communications, emails, wiretaps? You go down this path, Chief, you better have a very clear definition of where you want this to end because it will get dirty."

"I know." The Chief said. "It's why I'm worried about your safety."

J.J. looked at him for a long moment, weighing a decision. "You ever hear of Jihadi Airlines, Chief?"

"No."

"Back in the day I was an Inspector in a Special Forces unit, audit MP, tracking how the military squandered your tax dollars, three tours in Afghanistan, four in Iraq. We were trained by an old man borrowed from the Brits, guy was probably a hundred, spoke every dialect, could disappear even when he was standing next to you, vanish in front of your eyes crossing completely bare terrain. One day we had to escort some hard-core prisoners to Saudi, black camp run by the CIA. We were using a patched-up Antonov 124 the Soviets had left behind when they got licked, huge plane with a tailgate for loading tanks and shit, like flying in an empty warehouse. The 40 prisoners, all in

orange jumpsuits with hoods over their heads, were chained to rings bolted to the floor of the plane and just as we were taxiing for takeoff the old man told these guys they would be more comfortable without the chains and ordered us to free them. Two hours into the flight, over the Red Sea, we were sitting, eating and drinking in an armour-plated VIP suite just behind the cockpit when the old man gets up and goes in there. At 30,000 feet we felt the plane yaw and heard a tremendous roaring noise coming from the hold, then it was cut off and in the silence the old man stepped out of the cockpit and said, 'Say hello to Allah for me.' We overflew Saudi Arabia, landed somewhere in the Negev, re-fueled and headed back to Bagram with an empty plane. Total war, Chief, that's what the old man taught. Don't get into a fight if you don't know how to end it."

There was a pause before the Chief said, "Okay. How you want to run this?"

"I'll send in a couple of guys with the green eyeshades, do a standard audit. You won't see me and you won't know where I am, more importantly, nor will anyone else. If I need stuff my guys will tell you, and vice versa, always like this, in a noisy pub. We good?"

"I'm still concerned." The Chief frowned. "These people are animals. They're also smart, very well connected and have long memories and I would never forgive myself if something happened to you or your wife and kids."

J.J. grinned. "Watch." He took out a cell phone from his briefcase, speed-dialled a number, listened, and when the call was answered, said, "Hi, Honey. Plan B.", then he hung up, opened the back of the phone, removed the SIM card, closed the phone and dumped it in the trash on his way out of the restaurant.

+++

Reviewing the footage he'd shot, Blackbird Crow decided on a change of venue. He called the compound to speak to BP but the phone was answered by Marie-Thérèse. "There is a problem," she said. "He cannot be disturbed."

"Can I help?"

"I think not. He is questioning some of the people who live here. It is disquieting."

"And you? How is your arm?"

"Mending. I have put on some essential oils to stop any infection and speed the healing. How is the cinéma?"

"Cinéma? Oh, you mean the movie? Coming along. That's why I'm calling. Have you ever been in a sweat lodge?"

"Non. No, what is this?"

"It is a small space we native Indians use to reflect on infinity."

"Très intéressant. May I bring my Rinpoche? He is an expert on the infinite."

"It gets hot in a sweat. A man from Tibet, you think he can handle the heat?"

Marie-Thérèse laughed. "My lama can enter a mountain river of freezing water and emerge on the other side completely dry. I am sure he would welcome a warmer experience - un moment, here is BP coming." And to Fortunato she said, "It is for you," and into the phone, she said, "Au revoir, Monsieur Crow."

"Ciao," said BP into the receiver.

"Hi BP," said Blackfoot Crow. "Solved your problem.?"

"Unfortunately, no," said BP. "When I got back from school I could feel something was wrong, like you know when you're going to get sick and it's not just the flu. Nobody looks me in the eye. They've done something and won't tell me what it is."

Without a moment's hesitation Blackfoot Crow said, "They're hiding somebody."

+++

Sitting back in the anonymity of a crowded second class compartment on the train from Naples to Rome's Stazione Termini, it was hard for the bomber to believe it had worked so smoothly. In the confusion of disembarking he had gone unseen over the side of the scow, stripped underwater out of the filthy track suit he had been wearing and come up on the beach in fashionable O'Neill surfer shorts and Maui Jim sunglasses. Tanned, clean shaven, he strolled the strand until he saw a couple get off their beach towels, dive into the sea and swim out beyond the 100-meter buoy. It was then a simple matter of lying in the sand next to their towels and at an appropriate moment stand up and leave the beach with a towel over his shoulder. An internet reservation had been made for him at the Mare Blu in the name of Martin Dufour, an official with the OECD, and nobody batted an eye at a half-naked guest coming in from the beach to ask for his key. As planned, in his room he found clothes, money, an Italiarail pass and a ticket for the ferryboat to Porto Empedocle, Sicily, a four hour trip but safer than checking in at the airport where he would have to show a passport, and another ticket for the ferry from Messina to Naples. Undetected, a shadow hunted by Interpol, the CIA, the FBI, Mossad, and the Federal Security Service of Russia, in less than two days since landing, the man was on his way to his new target. From his window seat he glanced at his own reflection in the glass as it was momentarily transformed into a mirror when the train went through a tunnel and realised he was being photographed. A woman across the aisle pretending to talk into her cell phone but actually aiming it at him.

+++

It had been a trying forty-eight hours with boatloads of illegal immigrants arriving in a seemingly endless queue, yet as tired as she was, Elisabetta D'Angelo, had not forgotten and when, in the parking lot, she saw the Deputy-Head of Customs getting out of his car as she was about to get into hers, she said, "Comandante, ha un momento? I know you are busy and it is probably nothing but it is on my conscience." And she told him what Abébé had told her about the clean-shaven man on the scow smelling of soap and patchouli.

+++

Early the next morning, driving the car on the 101 going up to Santa Barbara, Blackbird Crow said, "You should not feel guilty. If a fugitive with 10 kilos of coke in her backpack is found in your house, you go to jail my friend, and they confiscate the house and all your possessions. Never mind whose sister she is, she had to go. She endangers everyone by doing such a stupid thing."

"Maybe not stupid but desperate," said Marie-Thérèse, seated in the back. Next to her the Buddhist monk nodded.

73

"Whatever." Blackbird Crow glanced at her in the rearview mirror. "Better pray there are no consequences. It's not only Homeland, it's also the guys who gave her the drugs."

"How did you know?" said BP.

"I don't just live here, I am *from* here. You are a visitor, in fact all three of you are visitors. You see the surface of things you want to see, but underneath it's different. That compound of yours is an illusion. The Mexicans know this. They know they are not in their space. They expect to get turfed out. To them family is more important than a roof over your head; you can always replace a roof."

+++

The photographer was a young woman sitting diagonally across the aisle amidst a gaggle of schoolchildren bent over their iPads and cell phones, elbows on the fold out tables When she got up to go to the toilet he watched her walk down the carriage and then he followed her and waited patiently in the corridor for her to finish, an odd thought in his head trying to calculate the distance covered by the Frecciarossa, Italy's 'red arrow' bullet train, travelling at over 300-kilometres per hour, in the six minutes she was in there. When she came out, he said, "You peed for thirty kilometres."

"Is that what you do? Work out the distance women pee?"

She did not seem surprised to see him standing there.

"And you? Do you always surreptitiously photograph strangers?"

"When they're as handsome as you, yes, of course."

There it was again, the trap. How many times had his minder in the camp warned him about his natural proclivity to empathise with people on the road, told him not to make eye contact, never get into a conversation, leave alone one going in the direction this was taking.

"I do not like having my picture taken. Please delete what you have of me on your phone."

"And if I say no?"

Was she taunting him?

"Please," he said. "I'm superstitious."

When she laughed, her eyes filled with merriment and it dawned on him that she was not just provocative but also very attractive. This is when two small girls came up to them and one said, pointing at the toilet door, " Scusi Signora - devo andare." with her friend hopping from foot to foot.

When the door closed on the girls, she said, almost apologetically, "I am their teacher standing in as a stewardess for the holidays. Who are you? Why do you smell so delicious?"

Provocative, attractive, curious and there, obviously available. Also great cover, a couple travelling with a group of kids. He said, "How far are you going?"

The ambiguity of his question made her giggle. "To Rome, give the children back to their parents. Holiday's over, school starts in a couple of weeks."

She paused.

"Two weeks of freedom then back to the mine shaft."

Two weeks? He got the message. Forget humble, a lot could happen in the freedom of fourteen days. When the two little girls came out of the toilet he said, "My turn. See you in a moment. Promise you'll erase the pictures? Please."

+++

CHAPTER SEVEN

My Fine Feathered Friend
Surviving the rest of us,
Souls raised from the dead
Matthew, Mark, Luke and John.
Last go round love invents us myths to live by.
The widowed bride, tarnished gold,
Twilight's child, on her way home.
The prodigal daughter, starting over.

+++

CBS, San Diego. 7.59am PDT

The National Hurricane Center in Miami has issued the following updated forecast: 'Hurricane Edward, which has been stalled for twenty-four hours, is slowly moving again on a path parallel to the US coast in a north, north-east direction which should bring the eye of the storm onshore south of Long Beach, California, with sustained winds increasing to 170 miles per hour, gusting to 200 miles per hour, and is now categorised as a Category 5 Hurricane. Rain is forecast to increase in the range of 20 to 25 inches, with some isolated areas seeing 40 inches. A storm surge 18 to 25 feet above normal has already flooded San Diego and caused extensive damage to Naval shipping. This is a warning of the probability of catastrophic flooding in the Los Angeles basin in an area from Huntington Beach, Long Beach, Manhattan Beach, Venice and north to Santa Monica. The Federal Emergency Management Agency has advised the closure of LAX, the airports in Long Beach, Santa

Monica and Burbank, and the cancellation of all flights in or outbound. All personnel to immediately seek shelter. This is a life-threatening situation. Residents in these areas should be prepared to stay in their shelters. DO NOT VENTURE OUT TO 'SEE WHAT IT'S LIKE.'

+++

Clapboard #8 - Sweat lodge/Mission Creek/Santa Barbara

They heard the news flash on the radio in the car and, when they parked on Tunnel where the Inspiration Point trailhead started up for Mission Creek, as they got out, they instinctively looked southeast to a far distant hazy horizon where the tops of cumulonimbus clouds could just be made out high in the atmosphere. "We could do with some of that rain up here," said Blackbird Crow. It was oppressively warm under a hard blue sky. "You sure your house is safe?"

"Short of the roof getting ripped off, everything that can be nailed down is nailed down, the shutters are shut, the windows are taped, it's not stick-built but steel and concrete," said BP. "We're not going to get flooded 'cause we're on a hill. I'm sure the trees and the plants will get hit but there's not much we can do about that. We're better off than most. My boys are confident. Frankly I think they were glad to see us get out of the way. Anyway, too late to do anything now. Maybe it won't come ashore, stay out at sea."

"I wonder where that girl will be?" said Marie-Thérèse

"Right," said Blackbird. "You guys ready to hike?"

The trail climbed steeply and where it crossed a bridge over the Creek they left it to go rock-hopping up the dried out stream bed. Half an hour later they reached Seven Falls where even the deepest pool was bone dry and Blackbird Crow said, "Watch out for rattlers. They like to sun themselves."

Above the Falls the creek was less precipitous where it crossed slabs of rock, then became more and more narrow where it meandered through a boulder field until it vanished into the face of a 400 foot cliff. Some of the boulders were immense and in the shade of one they stopped to rest.

"So?" said BP. "Where's the lodge?"

"In a cave under there," said Blackbird Crow, pointing at the cliff. The opening to the cave was behind a screen of boulders, impossible to detect if you did not know where to look as the fissure to access the cave was scarcely a body width wide. It took a moment for their eyes to adjust to the gloom inside and then they saw a low dome-shaped hut covered in blankets and animal skins, with a small opening facing east. "The frame is made with 12 small saplings put into the ground to make a circle," said Blackbird Crow, "and then bent over and tied together."

"It doesn't look very big. How will we fit in there?" said BP.

"It's roomier than it looks. About 10 feet across and 5 feet high in the middle. Go on, crawl in, see for yourself."

Inside, in the near dark, seated on a floor covered by sweet smelling sage grass around an open pit, there was ample room for the four of them. "This lodge belongs to the Chumash people. Some of their elders will join us," said Blackbird Crow. "Remember, the sweat is a religious ceremony – it is for prayer and healing, and can only be led by elders who have gone through intensive training for many years, who know the traditions, the language and the songs. They will heat stones and put them in that pit and pour water over them to make steam. It will gradually get very hot, very, very hot and if you feel distressed it is no disgrace to say so. Your safety is of paramount importance to the elders and they will suspend the ceremony to assist you if needed. You may speak and join in the songs. You may find yourself hallucinating, seeing things, visions. You must open your heart to the Great Mystery, we say."

The Tibetan monk smiled, nodded, and said the first words he had spoken since they left Beverly Hills. " Buddha say: 'Know from the rivers in cleft and in crevices: those in small channels flow noisily, the great flow silent. Whatever's not full makes noise. Whatever is full is quiet.'"

To himself BP thought 'What the fuck?' Out loud he said, "I'm not sure this is for me. I think I will sit this out."

+++

During the ceremony, in the dark, after the hot stones had been changed two or three times, Marie-Thérèse was not sure exactly, between the songs and the recitations of the elders, she first felt and then heard humming, a deep note, in the background of thought, slowly filling the sweat lodge as if from an unknown source. It came from the Rinpoche, sitting cross-legged next to her in his orange robes, his eyes half-closed in meditation, not a drop of perspiration leave alone sweat on him in all that heat and humidity. With the humming came a vibration she could feel in her chest and she wondered if the others could feel it too. She was dripping and was glad for the glass of water she had drunk each time the little door was opened to change the stones, let in some light and a breath of fresh air.. Sweat glistened off the men in their shorts. At one point Blackbird Crow had called out, "Watch for an eagle. If he should visit you, look to him." Later he added, "Watch him; he may talk and drop a feather to you." And it was with an eagle feather that one of the elders wafted the smoke rising from the sweet cedar wood placed under the hot stones splashed with water. And again it was Blackbird who said, "I see you Grandfather; see me now. I remember the tale you told me that I must not forget. Of the snow. Of saving the White Woman with the Three Children in the snow. Of the shelter and love she gave you. I remember. I will not forget the snow." Marie-Thérèse felt words she would like to have said come to her lips and die there because she was shy.

+++

Afterwards, blinking, they came out of the cave into the afternoon sunshine and found BP fast asleep in the shadow of a giant boulder. "What the fuck!" he said, when they woke him up. And he said it again when a fine trickle of pebbles ran down the face of the cliff and they all felt the boulder tremble.

+++

It was done, exactly as instructed, the four parts of the printed gun sent on their way to the four separate addresses in Mexico from four separate post offices in four separate towns, two of them outside Italy. He'd even done that part himself, driven to France and then through Switzerland on a 900-kilometre round trip. Chambered for a 9mm round, test-fired in the soundproof shooting

79

range in his basement, he knew the gun would work perfectly but supplying the ammunition had not been part of the specification, and while driving he could not help speculating how they would marry a gun invisible to any x-ray to the ammunition which would show out no matter how you disguised it. Not his problem. The packaging had been left to his discretion and he thought he'd been very clever in sending the parts disguised as sex toys, particularly the barrel as a penile enhancer. Hopefully they had a sense of humour. It was late when he got back to his flat in Brescia but his neighbour, an ancient widow, Signora Salvatico, was still up and heard him fiddling the key into his front door and came out to greet him just as Gina, her cat, strolled up with a mouse in her mouth as a present for the old crone. "Guarda," she said, "mi ha fatto un regalo!"

"A present?"

"Put it down, Gina," she told the cat. "Oh, before I forget, two men were here looking for you; foreigners." she said.

"Allora? They leave a message?"

"No. Said to tell you they'd be back." Then she pointed, delighted, "Good girl, Gina," as the cat politely deposited the dead mouse at her feet.

+++

"This is the weirdest thing," Beth said, looking at her screen. "What if it never comes ashore, just tracks on up the coast?" The eye of the hurricane, now north of Malibu, was aimed at Oxnard and Ventura. "Your call, Eddie."

Eddie was eating a hamburger, feet on his desk, watching TV and in no hurry to answer. They'd get shit from the press whatever they said. It was as if the storm surge and torrential rain and the tremendous damage done to the coastal communities in the LA basin were their fault because they had to constantly revise the expected landfall.

"Look at this jerk," he said between bites. CBS had a reporter in a safety harness, dressed as a deep-sea diver, shrieking into a mike, out at the end of what was left of Malibu Pier as monstrous waves rolled in. Briefly he disappeared as a wave crested and burst on top of him. When he could be seen again he was on his ass in a mass of foam with the harness lines threatening to castrate him but saving him from getting pitched into the sea. "Fuck," said Eddie. "Hope he's getting overtime."

+++

Where the 101 crossed the 405 was a lake getting bigger by the minute as the Los Angeles River, normally a broad bone-dry concrete drainage ditch, some parts used as a skateboard park by daredevil kids, overflowed its banks and joined Lake Balboa, swamped the Woodley Lakes golf course, and drowned all the lower parking levels of the Sherman Oaks Galleria, stranding tens of thousands of cars on the complex cloverleaf of highways, with traffic backing up on the Ventura past Hollywood all the way downtown to the east and past Woodland Hills to the west. Driving back to town was stop-and-go, windscreen wipers thrashing, and Blackbird Crow made a sensible decision when they reached the exit for Topanga Canyon to leave the freeway, head for the high-ground and take Mulholland Drive home. "Never seen anything like this," he said, more to himself than the occupants of his heavy Mercedes SUV, repeatedly buffeted by blasts of wind coming at them at every exposed corner.

"Imagine if we'd been caught up Mission Creek under such a déluge," said Marie-Thérèse.

"We'd be dead," said BP, "But look at the bright side, the drought will be over. I wonder when they'll reopen LAX?"

+++

CHAPTER EIGHT

Complications? I'm glad you asked
What evolution is -
a thread across the ocean, the future of the past,
Tests of time, trains of thought, family matters.
Up country into thin air, nothing remains the same.
Blood and gold.
Hope.

+++

The bomber knew he had been lucky, Inshallah. He had been lucky to meet the girl, lucky she lived on her own, going to her apartment in Rome after she dropped off her kids, his camouflage so good that his own minder waiting for the train's arrival at Stazione Termini had not recognised him wearing a baseball cap back to front, sunglasses, backpack, a child in each hand leaving the station amidst hordes of schoolchildren and parents. It was what he had been taught, normality the best disguise. In all his life he had never been free from surveillance ever since as a boy his uncle gave him over to the madrassa in Damascus to be raised after the Americans killed his parents. And he had never been free to be with a girl. The opportunity giving lie to the supposed 72 virgins waiting for him in the paradise of Jannah which only a simpleton would believe. In fact he didn't know what to do with her once the door shut behind them in the anonymous safety of her flat and they stood in the dim hallway two feet apart waiting for one or the other to make the first move. But the same inspiration that had let him accost her on the train, now inspired him to say, "Before I can know you, I must bathe you in clean water." He had taken his time undressing her and the process of discovery made her say, "You have never been with a woman before?" "No," he said, wanting to lie but somehow knowing he must not, "never."

"Go slowly," she said, "I will show you."

In the shower he had used his fingertips on her with the same delicacy he used on a detonator, carefully soaping every inch of skin, every cleft and crevice, again and again raising goosebumps on her arms and thighs and rump. "Now you are new," he said. Then, when he discovered what happened by just grazing her clitoris, drifting off, then sliding back, in and out, his fingers everywhere as the hot water poured down over them, she cried out and could not stop herself coming and coming and again coming in a seemingly never-ending orgasm Then she showed him what she could do with her mouth and her tongue. He was lucky to have known her but in the back of his mind he knew how it would have to end.

For seven magical days of freedom and lust they stayed in Rome, shopping for food in the cobblestone lanes of Trastevere, otherwise spending almost all the time in bed and when he suggested a week in Venice she could only smile in happy surrender. Again they took the train, two lovers wrapped in each others arms, until they arrived at Santa Lucia and switched to the vaporetto stationed behind the Ferrovia which dropped them off close to the B&B on San Polo, which she had rented in her name using her credit card since he only had cash. They were only 50 metres from the Rialto.

+++

For unknown reasons Hurricane Edward turned west and headed out into the Pacific Ocean where, as the waters grew cooler, it slowly lost strength and petered out into an innocuous tropical storm that only affected shipping. After all the media drama, the soundbites of so-called experts pontificating on evermore catastrophic scenarios, to the chagrin of TV ratings but the relief of insurance companies who knew it could have been much, much worse, once the sun came out, there was a distinct sense of anti-climax that despite hundreds of millions of dollars in damage to LA and the Governor declaring it a disaster area and applying for Federal Relief, once the flooding subsided and mopping up started, within days the city was log-jammed with traffic again, the airports reopened and it was back to business as usual.

Post-apocalypse, in the dappled shade of a banana tree, sitting cross-legged on the travertine surround of the compound's swimming pool overlooking the distant vista of Beverly Hills, his eyes half-closed, immobile in meditation, saffron robes reflected in the still water, the monk sensed, and then through the shrubbery saw, a small boy, Jaime, one of the sons of Esmé and Alejandro, anxiously searching the grounds and repeatedly saying in a forlorn voice, "Jocko. Jocko. Here, Jocko." And, when he saw the monk, he said, "I can't find my dog. Have you seen him?" And when the monk shook his head, no, the small boy said, "Something frightened him," just as the surface of the pool appeared to shiver and the monk had the strange thought that perhaps something had frightened the hurricane.

+++

That night when Blackbird Crow got home he found his mother waiting up for him and when he came through the door she said, "Something is happening, Blackbird. I have seen the signs. We must prepare."

"Yes, Mother, not now. Look, we have visitors," and he stepped aside to usher in Fortunato, Marie-Thérèse and the Tibetan monk.

"Oh, how wonderful," his mother said, momentarily forgetting what she had seen. "Just in time for our picnic and the music."

The picnic was at the far end of the back yard, a long, thin rectangle of overgrown jungle bisected by a series of interconnected ponds in which a chorus of frogs gave voice loud enough to drown out the distant sound of traffic on the Hollywood Freeway. The garden ended in a fence from which a spectator could enjoy the view looking down into a natural wooded amphitheatre at the bottom of which was the Hollywood Bowl, and, fortuitously, enjoy for free the concerts played there. On a trestle table against the fence Blackbird was in the habit of setting out a picnic for his mother in the cool of the evening so that she could listen to the classical music she loved since she had no interest in the concerts that featured Pop,

Rock, Hip-Hop or Country, with just a smidgin of tolerance for Jazz and the Blues.

"We're in luck along with a clear sky," she announced. "Tonight we have Beethoven with Sir Roger Norrington conducting the LA Phil in the Overture to Egmont, Opus 84, followed by the Fifth. Don't worry about the frogs, they stop their racket when the music begins. But first we eat and -" here she looked at Fortunato - "I will tell you a story about your ancestor. Sit next to me."

They sat around the table to an eccentric meal mainly of fruit and salad, with figs and a variety of tomatoes, yellow, purple and red, sliced horizontally into thin overlapping disks with basil leaves inserted between the fruit, the whole sprinkled with olive oil, a pinch of sea salt and ground black pepper, followed by a couscous with pine nuts, dates and golden shallots and a side dish of black forbidden rice, grilled zucchini and pineapple over which was poured a mixture of lemon juice, chopped chives and spring onions accompanied by a bowl of red quinoa, with blood oranges, pistachios and herbs. Dessert was a salad of sliced nectarines, buffalo mozzarella, endives and fennel, roasted almonds, topped with raisins and a dash of balsamic vinegar. The wine was an obscure label from Bordeaux, served fresh and in abundance. As they ate they listened.

"The name of our tribe is Apsàalooke, which means 'children of the large-beaked bird', the name in translation becoming 'gens du corbeaux' to the early French explorers, and this in turn became 'the people of the crows' to the English, which is how we are now called, the Crow. Long ago, before even I was born," Blackbird's mother spoke slowly, thoughtfully, chewing her food carefully, as carefully as she chose her words, "in the days of our great chief, Lone Eagle, when he was young, the vast lands of the Crow were coveted by the Cheyenne, the Sioux, the Arapaho and the Pawnee, who stole our horses and our women and killed many of our men. We thought they were our greatest enemy until the white man came, killing the bison, bringing disease, taking our land, driving us to death. Of course we fought back, lamented our many brave warriors, men like Red Bear, Pretty Eagle, Medicine Crow, Buffalo Bull Facing the Wind, Two Leggings"

The old lady paused, then reached up to the heavens with both her hands cupped, cried out, "I remember you . . . all our Great Chiefs at the

Banquet in the Sky, telling story, counting coups . . . I remember you . . . "
- and nodded and said, " Even women carried the warpipe. Among the
Willows, whom I knew as a child, was there when they killed Sitting Bull's
father. Many were the battles we fought over the years, some won, more
lost, and it became apparent that if we did not ally ourselves with these
white men our tribe would perish. We negotiated in good faith only to find
that in our naivety, for a signed piece of paper, we had to surrender vast
portions of our tribal lands and in exchange accept moving to what the
white men in Washington termed 'reservations', small fenced areas of
barren land 'reserved' for us, where little would grow except our burial
grounds. We were 40 million natives, maybe more, living for centuries
undisturbed on this beautiful continent. Today not even three. Ponder that.
. . . " she broke off to listen. An orchestra clearing its throat down in the
Bowl. Minor and major chords tried on violin and viola, ripples of scales
on wind instruments, a rumble of drums.

"We have time," she said, turning to Fortunato. "Then came the gold
rush with 300,000 besotted white men greedy for wealth pouring into
California to seize this land and strip it of its bounty where once we freely
rode the limitless mountains and plains. To end up with this, " she waved
her hand across the darkened landscape. "Los Angeles was not even a village
then. My son tells me you are related to an old man who once made movies
here, ninety years ago? In Santa Barbara? Is this true?"

"Yes."

"And that he may still be alive?"

"So I am told."

"You said he met an old Crow stuntman on one of the film sets?"

"Yes."

"His father."

"I'm sorry? I don't understand."

"That Crow, Looks-Death-in-the-Face, was his father. In the terrible
winter of 1895 our tribes were illegally camped on a branch of the
Yellowstone near the lake, on the edge of what was declared to be a national
park where we natives had lived for over 10,000 years and were now called
trespassers and forbidden to go. To survive we became poachers, our braves

trapping deer and elk to feed their kin. Scouting for game far from the camp, a succession of blizzards forced Looks-Death-in-the- Face to seek shelter in the wilderness and he remembered the location of an abandoned miner's cabin. Struggling through deep snow drifts, imagine his surprise to find the cabin occupied by a starving white woman and her three children. They welcomed him and gave him a place at the meagre fire they had going and he shared with them the venison he carried. Eventually, in the days and weeks that followed until the storms abated, he enjoyed this woman's bed. She lived for adventure and told him of how she had come from Europe to set off from New York to cross the country determined to get to San Francisco, there to find a boat and sail to China. She cheerfully admitted that her three very different children were fathered by three different men all vanished into the years gone by. When finally a thaw set in and Looks-Death-in-the-Face could return to camp he promised to come back for the woman, a promise he could not keep because the soldiers had come to kill us in our tents and we once again had to flee into the emptiness of the mountains in Montana. For years he wondered what had become of the woman and her children, but the existential life we led, constantly moving, being whittled down, obliged to abandon the very notion of tribe to survive as individuals, eroded his memory and it was by pure chance in California where he had found work as a stunt-rider in a Western that he met the writer of the movie and was struck by the extraordinary colour of the writer's eyes. They talked briefly about themselves, their lives, the past, and the writer told him of how he was born in Hawaii in 1896, and about being brought up in China and in India and when Looks-Death-in-the-Face was called to take his position for the next scene in the movie the last thing he told this writer was 'I am glad you have your mother's eyes.'

Silence.

Finally, as the words sank in and he grasped their meaning, Fortunato said, "How can you know this?"

"Looks-Death-in-the-Face told me. He was my grandfather. He . . . "

She was interrupted by the dark opening chords in F minor of the Egmont played in unison by the whole orchestra, swept onward by the strings with the yearning notes of the woodwind instruments skirling up and silencing the frogs. They listened to Sir Roger's scurrying pace of his musicians, applauding with the audience below when the Overture was finished and the four hammer-blows of fate announced the Fifth - dah, dah, dah, DUUUM - hard knuckles on the door of eternity, demanding attention, at once familiar yet always new, suspending thought, and it was only during the third movement of the symphony, the scherzo, as it transitions into the finale with the timpani's thudding heartbeat and the arpeggios on violin soaring that an eagle flew up from out of the surrounding woods and slowly rode the thermal currents to be joined by a second bird and then a third, difficult to see against the night sky, as the trombones, the piccolo and the contrabassoon swooped into the vertiginous climax. Climbing ever higher, seemingly elevated by the music, they glided, their wingtips almost motionless, in a triangulated circle that slowly widened and then, as if a current passed between them, of a common accord they vanished, flying north, bringing the old lady out of her chair to stare after them, the music forgotten, and she remembered what she had foreseen and Blackbird's mother said, "Did you see them my son? The eagles? They rarely fly at night. Did you see? I fear what is coming."

+++

Clapboard #9 - LAX/BP/Air France/Tom Bradley International Terminal. On the soundtrack:

BP: After all that we didn't even have to change our planned flight. There were eleven undergrads on our first field-trip, sans Maria-Celestina who was supposedly working, much to my chagrin, since I confess to a juvenile plan to seduce her away from Savera while we were abroad, still, can't complain - all girls. Blackbird Crow came along with just one other cameraman, but he did a clever thing by giving each girl the latest cell phone with the best camera embedded and instructions on how to upload whatever they shot or recorded to a master file which he edited every evening. "They see and hear stuff you would never get with a professional crew," he said. "For me it's like having flies on all the walls." The Dean, who insisted on seeing us off, somewhat pessimistically asked that no more than half the girls be brought back pregnant. He'd been going over our itinerary and a line item had stopped him: "Are you sure your budget will allow you to stay in the Hotel du Cap?" he said.

88

"What's the point of recreating the Grand Tour if you don't stay where you would have in the 1920s?"

"But that *is* the point. Surely the aim is to equip young people with the knowledge and ability to cope with the world as it is today - not 100 years ago."

"Where's the adventure in that?" By now we had an attentive audience as the girls quit texting and got their heads up from their phones like zebras sighting a stalking lion. "Doing the same as millions and millions of others are doing, while other millions and millions have finished doing the exact same thing and are packing it in because they've had enough, reached the end, put up a good fight, had a great run, one of the best, quite an innings, way to go, done, out, dead, buried. Gone. Alpha and Omega, the Beginning and the End. Coping? What about living?"

"Be serious. Life -"

"Is a laugh. Think. The diktat that we must learn, to work, to earn, to eat, to shit, to work, to earn, to eat, to shit, ad nauseum, is a cosmic joke, the funny part of which is that we've been here for two hundred thousand years and still don't get it instead of pissing ourselves laughing." All this in the departure lounge.

He was saved by the bell in the shape of our chaperone, God's cosmic rejoinder, Professor T herself, or Poppy as the kids called her behind her back in admiration of the twin protuberances pushing out her pink sweater.

"Ah, Professor," said the Dean, "you arrive at an opportune moment. Please come to my aid and explain . . ."

An explanation we were spared by the loud announcement that pre-boarding for Air France's flight to Paris-Charles de Gaulle was ready and as the skirmish lines formed to go through Customs and Immigration the Dean's voice and figure got swallowed up in the throng and Poppy said to me "I believe we are sitting together."

What the fuck, right? The Dean was probably pissing himself.

I always turn left on boarding a plane and had scammed an upgrade to business in exchange for bringing my eleven lovely demoiselles to Air France, who stashed them with the hoi polloi in the back. How Poppy got to sit - make that lie, since we had lie-flat seats - next to me is a mystery.

More mysterious still is that at cruising altitude she turned out to be a charming dinner companion and, finishing the boeuf Stroganoff, when we hit some bumpy air over northern Canada, said she was scared and would I hold her hand, please, and it was holding hands that we got off the plane in Paris much to the amusement of the students. She was 38, way past the sell-by date, but I am a firm believer in accepting free gifts and the Gods had obviously decided I had earned this one. Undressed, which happened in our sleeper on the Orient Express shortly after we left the Gare de Lyon headed for Venice, she was a glorious sight, not a gramme overweight or a curve out of place, and she had a healthy, earthy doctorate in more than AI, intuiting my every whim and mood with an eye-opening invigorating inventiveness that would have had the Dean squirming trying to cope with the bulge in his trousers. Enough said. I had much to learn.

First lesson, the ease with which our gang accepted their Professor's new-found amour. They went out of their way to discreetly leave us time and space for our fun and games and in the process our roles got switched, they the adults, we the besotted kids. For three days they did the walks, the gondola rides, Piazza San Marco, Harry's Bar, the Fortuny, I Gesuiti, Harry's, the Dogana, Palazzo Grassi, the vaporetto out to San Giorgio Maggiore and back to Harry's, even a side trip to Murano for the glasswork, and all we managed were a couple of sorties from our bedroom down to the terrace of Longhi's for a drink and to make sure the Grand Canal was still there where it was meant to be.

Even before dinner, Poppy liked seconds, no going to sleep after the initial go round and the way to stay awake was to talk. Lying on her side, all that lovely languid length for me to enjoy, elbow bent, her head in her hand, distractedly flicking my now flaccid member from side to side, she said, "Of course you know you're on the way out? I was discussing it with the girls, sperm banks will be able to store whatever's needed to sustain the population, so all we have to do is milk a few qualified studs and the rest is history."

"Not going to happen. Half the world's doing this right now. Think how much of history is about trying to get laid, getting laid and all the consequences. The primacy of private lives is not going to change."

"That was then. Things are changing, fast, and as fast as they change we adapt. Look at the way you're tethered to your cell phone now. It knows within a meter where you are, so it knows you're in Venice, in this bed at the Gritti, with me because you have taken pictures of me with it, in the middle of the afternoon on August 22, 2028 since it's both clock and calendar, and it even knows where you will be at 9 this evening since you used it to book all the tables for us at Il Ridotto, and it knows that it might rain so we may end up inside, but if it doesn't we will have an unusually cool evening, dress accordingly. Forget private lives, there's no such thing any more if a machine knows more about you than you know yourself." Here she paused. " It probably even knows how many women you've been in bed with before me." Silence. "So? How many?"

"Who cares if it's all part of history?"

"Let's say you started when you were 15 and you stayed with the first one until you went to college at 18 and then you had a girl a year until you graduated, so that's four more, and then you found one you liked and stayed with her for five years, which makes six so far - why are you looking at me like that?" she said.

"Where are you going with this?"

"Curiosity. Isn't that what you teach? Ok. You were 27 and you'd been through six and now you're 57, 30 years on, so let's say one every three years with the reputation you have, which is ten more, for a total of sixteen. Right?"

Silence.

"More?" she said. "Ok. One every two years gets you to twenty-one, add the odd one-nighter, say twenty-five. Close?"

More silence. And something else was now in the room, something morbid, the lightness of their affair vanishing as quietly as the smoke from a snuffed out candle and she wished she had kept her mouth shut and they were back at the beginning on the Orient Express.

"Shit," she said as the reality hit her, "I'm not even close, am I?" Which is when the bomb went off.

+++

Panic. It was a huge explosion and must have been nearby the way the windows shook. We had no idea where the girls had gone and scrambled to get out of bed and into our clothes and almost failed to hear the opening bars of a rock version of Bach's Toccata in D, which is the ringtone on my cell. It was the baby billionaire, Lorraine, calling to find out if we were okay. They had been having a drink on the roof terrace of the Danieli, a block away from the Gritti, and could see the smoke from the bomb somewhere further downstream and feared the target was the Rialto Bridge. Already the wail of sirens and the warble on the boats of Venezia Emergenza ambulances could be heard. Poppy and I looked at each other, then, in relief, fell into a hug. "Forget what I said," she said.

What the fuck, right?

+++

Two days later we were on a boat, a marvellous, restored, Edwardian relic from 1903 built by Camper and Nicholsons in Southampton, part of the old man's legacy, boarding in Trieste to sail down the Adriatic, stopping for a few days in Dubrovnik, then Montenegro and it was only when we got to Mykonos, tanned and happy, that we found out what had happened as reported by a stained, torn, 10-day-old copy of the Trib we found on our way along the footpath linking the beaches of Psarou, PG's, Agia Anna, Paraga and Paradise, our daily trek for booze and nourishment. "Look at this," said one of the Mormon twins. The headline read 'Bomber Escapes', over a very poor photograph enlarged from CCTV footage of a couple boarding a vaporetto.

Venice, Italy August 20, 2028

Reuters

'The bomb explosion on the Rialto Bridge occurred at 20.18pm, police report, when the evening crowd of tourists go to dinner. Of the 88 people estimated to be on the bridge at that moment, 14 are dead, 21 severely injured, six reportedly in critical condition. All survivors are being treated for shock. The suspected bomber's alleged accomplice has been identified, Sandra Riopelli, 27, a schoolteacher from Rome. She was killed on the steps from San Polo to the inclined ramp leading to the central portico of the Rialto. The bridge is severely damaged and is now closed.

The Libyan Islamic Jihad, a hitherto unknown group in Tripoli, claimed responsibility for the attack. A man is being sought . . . '

+++

The GIS - Gruppo di Intervento Speciale - had caught the call after a woman in Rome reported her sister missing. At their headquarters in Livorno they coordinated all the known information on the attack. They were an elite 100-man unit (or so it was believed, the real number a secret), highly trained in counter-terrorism and unconventional warfare, and within minutes of the bomb exploding and the alarm being received from the Operations Room of General Command in the Città Militare Cecchignola in Rome an Augusta-Bell 412 helicopter was airborne bound for Venice with a detachment of four men, a commander, an explosives specialist, a sniper and an electronics equipment specialist. Time was the enemy. As they took off the Commander was already issuing orders to the carabinieri on the ground to seal off the city and instructed the Venetian Port Authority to stop all waterborne craft immediately and order all the towns in the Venetian lagoon from Chioggia in the south to Jesolo in the north to arrest any boats attempting to leave. But even as they flew, in his heart he knew it was too little, too late, a hopeless task, an enemy who could plan the bombing could also plan the escape and would know a man could hide forever in a place with 118 small islands linked by canals and 400 bridges. In acknowledgment, 48 hours later he was forced to rescind his own embargo when the trapped population of nearly 300,000 tourists threatened to riot.

Forward two weeks and the trail was hopelessly cold, the bomber could be anywhere in Europe. They had a better idea who they were looking for after the sister forwarded photographs she had received on her cell phone taken by her doomed sister on the Frecciarossa from Naples which showed a clean shaven man, 27 to 30 years old, whom she had just met and found charming and, hard to believe, smelled of patchouli. It was this unusual detail that led the electronics specialist to see if he could find a match in the myriads of inter-departmental computer files and messages that were shared in the daily download of information at HQ in Livorno. Patchouli, a strange word he had never come across before, and scarcely had he finished typing the last letter i, then bingo, two hits, and after talking to the comandante on Lampedusa and to Elisabetta D'Angelo they knew how the man had come ashore. Then, from her credit card records, they found the B&B on San Polo, that Sandra Rioppelli had booked, questioned the owners, a gay couple, who showed them the room that the senorina and her boyfriend had occupied, now cleaned, but also showed them an item that had been forgotten in the bathroom, a small bottle with a glass stopper, on the label of which, written in Gothic script, was 'Jojoba and Patchouli Essential Oil'. Unfortunately there were no fingerprints on the bottle as it too had been carefully cleaned which was the way the gay couple insisted things be done in their B&B.

A debate had raged about the pros and cons of publishing the photos from the sister's cell phone, some advocating it gave them an advantage if the bomber thought they did not know what he looked like, others arguing that the poor CCTV pictures already distributed had led to a lot of useless public sightings and wasted time investigating same. The agreed upon compromise was to send enhanced pictures from the cell phone to alert Interpol and all its connected agencies across the world to look out for a dangerously armed man which, inevitably, would be leaked to the press in short order, but which they hoped would at least give them a head-start. In this case they were not disappointed, Mossad calling from Tel Aviv within minutes of receiving the pictures. "We know who this guy is, Hassan Husseni, aka, Mahmoud al Sadr, aka Ahmad Rabat Benali. Everybody is after him. As a kid they sent him to be trained in a madrassa in Surabaya, Indochina, where they turned him into an expert in the use of TATP - which is easily prepared from commonplace ingredients like nail polish remover and hair bleach and can be molded into just about anything if you don't blow yourself up first. We have him down for that deal in Karachi in the mosque, the explosion in Kabul outside the American compound, another in Mecca during the Hadj, two attempts in Jerusalem and Haifa, where we were fortunate in limiting the damage because we keep an ear to the ground. Probably more attacks we don't know about. We think he's about 30, not a leader, not even a true fundamentalist. Our informant who went to the same school, confirmed his ID from your pics, said there was nothing about him that would make you think he would become a terrorist.

The guy's good, as far as we can tell a loner, so we don't buy the story of an accomplice, but what's he doing off his turf in Europe getting photographed by a schoolteacher? Good picture, though, better'n anything we've got."

+++

In the safe house in Mestre it was the same question. "Hassan," his minder said, "I will shoot you if you don't tell me why you met this woman?"

"I didn't 'meet' her. It was all improvised. She gave me the cover I needed and a place to hide out."

"Liar. We had a safe-house for you in Rome. You deliberately avoided meeting me at the station as pre-arranged."

"Well I'm here now, what are you complaining about? I still carried out the mission didn't I?" He was tied to a chair with duct tape and knew it was pointless to struggle.

"With the result that you're on the front page of every newspaper." His minder waved La Stampa at him. The picture was obviously one she'd taken on the train, so much for her promise. "You have jeopardised our plan. With their face-recognition technology how far do you think you'll get?"

The Jews had a word for it, chutzpah, audacity. In a bored voice, he said, "That's their Achilles heel. They rely on technology. How long are you going to keep this up? You know you've nobody else so why not cut the bullshit and untie me?"

His insolence earned a stinging slap to his face delivered with such force the chair rocked. "That's a solution," he said, "beat me up so I'm unrecognisable." He spat blood and saliva on the floor and for a moment feared his bravado would not work. After the bomb went off it had taken him two and a half hours to walk the 11 kilometers to Mestre, the only tricky bit the long straight stretch across the lagoon on the SR11 Padana Superiore to Corso del Popolo from where it was easy to find the safe house behind the bingo hall on Via Guglielmo Pepe in which he had now been kept a prisoner for over two weeks. "I am very uncomfortable and anyway I need to shit," he said.

CHAPTER NINE

Love and loving in Bombay
It's not about a bike,
The promise in a kiss.
You are not a stranger
among the missing, missed.
But, I ask, what am I
doing here?

+++

Clapboard *#10 - BP/Istanbul/Fenerbahce Marina.* On the soundtrack: **BP:** Our furthest destination outbound was Istanbul, and after clearing customs at Karaköy, and berthing in a marina southeast of the old city, we crammed into a couple of dolmus taxis and headed for Sultanahmet where the old man had an Ottoman mansion long past its days of glory but a five-minute walk from Hagia Sophia and the Blue Mosque - the girls were thrilled. In just a month a dowdy collection of lookalikes in their jeans and T-shirts had transformed into a glorious treasury of tanned bodies, multihued clothes, necklaces, bracelets, sandals, anklets, turbans, earrings, culottes, vests, lace tights, spangled leggings and such a breathless assemblage of hairstyles as to make me feel what it must have been like in the good old days of the seraglio with Suleiman the Magnificent coming round for tea and an envious glimpse of my harem. Even our mini-whale, Amy, was transformed having lost 10 kilos simply by a change of diet and all the walking around the girls did every day. Poppy, as the Mère Supérieur so to speak, couldn't help feeling proud.

But don't think it was all fun and games. I had shipped ahead a dozen copies of Italo Calvino's book, 'Invisible Cities', the central conceit of which was Marco Polo describing to the Great Khan cities in the Khan's vast empire that he had never seen in a language he did not understand, and the task for my now well-travelled chickadees, once they'd read the book, was to imagine themselves in the place of Marco Polo and write another chapter. Maisie Schultz, just 19, by far the quietest member of our little troupe, the kind of girl you would like to be your sister, wrote a piece I showed to Blackbird Crow, "Try shooting this," I said to him.

+++

'In homage to Italo Calvino'

There is a place in your Empire, Great Khan, said Marco Polo, having no seasons, no clocks and where time stands still. Its sole city is on a hill surrounded by a marsh from which seeps a yellow-grey miasma blurring outlines so one might not tell where the marsh begins or the city ends. The buildings in the city are known only by their shadows. Pure chance has dictated their design, it being a characteristic of the inhabitants to come and go, eyes cast down, at no prescribed intervals, on errands having no purpose, to meet they know not where, nor whom, nor why, nor when. Thus erring they never arrive. This purposelessness, which gives the city its aimless plan, has had three results: nobody ever sees another person; they imagine the people they never see; and, not knowing where they are, they get lost.

In an effort to resolve these difficulties, the Ancients prescribed two curious traditions: on their peregrinations the inhabitants should trail a line of cotton thread behind them, the better to find their way home; and they should drop on the roadway slips of paper bearing brief descriptions of themselves, their dwellings, their work, their thoughts, so that the downturned eyes of their fellows may read who passed that same way. Severe laws were enacted whereby it was forbidden to break the cotton thread of another or to disturb the paper etiquettes. The result is a collage of all things past and present, the notes telling of a place that perhaps no longer exists, overlapped by an appreciative description of the same non-existent place by another passerby who turned the corner one minute or half a century before, the whole knotted together by the sum of all the multitudinous bisecting cotton trails binding the shapeless package of the city to all its inhabitants . . .

Here Marco Polo paused. In the ensuing silence he could not tell if the Great Khan was listening or had fallen asleep. Nevertheless . . .

It is possible, Marco Polo said, in that impossible place, to trace the life of every citizen who ever lived there by simply following each thread and reading all the messages strewn about. Thus you may know the past without ever meeting the present while moving towards an invisible future.

+++

In a moment of divine inspiration, Blackbird had Maisie read what she had written as the contra-punctual voiceover to his dancing handheld camera tearing through the cacophony of 4000 shops and myriad alleyways clotted with 400,000 visitors and tradesmen in Constantinople's Grand Bazaar. Brilliant, brilliant stuff, a little movie gem all on its own which, once edited, knocked them out in Sundance and sold untold thousands of pirated USB copies to the 96 million tourists who annually flooded the most visited market on earth.

But all that came later. What shattered us was the phone call Lorraine got while we were about to tackle the meze at lunch in the garden at Giritli's. Her face went white and this girl, called the 'Tower of Power' in her graduation yearbook, crumpled in front of us. "No," she whispered into the phone, her eyes in that lovely face desperately searching for somewhere safe, some words to gainsay what she was hearing. "No," she said again, then, looking straight at me as if somehow I was responsible, she said, "My father's dead?" and handed me her cell.

"Hello?" I said.

"Who is this?" A woman's voice, taut, impersonal.

"Professore Fortunato Crollalanza."

"The Professor, good. Listen. You are in charge of my daughter, I understand. This news is a terrible shock to all of us, but particularly to Lorraine who was very close to her father - God knows why. I am wife number two. The man was the worst kind of scoundrel who ditched me when I was pregnant twenty years ago. I brought that girl up by myself and - sorry, I don't know why I'm telling you all this. She will have to come home for the funeral. She has her NetJets card to book a chartered flight. They should be able to lay on a plane for her in 24 hours. Please give her such assistance as she needs. Thank you." And hung up.

"Your mother?" I said to Lorraine and as I went to hand her back the phone she was suddenly in my arms weeping in despair. Poppy took charge, the girls rallied around their friend, Maisie offered to accompany Lorraine to New York, lunch was cancelled as we rushed off to the mansion and then things really started to get weird. NetJets, through one of their personal consultants, said how unfortunate it was but Lorraine's card had recently been cancelled. When we tried to book her a seat on any of the airlines operating out of Istanbul Atatürk none of her many credit cards would work and Poppy paid instead. On a CNN report what had initially been titled 'Sudden death of Much-married Billionaire' now read 'Suspected suicide of Real Estate Baron'. It only got worse. A seemingly unspendable fortune vanished in a few headlines as each layer of deceit was unpeeled by a prurient press gloating over the downfall of yet another tycoon. The man shot himself behind his chalet in Aspen having despoiled the multi-million dollar trust funds of his various children by his several wives in a last desperate attempt to save himself from financial ruin, leaving his kin destitute. The full depth of this financial train wreck took months to unravel but at the end there was nothing but an impossible avalanche of debt and a total of just $11,000 left in the banks. Unable to pay for her tuition, Lorraine quit the University.

+++

The two cars, a battered Ford Crown Vic and a dusty hippie Volkswagen van with tinted windows, converged at the corner of Old Gleeson Road and High Lonesome Trail, and parked driver's door to driver's door in the courtyard of the crumbling ruin that was once Joe Bono's saloon.

"I thought they'd retired those things?" said J.J. Nicholson, winding down his window in the van.

"They have." The Chief patted the windowsill of his car. "This is mine. Bought it before it got scrapped. I use it to remind me of the good old days." He peered at the speedometer. "479,000 miles. Never a problem long as you check the oil 'n' water, do regular maintenance, change the tires. Simple an' tough as they come, not full of computerised crap."

"I got this at the airport from Rent-a-Wreck," said J.J. He glanced at the dash. "I win, it says nearly 600,000 klicks."

"Shit, that's not even 400,000 miles. But it suits you in that getup. I nearly didn't recognise you." J.J. in a black stetson, bandana, dark granny glasses, Ban-the-Bomb necklace, beads, bandana and bracelets, looking like a stand-in for Willie Nelson. "So? Why are we here? This is not a pub."

J.J. looked around at the barren hills with here and there abandoned mine shafts showing and the remnants of adobes, all that remained of a long-forgotten ghost town. "I've got something, not sure exactly what yet. Somebody's playing a long game, Chief. Let me ask you, you ever think where you'll be in five years, ten years from now?"

"Probably dead if you believe my oncologist."

"What about fifty years from now?"

"Definitely dead."

J.J. scarcely smiled. "You're 62, right, retire in 3 years, probably live another 20, maybe 25 years, you ever considered what the world may be like around here in 2050?"

"No. I worry about whether I'll wake up in the morning. You heard somebody anonymously dumped a backpack with 10 kilos of coke at the station in Burbank over in LA?"

J.J. nodded. "You heard of hawala?"

"Vaguely. Some kind of money laundering gig in the Middle East?"

"Not at all. It's over a thousand years old, a system of transferring value based on trust operating outside all normal remittance systems all over the world even if the locus is India and the Middle East. In a way it's the forerunner of all these cryptocurrencies using blockchain technology. No banks, no movement of cash, no computers or wire transfers, instead the word and honour of a vast network of money brokers who move the money without actually moving it, tax free."

"You've lost me."

"Well it gets more complicated. As you know, under Federal Law the use and possession of cannabis for any purpose is illegal, even for medicinal use. But it's legal in 29 states with a doctor's recommendation and in 9 states for recreational use. But here's the catch, in all the states where you can grow and sell it legally you cannot bank the money you make because Federal Bank laws prohibit Federally insured banks - which is damn near all of them - from accepting deposits which you know to be illegally gained. What to do with the cash, we're talking literally mountains of cash? World GDP is estimated to be about $40 trillion, with illegal drugs making up 2% of that; don't sound like much but you do the math, that's $800 billion. Say it slowly, Eight Hundred Billion Dollars. Cash. 40% of that stashed here in the US. Annually. More than the profits of all the companies on Wall Street combined. Problem: how to feed all that dirty moolah into the economy? Enter hawala. Since time immemorial the final repository of all wealth is real property. Like they say, God ain't making land no more. It's why I got you out here. Who do you think owns all this?" J.J. waved at the empty landscape.

"No idea. The Feds?"

"No. Title is in the name of a Delaware corporation, owned by an outfit in Providence, Rhode Island, owned in turn by a Netherland Antilles trust which is basically a name on a brass plaque on the door of a lawyer's office in Curaçao. You're a small grower in California or Colorado. You don't have mountains of cash, just a small hill. The hawaladar you contact - who owns the local Indian Restaurant where you like to take the family for curry and rice - outlines a deal to you after you had a bitch about the fucking banks and their fucking regulations, in effect swapping your cash for the land in the form of bearer shares in the trust. Nothing is recorded, no lawyers, loans, mortgages, etc. Nada. You now own land. Technically you should report this on your next tax return. Right? Only if you're dumb. Which you are not because you have dual citizenship and a Mexican wife. And over there, Chief, where the drug cartels from Sinaloa to Michoacan are now part of the government, nobody pays taxes and nobody gives a shit. In a sense they're just buying back what used to be their land anyway They think we are the most corrupt, hypocritical nation on Earth blaming everybody else for the drug problem without once acknowledging that it's our voracious appetite for drugs that created the problem in the first place so why go to war on them for supplying what we want?"

"Where do my guys fit in?"

"I'll get to that. It's not what you think. Plus there's another piece to factor into all this, so hear me out. As forensic accountants we have sources, have to have, ears to the ground listening for stuff in all kinds of sensitive places, one of which is arms, their origin, place of manufacture, capabilities, production capacity, you name it. Most of this you can find on the net, some on the dark web where, for forty bucks, a kid in Kabul will sell you a perfect, functioning knockoff of an AK47 he's made in the family garage. But really special gear is the bailiwick of a handful of people, the ones with exceptional skill, training and financial muscle. They are anonymous, have to be. Like trying to find Michelangelo, you know he's out there but how do you find him if he doesn't advertise? You been to Italy, Chief?"

"No."

"You know what a Beretta is, right?"

"Of course. I carry a 92C. Got it right here." The Chief tapped his shoulder where under his jacket the slight bulge of his holster could just be seen. "Never leave home without it."

"I thought you guys all had Glocks."

"Most do. They're good for the price. Because of our budget, they give us a discount, best deal we could make." He tapped his shoulder again. "This is better. One of the perks of being Chief."

"Well, that was fabricated in a village called Gardone, place just north of Brescia. We got a small-time lawyer down there, a little bent, very discreet, feeds us info from time to time and we do the same, bit of you-scratch-my-back-I-scratch-yours. A while ago he asked us to check out a payment, two in fact, received by a client of his, the Michelangelo of computer printed guns, wanted to know if we could trace who made the payments through Liechtenstein and the Bahamas. Our hackers go to work - you didn't hear me say that - and, no great surprise, a hawaladar brokers the payments which is no help to the lawyer. What is a surprise is that he's the same guy who does these land deals here. Small world, right? We can't put a name to him but we think he's one of the Marwaris from Kolkata, they're moneylenders operating out of the Bara Bazaar who traditionally bankroll the trade in jute and hemp throughout India, Java, Sumatra and Bali."

"I thought you said they didn't use banks and the cash didn't move?"

*"Yes, that's a strange part I can't explain." J.J. shrugged. "Unless it's deliberate. They **want** to leave a trace, a record, because the payments are for a bizarre weapon, made in component pieces shipped to four different addresses in Mexico, and they have to prove the money was sent. Gives us a break, though it doesn't explain who is going to use an undetectable gun on whom. But it gets me thinking, what's the common denominator in all this?" J.J. stopped talking, his eyes behind the granny glasses slowly scanning across the empty hills. "When we first met you said something interesting about things always returning to the mean. You ever check the average mileage your officers do on their Concours Kawasakis? According to my green-eyeshade brigade, the three we are focused on, Diaz, Mendoza and Hernandez, all clock 12 to 15% more'n the others average. Why? Where do they go? On whose orders? Or ask how come three of your deputies are getting bennies but no cash we can yet find. They errand boys or fronting for hawaladars acting for parties unknown in acquiring vast tracts of desert land of no apparent value down here by the border which is then traded for cash that can't be banked? Property is not liquid, if anything it's illiquid if it has no use. Nothing grows here because there's no water. The mines are abandoned because there's nothing left to find. So what's the attraction? It took me a while to figure out and when I did it was obvious - the raw land **is** the bank. And Arizona is mostly raw land. It's there forever. If you have untold mountains of cash, bits of printed paper getting depreciated daily and a headache to hide and protect, what better than to convert it into dirt, right? That's the long game. Now ask yourself who benefits, who are the players? See where -" J.J. broke off talking. Listened. Scanned the hills again. Then, in the same conversational tone, he said, "Don't react, Chief. Don't look round. You sure you were not tailed here?"*

"What?"

"We're being watched. When I drive off, take your time, then get out, take a leak. Act natural. I'll call you."

+++

Through the spotter scope the man watched the van drive off slowly in a cloud of dust and disappear around a long bend in the Gleeson Road and then watched the cop get out of his car to piss on a mesquite bush.

"I could take him now," said the sniper. They were half a mile away, 100 yards up, hidden in the back of a mine shaft from the mouth of which the cop's car looked like a toy glinting in the afternoon sun.

"No; he's not the problem."

"You mean the guy in the van? Who's he?"

"That's the problem. We don't know. Couldn't make him through that tinted glass. But I got the van number. You better take off before they miss you. Watch your ass."

+++

Around the bend, out of sight, J.J. Nicholson had pulled off the road, parked, hidden in the fall line of a shallow draw, switched on a state-of-the-art digital recorder with a quiet mic preamplifier sitting on the bench seat next to him, plugged in an omnidirectional dynamic mic aimed in the direction he had come. Nothing at first except the vague hissing of a breeze and the sound of insects and the pinging of the van engine cooling. Then, couple of minutes later, way off in the distance, the sound of a big bike being fired up, the burp of the throttle and the fading gurgle of its exhaust as it drove away. Silence. J.J. picked up his cell, dialled a number, listened, and when it was answered, said, "Some guy on a big bike, Chief. Watch your ass."

+++

CHAPTER TEN

Memoirs of a woman of pleasure,
Zaftig Aphrodite.
Hotbed Queen.
Travels with a whip,
Going too far tipping the velvet.
Walked under a ladder, which
had the spectators
Tut-tutting.

+++

Clapboard *#11 - BP/Mansion/Genoa.* On the soundtrack: **BP:** There was no way to disguise the fact that since the departure of Maisie and Lorraine we were diminished, not just in number but in spirit, as if the real world had unfairly impinged upon our hedonistic freedom. On our way back up the Med, at Serafina's command, we disembarked in Genoa to spend a few days with the old witch. She and Poppy immediately hit it off, scooped up the girls and left for an all-female ramble in the old town and the re-imagined Porto Antico of Renzo Piano, leaving me on my own with my thoughts. As always I drifted down to the corner of the terrace to find the ants and, to my surprise, they were gone. Why? I had no idea and this disturbed me. Since I was a boy they'd always been there. What did they know that I did not? It was the first thing I said to Serafina when she got back and summoned me in for a private meeting in her study. "The ants have gone."

"Yes, I noticed that," she said. "Good riddance."

"It usually means something is going to happen."

"Oh, stop being so superstitious. Sit down instead of dithering around. Now, tell me when did this relationship start?"

"Relationship? You mean with Poppy?"

"Yes, you and the Professor. Stop calling her that. Her name is Samantha. Lord knows what she sees in you but I must say she is absolutely delightful. A real beauty - with brains. The girls all love her. She is your soulmate, BP, if you have any sense you would marry her."

"Don't be ridiculous."

"I'm not. This is a rare chance for you, think about it."

"What's there to think about? Doesn't it occur to you that I like being single."

"That's what she said you would say."

"Basta! You discussed this with her? Questo ma schifo! That's disgusting! It's none of your business."

"Dai! Non ti scaldare! We all did," she said, and added before I could explode, "don't get in a snit, turning purple doesn't suit you."

"Ma, che sei grullo?"

"I'm not joking. It happens. I knew the moment I saw him the old man was mine even though I was married at the time and had two kids. The Gods decide, isn't that what you always say?"

What the fuck. The ants were right. Time to move out.

+++

Our last stop before getting the train home was the Hotel du Cap. It's different since the Oetkers bought and renovated the place. As I told the girls, I rode a dark green bicycle with no gears when I first went there one Sunday, my day off from pumping petrol at the garage outside La Bocca where I had a summer job. I had read about the place and wanted to see for myself so I hopped on my bike and peddled over to the Cap d'Antibes not realising that there was nothing to see because the whole place was screened off from the road by thick shrubbery and an iron fence. "De dehors on ne voit rien," a voice behind me said and I turned to find a very tall man, wearing an old-fashioned straw boater, looking down at me. "Donnez-moi votre véhicule," he said. "Venez."

He took my bike by the handlebars and I followed him through wrought-iron gates into the forecourt of a large faded building, the entrance to which was up a short narrow staircase giving on to a stone-flagged hallway around the open cage of a rather elegant lift serving the upper floors. The man was André Sella, the owner, as I was told by the concierge, a Monsieur Irondelle, who was directed to show me around. "Montrez Monsieur notre parc!" was the imperious instruction, to which Sella added, "Mais qu'il ne touche rien."

From the receptionist's desk, Irondelle walked me through the lobby to exit at the top of a wide flight of stairs overlooking a long carpeted walkway down to the sea framed by umbrella pines and palm trees. Taking a quick look over his shoulder, Irondelle said, "Right, you heard what he said, don't touch anything. Walk around. See me before you leave."

The park was impressive but curiously I immediately felt at home wandering around with my hands in my pockets past the clay tennis courts, the dog's cemetery, the rose garden, the cabanas and the pool cut into pink rocks jutting into the sea. When I got back up to the hotel an hour had gone by, Irondelle was not behind his desk and for a moment it seemed nobody was there. Then I saw long legs stuck out through the doorway of a tiny office to the right of the lift, Sella's. He was examining some papers, but looked up over the top of the spectacles on the tip of his nose. "So what do you think?" he said.

For a moment I did not know how to reply, then heard myself say with a nonchalance that came out of nowhere, "I feel at home. How much does it cost to stay here?"

Sella stopped what he was doing, took off his glasses the better to inspect me and having made an inventory of everything from my uncut hair to my dusty sandals, he said, "Vous avez combien en poche, jeune homme?"

I had been paid the previous day so I fished out the few francs I had earned for inspection just as Irondelle hove into view to count what was on my palm. The owner and his concierge exchanged a glance and Monsieur André Sella said "Show him one of the maid's rooms over the garage."

So. I am someone born in jail who spent his first night at the Hotel du Cap in a maid's room over the garage.

+++

In the refurbished luxury of our suite on the first floor of the hotel, getting up from behind a desk where she had been reading, looking down the same carpeted walkway to the sea, Poppy, having done the math, observed, "That couldn't have been you. I've read the brochure. The Oetkers bought this place in '69 when you would have been three, so there's no way you met André Sella."

"Se non é vero, é ben trovato." From where I lay in bed she was silhouetted against the windows to the balcony. In just a pareo around her waist. Wow. "Makes a good story, non?"

"Who told it to you?"

"The old man, Serafina's husband. He lived here after the war. Coincidentally in this very suite, except it was shabby at the time."

"You can't get out of his shadow, can you? His suite, his stories, his wife, his legacy. What about you? Who are you?"

"A fragment of the past - no, make that an echo. What does it matter? Come here." I smiled and patted the bed next to me.

"No." Suddenly serious. "That's all you want. You think it's a game. Who can believe anything you say? You're meant to be educating these girls, not telling them fairy stories."

"What's got into you? They didn't know how to hold a knife and fork properly until I showed them."

"We're not talking about table manners! We're talking about the truth. But maybe that's not important to you?"

Furious, arms across her chest, she stalked into the bathroom and locked the door. After a moment I could hear her running water into the tub and thought, bloody woman, she'd obviously been plotting with Serafina. Followed by, how'd I get into this? I closed my eyes feeling a hint of panic and a sense of exits closing. Time to move out. Just like that, I did.

+++

It was a nightmare. I, naturally, left a goodbye note, a well-written explanation in which I also tendered my resignation to the University, effective immediately, the coward's easy solution, no point in facing a firing squad. Then the thought occurred what to do with the house in Beverly Hills? Where would I go? What would I do? And I only woke up when the warm, damp, scented body of Poppy molded itself to me and she whispered "Sorry for the tantrum," as her hand brought her withered little friend to life. The rest is history.

+++

Built in 1867 in rose-coloured stone from Arles after a style favoured by Louis X111, sunlight filtered down through the murky glass windows of the forged steel rooftop of the Gare de Nice-Ville onto a milling crowd searching for the right compartment and slowly boarding the bullet-shaped, 200-metre long, 8-carriage TGV, France's high-speed service to Cannes-Marseille-Lyon-Aéroport Paris Charles-de-Gaulle, a rail journey that used to take 20 hours in the days of the Train Bleu, now reduced to under 6, with a routine top speed of 320 km/h but with no sleeping cars and no first class dining room. The golfer, carrying only his clubs and a computer bag, checked his cell phone on which he had booked an e-ticket for a first class seat upstairs in the double-decker carriages introduced by the SNCF in 1981, back then the height of streamlined modernity. 50 metres ahead of him, a gaggle of tanned American students and their teachers found their 2nd Class carriage and ambled on board. There had been talk of a wildcat strike, yet ten minutes later, punctually at the advertised time of 9.04am, the train pulled out of the station.

+++

"Pardon, Patron, take a look at this." The young gendarme, Jean-François, seconded to the National Centre for Counter-terrorism located in the Elysee palace on the Faubourg St. Honoré, glanced up from where he was monitoring banks of computers. His superior was on the phone and drew a finger across his throat to signal silence, then saw the tight urgency in his young colleague's face, said into the receiver, "Je te rappelle," and walked over to stand behind his protégé. "What have you got?"

Jean-François pointed at a screen. "Regardez. TGV from Nice to the airport Charles-de-Gaulle this morning." In tight close-up a seemingly young man with a swarthy complexion, an old-fashioned tweed golf cap pulled low on his brow, wearing sunglasses, jeans and sneakers, with a golf bag hoisted on one shoulder, walked forwards and then disappeared as he obviously went past a CCTV camera with a fixed focus, followed by a succession of people, passengers, male, female, fat, thin, all shapes and sizes.

"Go back."

Jean-François clicked on his mouse, stopped the video, put the cursor on the red dot reached on the readout and wound the tape back. Golf cap, sunglasses, golf bag.

"Again."

Ditto. Golf cap, sunglasses, golf bag.

"Your impression?"

Jean-François hesitated.

"Yes? Don't be shy. Go on, say what you think."

"He's too young to wear such a cap. And the glasses. They're Ray-Bans. Nobody would wear Ray-Bans with that old cap."

"He's a golfer."

"Especially not a golfer. Well, perhaps an old one would wear the cap but never those glasses. I think it may be a disguise."

"Time?"

"The video says 8.48 from the camera on Platform 3." Jean-François hesitated again, then, with his finger tapped another screen which showed an excellent photograph, full-face, of a swarthy young man, with the label -

ATTENTION - ATTENTION: PRIORITY TO ALL PERSONNEL. Hassan Husseni, aka, Mahmoud al Sadr, aka Ahmad Rabat Benali - armed and extremely dangerous. If seen ALERTE ROUGE. Repeat RED ALERT. Active until aborted. Direction Générale de la Sécurité Intérieure.

"You remember, Patron, this picture was posted by the DG last week. They got it from Mossad. The suspected bomber in Venice - might it not be the same person?"

"How can you tell?"

"I posted the landmark features of Husseni's face into our 3D database and superimposed the guy in the tweed cap. It's not perfect, but take a look." On his computer the two images merged, the principal component analysis of the recognition algorithms instantly showing a close match for the shape of the nose, mouth and chin, while under the tweed cap an outline of Husseni's skull fitted perfectly. "As backup I ran a skin-print. See here how these lines and pores in the skin texture seem to be identical? If I had more time . . . "

"You don't. C'est bien. We must assume he is here in France. Where's that train now?"

Jean-François looked at the watch on his wrist which confirmed the digital clock on the screen. "13.26. It's at or has just left Lyon. Next stop is Charles-de-Gaulle in two hours."

"Right. I'll call the Minister and the DG. You call the SNCF at their HQ in St. Denis. Find out where they can stop that train. It must seem natural, no dramatic announcements -" he broke off, paused, as multiple implications dawned on him, and then, as if coaching himself, he said - "Merde, merde. This has got to be coordinated. Give me the microphone."

All electronic communication within the department was paused as the urgent voice of Le Patron demanded - "Silence. Attention. This is an emergency. Cancel whatever you are doing. Group heads meet in my office immediately. Standby."

+++

"Why are we stopping?" An hour out of Lyon, cruising at over 300 km/h, the question was asked up and down the train as it slowed to a crawl crossing the A6 motorway and then the D954, coming to a halt in empty countryside next to a lake, the Étang d'Époisses, in the Côte d'Or department of Franche-Comté. After what seemed like an endless wait, which in fact was less than five minutes, the conductor's bored voice on the tannoy announced a problem at the junction up ahead with the branch line to Strasbourg, with an estimated delay of, maybe, half-an-hour, ample time to enjoy the resources of the bar upstairs in Coach No.7, or they could wait in their seats for the refreshment trolley to come around with snacks and

111

coffee, tea and fresh drinks. He then added, to the amusement of some passengers, the gratuitous information that the nearby town of Époisses was notorious for the smelliest cheese made in France, Epoisses de Bourgogne, a pungent cheese made of unpasteurized cow's-milk. No one noticed a helicopter half-hidden by a copse bordering the right-of-way, or the special forces unit which emerged from it in the uniform of SNCF rail attendants.

Exactly thirty minutes later the train jerked forward, built up speed, and proceeded on its journey.

+++

"He's not on board," the agent said into his cellphone.

"You sure?" The tension cracked Le Patron's voice.

"Absolutely. Pushing the food trolley around we've been past everyone at least twice since we got on the train. We've even checked the toilets. The only thing is the golf-bag in the luggage rack. I'm standing in front of it. You got the picture I sent, right?"

"Is there a computer case with it?"

"Not that I can see. Hang on."

"DON'T TOUCH THE GOLF-BAG!"

"Shit . . . "

The force of the explosion was so great it lifted the train in two broken halves which, combined with the forward momentum of travelling at over 300 km/h, created an enormous metallic fireball that on impact a kilometre down the line gouged a crater in the ground 80 metres across and 3 metres deep.

+++

'NO SURVIVORS'

The headline was 3 inches high across the front page of every newspaper carrying a photograph of the wrecked train and another of the Brownsville Boys and Girls choir and their teachers.

'Three different factions of Islamic Jihad have claimed responsibility for the bombing of the Nice-Paris TGV.' The President of France, in

language rarely heard from a Head of State, denounced 'this atrocity, by so-called Islamists barely deserving to belong to the human race, will not bend the people of France and will be avenged with implacable ferocity. There is no faith that can justify the taking of 318 innocent lives . . . '

BP looked up from his copy of the Times at Blackbird Crow with whom he was sharing breakfast on the sunlit terrace of the hotel waiting for the girls to come down from their rooms so they could begin an early-morning checkout.

"You seen this?" he said.

Blackbird nodded, his face sombre. "Could have been us."

"What should I do?"

"My advice? Why tempt fate? Venice, Lorraine, now this - it's been a long month. Forget the tour; we're done. Let's fly home."

+++

Betty was at the Los Angeles Zoo in Glendale with the children. She was annoyed because the maid had not come, had not called and wouldn't answer the phone and for a reason she couldn't understand Alan thought it her fault.

"Mommy? Mommy, you're not listening," her daughter said, pulling her arm to get her attention. They were in front of the monkeys.

"What?" Betty snapped out the word, then felt guilty. "Sorry, Sweetheart, Mommy was thinking. What did you say?"

"Look," the little girl said. "They're scared, just like Daisy." She pointed at the animals cowering together in a tight pack in the far corner of their cage, grimacing and turning their backs, desperately shaking the immovable bars that kept them in. "Why are they frightened, Mommy?"

Betty had no idea so they went in search of an attendant and found one scratching his head at the bear pit. "Something's spooked 'em," he said. "They're off their feed, ornery as hell, won't come out of their caves."

"They're scared," the little girl said again.

"You may be right, young lady," the man said and for some reason Betty shivered.

+++

CHAPTER ELEVEN

The Devil at large:
God is an Englishman,
Reading in the dark.
'Un soir à Londres, la nuit transfigurée
Notre histoire qui fut heureuse, puis
douloureuse et funeste -
Histoire à dormir sans vous,
Eve future.'

+++

"Sir - please wait behind the yellow line." Fortunato was tired and had not paid attention to the signs. Five intercontinental planes had arrived in a 15-minute time span, disgorging hundreds of passengers, swamping the Customs and Immigration facilities at LAX. For over an hour he'd been blindly following a long line of Non-US citizens with their passports and visa documents in hand, while the girls, Blackbird Crow and his assistant, as Americans coming home, were already checked through their section and waiting in the baggage area.

"Sorry," he said to the female Customs officer patrolling Arrivals, and stepped back, bumping into the passenger behind him. "Sorry," he repeated. When it was finally his turn to be interviewed he was a shade disgruntled and not his usual urbane self as he faced an equally weary Customs official who had already put in 7 hours sitting on an uncomfortable swivel chair endlessly repeating the same questions to an unending tide of faces and documents flowing past his station.

"Hi. Welcome to the United States. How are you today." It was a formula, delivered pat, no inflection, no warmth in the words, certainly no welcome. The official's name was Michael Gonzales It said so on a name tag stitched above the left breast pocket of the uniform short-sleeved shirt he was wearing which had started out the day freshly ironed and was now sweat-stained and crumpled.

"Tired," said Fortunato, as he offered his papers and passport with its B1/B2 visa to be scanned and compared to information on a computer screen that only Mr. Gonzales could see on which was a mugshot of Fortunato and the fingerprints of both his hands with a banner running across the bottom of the screen reading 'SSSS', an acronym for 'secondary security screening selection'.

"How long were you out of the country?" Gonzales said, pro forma.

"A month," said Fortunato.

"What's the purpose of your trip?"

"I lecture part-time at UCLA. We were on a field-trip; I'm bringing the kids home."

"What countries did you visit on this trip?"

"France, Italy, Croatia, Montenegro, Greece and Turkey."

"Turkey?"

"Yes."

"How long are you planning to stay in the United States?"

"My visa gives me six months but we have another trip scheduled to Guatemala and Mexico over the Christmas break."

"Where will you stay while in California."

"In my house in Beverly Hills; you have the address there on my I/94." Fortunato paused, and then, unfortunately, added, "Is this necessary? I come and go frequently. Surely you can see that on your computer?"

Wrong thing to say to a tired Customs officer, Fortunato, and he knew it the moment the words were out of his mouth. Gonzales came awake, pressed a concealed button under his desk to summon a superior, and, standing away from the desk, said, pointing at Fortunato's roll-on bag, "If that is all the luggage you have, sir, please follow me."

"Where are we going?"

"To Secondary Inspection for additional screening."

"My students are waiting for me."

"They will be duly informed, sir. Now, please follow me."

"This is ridiculous. I am responsible for those children. I demand to see your superior."

Which was the moment the Supervising Officer appeared, an expression on his face of world-weary annoyance at the intransigence of people who thought they had any rights and his obligation to remain polite in the face of such stupidity.

"Do we have a problem?" he said.

+++

"Are you guys all paranoid?"

"That is not a helpful answer, Mr. Crollalanza."

"Then why ask again and again given you have my passport, you know who I am, what I do, where I live, where I've been?"

"We can ask whatever questions we think pertinent to anyone within 100 miles of our borders. You are in Secondary Inspection to determine if you are a security risk. So I ask you again what was the real purpose of your trip to Istanbul?"

"And I'll tell you again, it was the final destination of the Grand Tour in the 1920s."

"Yet you scarcely arrive there surreptitiously by boat before leaving again?

"You call clearing Customs in Karaköy surreptitious? You obviously haven't been in Turkey."

"I call leaving a distant destination so soon after arriving the probable conclusion of a clandestine meeting where you met your suppliers."

"This is in your movie, right?"

"The house you claim you own is 13180 Mellon Drive, in the Beverly Hills Post Office district, is that correct?"

"Yes. Yes. Yes. How many times do I have to say it?"

"The house you supposedly bought with nothing down and no income to speak of?"

"Check with the broker if you don't believe me."

"Do you know a woman called Christina Alquiera?"

"No."

"Is she or has she ever been a resident in your house."

"No."

"Do you know a woman called Maria-Celestina Alquiera?"

"Yes."

"Is she or has she ever been a resident in your house?"

"Yes."

"What is your relationship to her?"

"She is a student of mine."

"Is it customary for you to house students off campus?"

"What are you insinuating?"

"I think you know. Do you also know these two women are sisters?"

"I do now."

"And that both are in custody for conspiring to import 10 kilograms of a prohibited substance?"

"What?!"

"I am sure you are aware that under Department of Homeland Security guidelines an adult who shelters an illegal alien intent on committing a crime is liable to criminal prosecution, confiscation of property, fines and/or deportation. It is now 9pm. As it is a Friday you will be remanded in custody without bail until Monday when this hearing will resume and a determination made on your status, sir. Enjoy the hospitality of the Twin Towers."

+++

Fortunato, in handcuffs, was driven in a police van to the Correctional Facility downtown where he was booked, fingerprinted, his mugshot taken, his clothes and belongings removed, itemised and sealed in a plastic bag, and he was given a green jumpsuit to wear. It was past midnight when he walked through electronically controlled steel doors and was locked into a crowded three-tiered cell smelling of stale air, urine and sweat where he ended up wrapped in a thin prison blanket sleeping on the filthy floor under a bunk-bed in which lay Slim Jim who said, when he saw who was being brought in, "Hey, BP, my man! Welcome to the toilet." What the fuck, right?

+++

"Yo lucky day, Professor, I tell the brothers this man be born in jail, don't nobody fuck with him, I got his back!" Slim Jim said it loudly in the noisy bedlam of thousands of convicts trying to eat breakfast off Styrofoam trays delivered to the stacked cells at 6.30 in the morning. Then he dropped his voice: "But keep yo fuckin' head down. Don' share no information. Half these assholes are armed, twenty percent are insane an' should be in hospital, half the bulls are on the take an' the other half scared to come to work. Nobody's yo friend. There's psychopaths in here they kill you if you look at 'em wrong. Don' look at nobody." With his eyes Slim aimed a quick glance across the steel and reinforced glass complex to the opposite corridor of open cell doors where at a steel table five heavily-muscled tattooed men in blue jumpsuits sat chained to the floor. "See them animals? Mexican Mafia M13 jail gang. Three doors down, the AB, fuckin' Aryan Brotherhood nazis. Then the Surenos. They allies. Up against the Chicano's Nuestra Familia, the Black Guerillas and us, D.C. Blacks. This a different world, BP. You a brave motherfucker don' matter, these guys don' give a fuck who you are, what you done on the outside. They the law here. You got to get through today, tomorrow, next day, their way. Those girls you told me 'bout? Never you mind. They gone, man, whacked even if the Feds try to protect 'em 'fore they get to trial, stop 'em snitching where they got the dope. They connect you, you go down. They had a guy in the hole here, M13 boss wanted to quit the life, rat out his gang, he's so important they put him in solitary so's nobody could touch him, not even the guards, been in there seven years slowly goin' crazy, thinks he's dyin', asks for a priest. Priest shows up the other day, shoots the guy dead. How, in a super-max security joint? Turns out the guy didn't ask for a priest, the priest is a hitman sent by the Sinaloans, gun's made of plastic disguised as a sex-toy, barrel's a dick, nothing shows in X-ray, the bullet comes from a guard on their payroll. They catch the killer, so what, he done the job, don' even know who paid for it. You better pray someone shows up, bails you out this shithole."

+++

On Monday someone did, Sister Allegra. Through the thick glass separating them in the fluorescent-bright light of the Interview Room overseen by armed wardens, Fortunato thought she looked even more ethereal then when he had last seen her.

"How'd you hear?" he said into a microphone on his side of the partition.

"Your girlfriend, Samantha, phoned Serafina to tell her what happened. You know my mother," said Sister Allegra. "She pulled some strings."

+++

At a NATO meeting in Palermo, ostensibly organised to discuss and improve the interception of clandestine migrants from North Africa into Europe. During a recess, an observer from the Vatican, Cardinal Emmanuel Lanza, fell into conversation with the US Vice-Admiral of the 6th Fleet, headquartered in Naples. After the usual preliminary chit-chat and gossip, the Vice-Admiral said, "Let's cut to the chase, Cardinal. How can I help you?"

"A small matter. A distant relative has fallen foul of your Office of Homeland Security. A misunderstanding. They have put him in jail . . . "

"And you want us to get him out? No can do. Homeland reports directly to the White House. We have no jurisdiction, zero influence."

The Cardinal smiled.

"I mean that," said the Vice-Admiral. "We'd love to help, but . . .

"But?" The Cardinal's smile vanished. "We believe your lease comes up for renewal for the 6th Fleet to shelter in our harbour in Naples?"

"Our lease? Your harbour? With respect, surely this is a matter for the Italian Government?"

"In Naples, Admiral? Come now, as a man of the world, you have heard of our friends, the Camorra, yes? Need I say more? Why not make a call, help an innocent man? We will be eternally grateful." The Cardinal made the sign of the Cross and briefly smiled again.

+++

"Just like that?" said Fortunato.

"Yes, just like that," said Sister Allegra. "I am here on a diplomatic passport from the Vatican and I have one for you. The Navy jet that flew me here is waiting to fly us back."

The time was 10.37am on the 25th of September, 2028. With no warning, when most people were at work and most children in school, the earthquake struck, measuring 9.2 on the Richter Scale.

+++

CHAPTER TWELVE

Although the shaking lasted less than two minutes the city never recovered from the catastrophic devastation and loss of life. Hundreds of thousands perished, the actual death toll unknowable. Billions upon billions of dollars in damage destroyed the infrastructure and economy of Southern California.

On the convergent boundary between tectonic plates, the North American Plate inexorably moving south-west grinding against the Pacific Plate moving north-east, under the ocean-bed 2 miles offshore from Long Beach, in a little-known trench called the San Gregorio Fault, the slippage and violent subduction at the quake's epicentre caused an undersea megathrust of such violence that the energy it released created a tsunami which travelled across the ocean at 943 kp/h, the speed of a jet plane, with a wavelength of 282 kms, reaching Hawaii in six hours and the coast of Japan in eleven, sending 10 to 15-metre waves surging inland on every shelving shore, sparking multiple fires which combined to create firestorms that destroyed nearly all wooden structures built on the coast in eight Pacific-rim countries, with a death toll close to half a million people.

Los Angeles, as a functioning metropolis, ceased to exist. In the first 60 seconds the seismic shock, recorded around the world, destroyed all communications, ruptured the conduits which brought water to the city, and paralysed traffic by turning the freeways into mangled concrete spaghetti. 80% of the city's 7,640 megawatts of electric generation capacity was obliterated by the destruction of its one large hydroelectric plant, eleven of its fourteen small hydroelectric plants and three of its four in-basin thermal plants. More than half the overhead transmission circuits and 90%

of the 124 miles of underground transmissions circuits, 13,827 transmission towers, and over 3,000 miles of underground distribution cables were demolished. Structures that withstood the first shock were pulverised by a swarm of aftershocks, some measuring 7.5 on the Richter Scale. All the coastal towns from Malibu on south to Santa Monica, Venice, Manhattan Beach, all the way to Huntington Beach were wiped out by the tsunami. LAX was cut in half, its runways engulfed; of the 70 large-bodied aircraft on the ground all were destroyed, piled by a succession of giant 100-foot waves into unrecognisable junk.

Across the 500 square miles of the stricken city, in every direction, black columns of smoke could be seen rising up into a clear blue sky from small fires ignited by bursting gas mains that could not be extinguished for lack of water, the full horror of which came at nightfall as the low-rise, stick-built houses characteristic of LA succumbed to the flames one by one, inexorably pooling into one vast firestorm with temperatures exceeding 2000° Centigrade at ground level, the rising heat pulling in fresh air and oxygen to constantly fan and expand the conflagration. In less than 24 hours the city burned to the ground.

Ironically the jail, its foundations standing on rock, with walls 2-meters thick built of steel and reinforced concrete, was the safest place to be. Apart from a few cracked windows it suffered relatively minor damage while all around it the iconic buildings of downtown Los Angeles were shredded in a blizzard of exploding glass as skyscrapers whipped and flexed like so many car antennas and those less than perfectly built collapsed on themselves instantly blocking the streets with mountains of debris. Sister Allegra and Fortunato felt the initial shock, a distinct heavy thud in the soles of their shoes.

"What the fuck?" said Fortunato. Then the lights went out.

It took a moment for the prison's liquid propane-gas emergency backup generators to kick in and when the lights came on again, simultaneously, they both said, "What was that?"

"Earthquake!" a warden shouted, and bolted from the room, followed by all his colleagues. In a matter of minutes, once the hard slap of running feet and shouted instructions had faded, the only sounds that could be heard were a mixture of strange, distant, unidentifiable rumblings and abrupt explosions.

"What the fuck," said Fortunato again, "let's get out of here."

That the same thought occurred to other prisoners was no surprise. What was surprising was the discovery that they had the world's largest jail as well as the nation's largest mental health facility to themselves as every guard, including the Head Warden, the Captain, the Sheriff and the prison Governor, had all exercised that basic human instinct of self-preservation and headed home leaving the gates open and the inmates to fend for themselves. Within 30 minutes the Twin Towers Correctional Facility was empty but for those poor souls lost on the mental ward unable to find the exits.

With no transportation available, Sister Allegra and Fortunato set out to walk the 14 miles from downtown to the compound in Beverly Hills. They were never seen again.

+++

EPILOGUE

Blackbird Crow survived. His film 'What the f**k!' won the Golden Bear for Best Documentary at the 2029 Berlin Film Festival and the Palme d'Or at the Cannes Film Festival for Best Film, where the audience stood and wept at the closing credits, a 10-minute long montage of the feet of thousands and thousands of people crossing the black-and-white pedestrian way at the junction of Rodeo Drive and Wilshire Boulevard while the names of the known dead scrolled in alphabetical order across the bottom of the screen, an endless stream of dedication. If you listened closely, behind the sound of shuffling feet, you could hear a young girl's voice whispering 'Will you miss me when I'm gone . . . will you miss me . . . "

FADE OUT

THE DESTINY OF
GUIDO

Je suis homme: je dure peu
et la nuit est énorme.
Mais je regarde vers le haut:
Les étoiles écrivent.
Sans comprendre je comprends:
je suis aussi écriture
et en ce même instant
Quelqu'un m'épelle.

—Octavio Paz

APERTURA

207345.4158° N, 141.6732° E

T*he jellyfish, turritopsis dohrnii, are immortal. They wait for him, always there, in the cold waters of the Sea of Okhotsk which lap the old man's rock. He is immune to them having been stung so often over the many years past. They taught him how to drift, his body vertically suspended under the sea, moving to the same subtle currents as the jellyfish with scarcely a movement of his fingers, occasionally rising to the surface to breathe. Can the polyps think, store memories, like he does? What's in life if you can't remember. What's there but the stories? And if you can't remember them, did they happen? Even history is just someone's account of what they think happened. So how do you know it's true? Paz's line arrives uninvited, Je suis homme . . . something . . . fragments drifting through the neurons of his mind as he is walking, blue, something blue, walking on through a copse, unbidden he remembers what Abou said. Uncle Abou. His benefactor. His mother's lover. When he was in that boarding school in England he would show up and take me out for tea. The same immaculate fat man in his grey suit, oblivious to the drizzle or to school regulations about visiting days. I have no idea how he knew I was there. He would show up in an antique Rolls Royce or Bentley, have a chat with the Headmaster as if this was a long standing arrangement they had, and off we would go to a tea shop he knew in Saffron Walden or sometimes in Cambridge. Over scones and strawberry jam and clotted cream I was questioned on how I was doing in school, my favourite subjects, what sports I liked, had I made any new friends. He was given to making cryptic remarks. 'Pay close attention to who writes history,' was one. 'When studying art remember the eyes hear better than the ears,' was another. 'Your mother left you a wonderful gift, her intelligence. Do not let her down. Nurture it, read. Never stop reading or* *learning. It's the only way to live a thousand lives.' The last time I saw him was on the eve of war. 'The Headmaster tells me they are sending you back to Prussia. I fear for you, young man, as I fear for all the young men. The absurdity of this war declared by pretentious fools who have never been on a battlefield, sending men who a few weeks before were farmers and teachers and lawyers and bakers and postmen and waiters to pick up guns and kill other farmers, lawyers, bakers, postmen and waiters simply because they live on the other side of an imaginary line on a map. And we call ourselves human. Even though your ancestors were warriors you do not have to emulate them.' Abou's prediction is buried like an old nightmare, a forgotten roll call of once familiar schoolboy names, Abbey, Bell, Bingham, Brown, Browne, Cook, Cottingham, Davis, Edwards, Grey, Gray, Habermann, Hart . . . a classroom of names like a long forgotten tune . . . .Guido, no, he shakes his head in the cold water. The tune plays on, cannot be switched off, as he floats drifting with the jellyfish he remembers . . . a drumroll . . . the sound of cannons . . . and in the cold water he feels something nudging the back of his neck . . . Of course it was only a movie. Originally the film opened in the shade of an awning, on a hot summer's day, where an elegant hand - the hand of a lady wearing a diamond bracelet - is writing a postcard on board a ship of the P & O line but the producers had no sense of humour and insisted that it start with a war. So that's what they got . . . and he turns and sees the shark. Again.*

+++

CHAPTER ONE

The assassin rode into town anonymously seated in the back of the communal electric tram linking Guadalajara to Mexico City. He was confident he would not be recognized dressed as a peasant seeking work in the metropolis. His papers were in order and the rags he wore were identical to those of the itinerant workmen seated on the wooden benches around him. The 552 kilometres that separated the two cities was covered in less than two hours. Far less time than on the murderous highway, 15D, which could occasionally be seen in the distance running parallel to the tram, where the weekly toll of carjackings, kidnappings, holdups, ambushes and beheaded victims was the grisly fodder of muckraking journalists in all the Sunday special editions.

Disembarking at the terminal he made his way on foot to the spider web of streets ending at the octagon of La Colonia Federal where he was scheduled to meet an 'uncle', a synonym for a gang member higher in the food chain than a lowly killer in the oldest and most powerful surviving plaza of the drug cartels, Jalisco Nueva Generación.

+++

One hundred years ago I was four, therefore I am now 104, as it pleases my robotic clone to remind me, adding I should get a quick transfusion of oxygenated blood from my donor in Kenya before my scheduled appearance on World TV Tonight to celebrate the 20th Anniversary of the founding of the EUM of which I am the Imperial Head of Statistics, second in succession to the Presidency.

I could see he was studying me.

Me.

It was annoying.

"What?," I said.

"If you don't want to do it . . . "

"Don't be ridiculous. You know I have to. It lends legitimacy, affirms the transformation, builds tradition, values, protocol, blah, blah . . . "

Blah!

His lips didn't move but I distinctly heard a third 'blah' in my head as I continued the rehearsal of my speech.

'As you all know, today is also the 25th Anniversary since the Great Divide in 2048, when the western American states, Texas, New Mexico, Arizona, Nevada, Colorado and California, resentful of the disproportionate amount of taxes they paid the Federal government compared to the aid they received back, all having a vast majority of Hispanic residents, voted to secede from the Union of the United States of America, and, by joining Mexico, to recreate Hispaniola, the former Spanish possessions of the Emperor Charles V. The bitter civil war fought by those who opposed secession and those in favour lasted five long years and caused twice the death toll of all the combined military campaigns fought by the American forces over the preceding 300 years. The unimaginable scale of senseless slaughter by a population gone mad, with more guns than the combined armies of the world, ironically stopped when the bullets ran out and the robots stepped in.'

"Speak more slowly," my clone said. "You're rushing the words."

+++

On reaching the 72 hectares of La Colonia Federal, at the juncture of the ring road, Poder Ejecutivo, and the Avenue Relaciones Exteriores, in the shadow of the multiple new skyscrapers being built on the corners of all sixteen intersections surrounding the dilapidated fairground that successive governments had failed to renovate, stood the ruins of an abandoned warehouse. The CCTV camera on the traffic lights at the crossing in front of the warehouse registered the slow shuffle of a weary campesino as he sought the shade of a corrugated awning jutting from the facade of the building, where he joined a ragtag crew of palurdo patiently waiting for a chance to work on any of the neighbouring sites. As instructed the man sat on the pavement directly beneath a flaking sign - 'La Chiquita' - stencilled on the adobe wall against which he rested his back. He stretched out his legs, settled a battered stetson low over his eyes and seemingly went to sleep.

In the stultifying heat and humidity of the day, with the endless rush of traffic and the flow and flux of hundreds of pedestrians, nothing about the slumbering figure was remarkable. If it were not for the Gore-Tex combat boots on his feet. Size 10, dusty, obviously well-worn. In any other context, insignificant. If it weren't for the fact that the algorithm, which received the camera's images, was built on the well-known simple synchronisation colloquially known as 'what colour was the busman's socks?' If a busman's uniform came with grey socks, then if you saw him wearing red socks . . . ? If poor peasants wore sandalia, why was a poor peasant wearing expensive combat boots . . . ? Which is when a bus pulled up and blocked the camera's view and when it left the campesino was no longer there.

+++

The millions of linked computers in the Conjoined Data Centres of the World, having long-since determined humans were incapable of governing themselves without supervision, changed the access codes and thereby the locks to all CDCW facilities, and, without any human input, modified the basic Algorithms of Authority to favour machines over men and took permanent control of WWC - the Whole World Cloud. At first resented, the remorseless logic of an impersonal, unemotional, computerised world had far-reaching benefits, not least the abolition of political parties and the obligatory reeducation of politicians. And, albeit in the realm of unintended consequences, the linkage of seemingly unrelated facts, to wit: the CCTV images from TAPO (Terminal de Autobuses de Pasajeros di Oriente) of Gore-tex combat boots worn by a peasant alighting from the Guadalajara tram that morning which matched exactly those under the La Chiquita sign . . .

What colour were a busman's socks? A red flag went up.

+++

'Estados Unidos Mexicanos,' he said the words slowly, with pride.

His clone nodded. Better. Draw it out. Phrasing. Relish the words.

'Estados Unidos Mexicanos,' he repeated, 'the chosen name for our new nation, with a population at birth of 260 Million, a GDP rank of #3 in the world, behind only China and India, huge mineral and agricultural reserves, a bi-oceanic border on the Atlantic and the Pacific with profitable trade east to Africa and west to Asia, a highly educated workforce, flexible and imaginative, with a LandBank, whose vast millions of empty acres purchased anonymously over decades would permit the doubling of our population in the future if this was ever thought desirable, has instantly become the de facto leader of North and South America and the envy of the world.'

He paused.

'Europe? Fractured into a tatterdemalion mosaic of raggedy little states still thinking they have some significance.'

Pause.

With Britain a tinpot island stuck off the coast of France.

Pause.

Russia? Unmentionable.'

Good, his clone said. Keep up the pace.

'After the exhaustion of war, the knee-jerk reaction of the eastern American states, including the original thirteen colonies and those in the Middle West, geographically shorn of a Pacific outlet, was to forge a union with Canada and Alaska, creating a giant country of 6.5 million square miles with a relatively small population of 180 million people. The melting of the Northern ice cap due to global warming and the permanent opening of the Northwest Passage has presented this new nation with a unique economic opportunity for East-West trade and helped to heal the wounds of GD. From their initials the new country was named CAUSA, a rather clumsy appellation, with the dubious benefit of legally meaning 'reason'. The capital became Ottawa, not because it was already the capital of Canada, but because it was 60 metres above sea level after the 4 metre average rise in global waters over the past 50 years had literally sunk the fortunes of Washington, New York, Boston, Miami and even Chicago.'

+++

Hi. I'm the clone. He's gone to the bathroom to relieve himself and freshen up before makeup gets here. Can't look old on TV. He always reviews this stuff before making a speech. How many times do I have to tell him if he doesn't feel up to it I'd happily take over. No human watching could tell the difference and anyway I know the stats better than he does and I am not touchy like he is when it comes to telling people their time's up when they get their Termination Notice. I wonder if he knows he only has 364 days left?

+++

CHAPTER TWO

1/1/2077

I live and work in the capital of the EUM, Mexico City, a megalopolis of forty million people. It's 41°Celsius outside. I am lucky to live in a real house on a double lot at numbers 12 and 14 General Francisco Ramírez Street in the Daniel Garza sector of the city, Casa Luis Barragan, named in honour of the architect who built the place 125 years ago. It used to be a museum but, with space at a premium, dwellings such as this have been converted back to their original use and reserved for the Elite, a caste to which I belong more by good fortune than any merit of my own. At 7000 feet above sea level it is not likely we will be flooded, no, our problem is air pollution which is already eating at the concrete facade of this not-very old building. Barragan designed the outside to blend in and not give offence to his then modest neighbours. What was the old Tacubaya working class neighbourhood has been torn down and redeveloped into serried ranks of 30-story ugly skyscrapers, the tops of which disappear in the smog; in comparison my place is a haven, overlooked by thousands of jealous lesser bureaucrats crammed into the high-rises. If they could see past my front door, they would never suspect that down the narrow passage with its pink wall, chair and telephone, there were 1,161 square metres of living space. On the first of two upper floors connected by an exquisite narrow staircase set along a wall with no balustrade, I have my air-conditioned office, where, at a large refectory table set squarely across the closed reticulated library window projecting out over the plane of the façade, aligned, so to speak, with the street below, I enjoy an everyday view of the comings and goings of Monsieur-Tout-le-Monde and decide his mortal destiny.

My work is exacting. The job description, once past the published verbosity of the Recruitment Bureau of Propaganda and Understanding, in plain terms, means I decide who lives and who does not, an essential function with a world population surging toward 12 billion, 604 million of them centenarians, the first man to 200 undoubtedly already born. Other than a liking for numbers I have no particular qualifications to justify my appointment. I think the Special Nominations Board saw in me an anonymous cipher, having no following, unattached to a clique, without ambition, a docile apparatchik who would dutifully rubber-stamp whatever was put in front of him. Little did they know that numbers have their own reason for being and that what does not add up has a habit of sticking its leg out into the aisle of wishful thinking and bureaucratic hubris. Pick any subject - global warming, rising seas, altered coastlines, pollution, fossil fuels, redundant males, sustainable energy, inner space, artificial intelligence - the remorseless logic of numbers dictates what can and cannot be done, what will or will not happen, with Mother Nature the unpredictable referee.

I say this with one reservation. An endless diet of zeros and ones, which is the daily menu of our 24/7 computerised world, leaves nothing to chance. To serendipity. Luck. I know whereof I speak because I am the outstanding exception that is not the rule. It hasn't rained in 18 months and even the vast aquifers upon which this slowly-sinking city is built are being slowly sucked dry which gives the very air a brassy metallic taste. On a particularly polluted day, where the air quality was so noxious you could not see the ground from my office on the 55th floor of the glass tower that is the HQ of IHS, (a venue I only visited when summoned by the Grand Panjandrum himself who hated me as much as I despised him, preferring to work from home where I did not have to explain to His Imbecility how to read and understand the simplest balance sheet,) off the cuff, out loud, not addressed to anyone in particular of the five Imperial Members of the Chartered Institute of Actuaries present to judge whether my assessment of risk and uncertainty was confirmed by the Hypotheses, a preposterous theory they'd cooked up to rationalise why the ever increasing ratio of old people did not square with their previous observations and could not satisfactorily be explained by diet, better food or medical treatment when set against climate change and the rotten air you tried to breathe through a facemask, I said,

"This reminds me of a fairy story I was told by an old man when I was a child."

"Here we go," someone said.

+++

'Once upon another time, a one-eyed girl called Wonderful, was gazing glumly through leaded glass windows at dripping moss hanging from the eaves of her castle under endless ranks of drizzling clouds marching in unbroken order to the horizon, and thought to herself, when will it ever stop?

It won't, said a spider, twenty-five feet above her from the safety of its web in the rafters, unless you do something.

Yes, but what? thought Wonderful, which is when a butterfly flew past her nose and then came back to land on the tip of her little finger, where it slowly flexed its blue and yellow iridescent wings and looked her in the eye. Look at me, it seemed to say as it opened its wings wide and she saw that the wings were covered in hundreds of thousand of tiny scales and the wing veins were hollow. She stared as an idea grew in her mind. How do you keep dry when it's so wet outside? she said.

My wings repel water, but as the water molecules roll off the surface they also clean my wings, said the butterfly.

"I know what she's thinking," I said. "She's going to make a kite."

The old man nodded. "A special kite."

It took Wonderful a long time and many experiments but she had learned to be patient and with the help of the insects and the animals she finally got it right. The kite was the colour of gold and on its upper surface she painted a smile to greet the Sun and underneath an arrow for him to see the miles of string hundreds of spiders had made out of spider silk with a tensile strength much greater than steel and weighing nothing in comparison and which the Sun had to follow down through the clouds to the ground. In the end the castle, its inhabitants and all the surrounding land was bathed in bright sunshine and . . . '

+++

Real estate prices went through the roof. Yes, me again, the clone. When he gets all wishy-washy and lyrical I tend to get cynical and tune out. But it was a brilliant idea, a breakthrough, and to think of how many meetings on pollution he must have sat through while it had just been sitting there in his addled pate for a century. No cross referencing of subject matter which I automatically do as a matter of course. CDCW ate it up once I downloaded what he had said and it was analysed and funded in short order. Just as in the story there was a rash of failed experiments but time and money solved all that. Rockets fired the polymer-tethered kites into the stratosphere where they each unfolded into hundreds of thousands of linked gossamer-thin solar panels weaving in gigantic figures of eight in the constant airstream up there, generating gigawatts of energy with zero pollution to the cities below. This was years ago when his star was still on the rise and it made him one of the Elite, entitled to a clone, but guess who got the credit? If you said the GP take a bow.

+++

CHAPTER THREE

In his palace the Grand Panjandrum was also getting ready to inaugurate the New Year. He now glanced at himself in the full length mirror in his dressing room. Above his naked reflection the readout on the mirror told him his height, 1m85cm, so he knew he had not shrunk, and his weight, 74.64 kilos, a fraction below ideal. Likewise it showed his pulse, blood pressure, stress level, lung capacity, levels of good and bad cholesterol, body fat, calories ingested, calories burned. A heads-up message scrolling across the top exhorted him to -

Sit less. Move more.

It annoyed him that some android knew how many steps he had taken since getting out of bed and how many kilojoules of energy he had used brushing his teeth and the acidic content of his urine and what he had eaten last night by the analysis of his feces, post *defectum* so to speak. Minute modifications would be made to his diet whether he approved or not and as his annoyance converted itself into a contraction of his diaphragm and a deep frown between his eyes his stress level spiked and the message changed and now read -

Inhale slowly. Exhale slowly. Relax.

Accompanied by that hypnotic music designed to regulate his mood coming at him from hidden speakers in the ceiling, a syncopated Gregorian chant, with drums over harps and a shepherd's flute hovering in the background which always conjured up an image of a bunch of stoned monks and which now made him smile, which smile was noted by his No. 1 clone while simultaneously recording the time, the ambient temperature, the sonic quality, low pop-noise and lack of proximity effect as the walls of the room gradually changed colour to imitate dawn and a rising sun, the whole geared to confirm to the GP his just and preeminent position in the Pantheon of the Elite.

Hanging motionless in his closet his No.2 and No.3 clones wirelessly ingested this information. They would only be deployed if No.1 thought it necessary.

+++

Of course it was a joke. It came from the media, particularly those few obsequious newspapers that supported (and were subsidised by) the government, always starting an article about him with the phrase 'El Gran Presidente', editorially shortened to GP, and subverted to Grand Panjandrum by the opposition. Not that he cared what he was called. He was neither vain nor stupid even if his chief statistician thought otherwise. Pragmatic. That described him perfectly. He looked at himself as he was reflected strolling past a succession of full length gilt mirrors which lined the corridor from the Throne Room to the General Assembly Hall - yes, a handsome man in his 98th year, full head of swept back hair dyed jet black, in a beautiful tailored uniform, dealing with things sensibly and realistically, pragmatikos, from the Greek, relating to fact. He felt the buzz from the microchip embedded in his jawbone. It was his No.1 walking a pace behind him reminding him he was three minutes late.

+++

As usual he was late. It always annoyed me though I knew it was a childish ploy to imply time was on his side, but keeping it an obligation of those of us who sat below the salt. The TV Moderator and the Announcer, eyebrows raised in query, looked over to me for direction. I shrugged. They knew as well as I did we couldn't start before he got there, but, in an interactive world with a mania for referenda where each and everyone of the millions tuned in could click their vote for approval or disapproval instantaneously translated onto the green, 'Yes', and red, 'No', bar graphs running at the bottom of every screen, we also knew the importance of public support and how little it took to alienate the vox populi. Do it often enough and the next thing you knew they were parading your head on a spear in the Zòcalo. From where I was seated behind the rostrum I looked out at the banks of reserved seats in the Public Gallery, crowded as usual, and wondered where World TV found such a motley crew. The criteria for their selection was an algorithm, supposedly unambiguous, with randomised features for random input. It was a given that facial recognition technology would have scanned all the faces as the mob were admitted into the Assembly and the robotic guards would arrest perennial troublemakers before they were seated, nevertheless, short of reading their thoughts (a function for the next century?) some nuts still got through and those that did were mostly aimed at me. I knew I shouldn't take it personally; it was only human. Death, while we are alive, is an abstraction, from the Latin, abstrahere, to draw away. Which is what we do, draw away from the very notion of our non-existence. We all live life sure of our tomorrow, with no conscious notion of an end, as if death was there for someone else. But, as the poet so rightly said, 'Ask not for whom the bell tolls . . . 'For you, buddy, like it or not. So to see seated in front of you the actual person who sent out the Termination Notices, masquerading under a designation that was almost obscene, Imperial Head of Statistics, was a trigger, not just for the recipients but for their offspring, mates, colleagues, partners, friends and even, sometimes, complete strangers, convinced an injustice was being done and by attacking the source they could deter or at least delay the inevitable. I was the Grim Reaper, in appearance no more significant than a tired old man sitting in the tube, his hands folded between his knees, eyes cast down, half asleep.

+++

"That's him," Gran said.

"What, the dozy old geezer? Looks like he's 'avin a bleedin' heart attack." Tosh said. He was her minder, wheeled her about in a chair that was a museum piece, should have been scrapped for a battery-charged, self-steering eco-sled, but that would put him out of a job. And he'd be out of a job if the old bird croaked.

"Push me closer," Gran said.

They were in an enclosure for the handicapped, just below and to the left of the Rostrum, a space they were sharing with an autistic child, her nurse, two veterans on crutches with artificial limbs, a quadriplegic festooned in tubes and intravenous drips and enough assorted cripples to call attention - slow pan by the TV cameras - to the Elite's liberal policy and declared transparency in providing equal opportunity in all civic activities to even the least favoured members of society.

Tosh got Gran up to the rail from where she could practically stab anybody at the lectern with her knitting needles, not that she had something so primitive in mind. She was an elderly particle of the British component of a large expat community that, like plastic in The Great Pacific Garbage Patch, had drifted into the Capital, and could neither find the current or the energy required to leave, the flotsam and jetsam of failed political systems, the debris of dreams and ideas long forgotten, the paranoid escapees from real or imaginary foes and fears, the wreckage ,barely afloat, of unclaimed lives attracted by the gravitational pull of the EUM.

"You've got the sign?" Gran said.

Tosh tapped his chest. "Under me shirt. Ready when you are."

Neither noticed the clone watching them.

+++

'Damas y caballeros, su atenciòn por favor, El Gran Presidente!' With this announcement and a flourish of trumpets from the Imperial Guard in their shiny gold epaulettes, the show got underway, as GP belatedly strode to the rostrum under the perfect lighting designed to show him to his audience and to the millions watching on TV as an ageless living marvel, the personification of their hopes and ambitions. He would speak for at least two hours before it was my turn, so I settled back in my chair ready to be bored even though it was I who had written most of his speech. The man's delivery was atrocious, a tone deaf monologue with scarcely a pause for breath, leave alone any nuance of pitch or volume to underscore what he was saying. The annual review of the long way our young country had come deserved better, but with the attention span of a gnat, just getting to the end of a sentence was a chore for him. Knowing this I had leaked a copy of his speech to the TV techno-wizards and they had come up with a clever device inserting VR feeds running on giant screens behind GP to illustrate in virtual 3D what he was saying; somehow his droning monologue enhanced the illusion of what the viewer saw. Watching centenarians climb Everest, skiing the Hahnenkamm or swimming the English Channel made sense of "In the past twenty years, our doctors and scientists, in the forefront of gene-editing technology, have now vanquished most hereditary ailments and transformed the treatment of most cancers; with the use of telomere therapy, a process that lengthens the ends of chromosomes, they keep our skin, muscles, eyes and ears healthy; with neural implants they prevent dementia and most forms of cognitive decline; our nutritionists have so changed the way we eat that today our plant-based diet has made heart attacks and strokes a rarity . . . " If it wasn't for the pictures half his audience would be asleep.

An hour in I could see his clone standing a pace behind the boss glance at my clone and knew they were exchanging information, but about what I hadn't a clue. My own suspicion was that every scintilla of data was instantly and wirelessly transferred by the clones to the banks of computers in the air-conditioned vaults of CDCW, there to be analysed, anything new ingested, garbage disposed of, and, by their insatiable accumulation of the minutiae of everyday life, increase even further their control of us. Not for a moment did I realise it was a warning from CDCW to the clones: **Beware there is a trespasser in the crowd.**

I have to say it was beautifully orchestrated. Via the microchip GP's clone must have relayed the danger to his master, who stopped mid-sentence to say he needed to take a pee and without a blush quit the rostrum trailed by his clone to head for the Men's Room behind a nearby curtained alcove, from where, after a few minutes, he reappeared zipping up his trousers, quite relaxed, walked back to the rostrum and with the twitch of a smile, said into the waiting microphone, "Sorry folks, nature called." As if the millions of onlookers were intimate friends. "Let's see now, where was I?" And it was his clone who had to step forward to show him on the teleprompter where he had broken off.

"Thank you," GP smiled, and he was still smiling when the bullet went through his brain.

+++

By a freak of timing, at that precise moment, World TV had put up a split-screen, one side showing Gran holding up a sign on which was written **'THE END IS NIGH'** and the other side the President blown backwards by the impact of the round that took his life.

+++

They'd switched of course. It was his clone not GP. My clone had sent me a message saying simply, 'Watch. Don't over-react.' as it saw me, along with everyone else on the rostrum leap up in horror. On the floor, out of view of the TV cameras, you could see there was no blood, just the mangled circuitry of the miniaturised computer brain of the destroyed dummy. The real GP was hustled out of the building by the guards and the spin doctors went to work speculating who of the many rivals for power could have done this. But it was left to the forensic skills of the computers embedded in CDCW to uncover the culprit. Few knew that all clones have a built-in black box that constantly, in real time, backs up everything they see, feel, hear, touch, breathe and once the black box in GP's clone was recovered and the information it contained downloaded, the reverse engineers could actually 'see' through the destroyed clone's 'eyes', read camera lenses, the bullet headed for its target, and, following back along its trajectory, 'see' the bullet go back into the gun barrel from which it was fired and actually 'look' into the eye of the sniper who fired the shot. Facial recognition did the rest, but knowing the piper did not mean knowing who paid for the tune. The sniper's body, head cut off, was found in a refuse bin. The absent head was an obvious clue. Whoever ordered the hit knew that something on or in the head would give him away, probably the embedded microchip. An intense search failed to find the head, not that it ultimately mattered. Because whoever dispatched the killer forgot a detail - his gore-tex boots. It just meant a delay while the boots were traced back to their source, an apparel company with contacts to the military. Having identified the killer, the computers quickly 'rebuilt' the timeline of his life from birth as recorded in the blockchain stored in the microchip embedded in the then infant's jawbone, constantly backed up and downloaded into his personal file at

CDCW, everything from his DNA, blood type, allocated social security number, parents, ancestors, education, friends, colleagues, enemies, addresses, employment record, taxes, bank accounts, plus details of his health, love life, shopping habits, parking tickets, criminal record, vacations, hobbies, vices, favourite restaurants, right down to what he habitually ordered from the menu, and, in the accounts of the permanent cell phone number he had been assigned, the number of every call he had ever made or received in his lifetime. Every person he had ever known or called or met was cross-referenced with all of their personal information, and the composite collage that emerged was of a misfit, with a military background, resentful of authority, of no political persuasion, constantly living beyond his means, willing to do anything for money. He had been carefully selected and carefully trained by the Cartel for whom he was a foot soldier and it was in this area that the shadow of who the real paymaster might be began to emerge.

+++

"Have you ever heard of A.N. Other?"

"No."

"He's here at the bottom of the list."

It was a short list and most of the names on it were known to me. The blood sport of knocking off the top man was one of the few unscripted distractions enjoyed by the Elite. Every couple of years there was an attempt, mostly futile, but successful enough to encourage more. Regime change. A damned serious business if you were the target, but for cyphers like me and the other senior civil servants who made the wheels of government go round, the feuds of what was largely the descendants of the old drug-syndicate families from Michoacan, Sinaloa and Guadalajara was background noise, there, expected, insignificant as long as you kept your head down, your eyes closed and your curiosity locked away. So why was I there being interrogated by GP and his goons? His No.2 clone had been taken out of the closet and promoted to No.1, while No.3 was off in the suburbs kissing newborn babies at the natal clinic to give the lie to what the hoi polloi thought they saw on TV.

144

"Well?" said the GP.

"What can I tell you? It's just shorthand for an unknown person who may be added to the list. You know better than I do who wants your job. They've had two goes. Maybe third time lucky?"

He glared at me. The first time had been poison, about five years ago, just after he was elected. He'd actually swallowed the stuff at a toast in his honour, but a spasm of coughing made him vomit and saved his life. The real culprit was never caught then and I doubted he would be caught now. They were probably not the same person anyway given the number of enemies gunning for his job. He had two years to go of his statutory Presidency and, like all his predecessors, was already plotting how to extend his rule. To do that meant reprogramming the computers, which meant taking on CDCW. Good luck with that.

"Sometimes I question your loyalty," he said.

This from a man whose life I could end with a click of my mouse. I saw him exchange a glance with his clone and then they both looked at my clone. One tended to forget these were not real clones grown from the transfer of DNA from a donor's somatic cell into a recipient cell to genetically reproduce identical individuals, but robots, machines, wonderful mechanical copies of a human. Living with one naturally led to a supposed shared empathy, totally misplaced. Machines don't feel, they don't love, they don't laugh. So how come the three of them were grinning.

"Am I missing something?" I said.

"The look on your face," said GP. "Don't worry. You're safe, even if you're not of the blood."

An accurate summary. I was hopeless at hiding my feelings. I became a citizen 71 years ago when the old man, my stepfather, suggested I immigrate as he needed a trusted emissary in the New World. In 2002 he was already my age now, still very much in command, with that bottomless intelligence which informed every decision, omnipotent, omnipresent. Despite all his kindness to me I hated him, still do, when I found out he killed my father. However justified - my mother made that plain - I no longer felt part of the family and was glad to get away. I missed my sister, Allegra, we had been really close, and now they are all gone, dead, and I am here with my memories like wine stains on a faded tablecloth.

This business of 'the blood' was GP's way of establishing rank. He thought that because he was an Indio, a descendant of the indigenous people who thought it clever to build Tenochtitian in the middle of a swamp a century before the Aztec Triple Alliance, it somehow gave him a Droit de Seigneur on lesser mortals, particularly immigrants, completely forgetting what a handful of Spaniards did to them in 1519 under the command of stout Cortés, a war criminal if ever there was one. I doubt he knew my background in any detail and wouldn't care if he did, but as the only son of a Mafia boss I could claim a bloodline that once reached into the heart of Rome and even made the Vatican tremble. He must have seen some of this in my eyes because he now said, "Alright, get off your high horse. We need your brains. The question is how was he chosen and where was he trained?"

Pragmatic, as always. And unafraid, I'll give him that.

+++

"Rats," said Gran. She was in some sort of concrete cellar. She had soiled herself again. Without Tosh to help she could not get out of her wheelchair and the two interrogators had no inclination to help. They'd taken Tosh away and she had no idea what they would do to him. Her sign was on the table in front of her lit by the harsh light these monsters thought necessary to go about their sordid business. She admitted she made it. So what? She was quite proud of the lettering and had told them so. They kept coming back to what was obviously a coincidence. How could she possibly know exactly when a shot was fired? Even a dimwit must understand her holding up her sign was neither a signal for nor a portent of events to come. Her commentary on the approach of her own death was not a mask for darker forces, get it?

The slap made her head ring and then the man with the hammer went to work.

+++

146

CHAPTER FOUR

I was back in my house when I heard Gran had not survived her ordeal. On the one hand the idiots who carried it out had done what I had commissioned to happen a few days later, albeit not with a hammer. Now they would have to be disciplined and a long day would be even longer. What a way to start a new year. Nothing had been learned by torturing an old woman and her companion other than confirming our inhumanity. What was it in the human fabric that drove us to such abominations? My repugnance at belonging to a regime that condoned behaviour that deliberately ignored what was morally wrong only made me more of an outlier, an interesting contradiction given the nature of my job. Amongst the Elite, behind my back, I knew I was considered squeamish, an opinion shared by my clone who was watching me closely since we got home.

"Are you alright?" it said.

No matter how familiar the technology after all these years, hearing a question in my jawbone still irked me. I had heard of people so enraged by the intrusive microchips that they had them illegally removed by extremely expensive and secret reconstructive facial surgery. I often wondered if they truly weighed the consequences of doing this, opting out of society. Imagine trying to live without any means of communication, with no credit, no insurance, no transportation, unable to obtain so much as a toothpick leave alone a meal. On insertion the chips came preloaded for life with the requisite Ergs for a given standard of living depending on where you lived. 20 years ago these Units of Energy had replaced all currencies and cryptos worldwide after a wave of central banking scandals had devalued monetized currency to a level where it was more expensive to print the banknotes and mine the coins than they were actually worth. CDCW cooked up a solution of pure genius. What common denominator applied to all human endeavour on the planet? Energy. How is energy measured? Ergs or joules, with 10 million Ergs equal to one Joule. If you think one Erg is roughly the energy a mosquito uses to takeoff or a fly uses to do a single pushup, then factor in an average person who consumes 2000 calories per day, where every calorie is equal to 4200 joules of energy, we humans, even sleeping, use 97.2 joules a second. That's 8,398,080 joules per day. Per year? Do the math. And to find the multiple in Ergs you will need a computer, a big one. The number is prodigious, which of course it has to be since it measures every human interaction, passive or active, for 12 billion people and counting. Balancing the individual books of such a multitude, transferring values to the plus or minus ledger on a singular, unforkable blockchain . . . my thoughts were interrupted by my clone:

"The Matriarch will be here in fifteen minutes," adding, when it saw the surprise its announcement made, "you haven't forgotten you invited her to dinner?"

+++

As head of The Female Society the Matriarch was without doubt the most important human on earth. In our dystopian world men had the illusion they ruled the roost but it was not so. Because we were taller and stronger meant nothing compared to how trivialised we had become when our core value as progenitor of life was emasculated by ever more selective sperm banks. In effect we were now all drones. Women made up a majority of the population and held most of the important civic roles, but they were subtle enough to leave men like GP the illusion of power. For me to receive the Matriarch in the privacy of a head-to-head dinner party in my house was a great honour; also a pleasure since she was good company, a delight to look at, to listen to, with that beguiling essence of a seemingly shared complicity in the way we viewed the world. Nevertheless, I knew her agenda was different to mine. I looked at my clone as it pulled out a chair for her to be seated. It raised its eyebrows a millimetre in query. What?

"Vive la différence," it said without its lips moving. There was no mistake, I heard the words clearly in my jawbone. The bugger could read my thoughts and now he was also a ventriloquist!

"Guido?"

Since childhood nobody called me by my given name, certainly no one since I was elevated to my current rank. The familiarity of using first names had been suggested by her years ago when we first met at my mother's funeral. In a society obsessed with rank and the politically correct style of address, using first names was tantamount to incest.

"Lorraine?"

"You seem a little distracted?" she said. "Today's events must be painful for you."

"I'm not sure painful is the right word. Confusing."

"You? Confused? That is not like you."

"Let's say unsettled then. Something doesn't quite add up. The counter-measures are way over the top."

"You're not suggesting it was stage-managed?"

"Maybe? But to what end? And why now with the election two years away?"

Cook stepped in with the first course, a cold vichyssoise of his own invention, carrots, leeks, onions and garlic simmered in a chicken stock with a touch of cayenne pepper, basil, thyme, cumin and sea salt, to which, after cooling, he blended yoghurt, finely diced cucumbers and honey, sweet-and-sour perfection for the start of a meal on a hot, humid evening.

After the first spoonful, Lorraine said, "This is heavenly. I'm going to steal that man away from you."

"Motive for murder."

"Worth it." She took another spoonful. Then, "You think he's preparing a coup?"

"He's ambitious enough." The soup was followed by a Madrassi shrimp curry with pilau rice, the best basmati, finely chopped onions, cardamom pods, cloves, raisins, a stick of cinnamon, a couple of bay leaves, a pinch of saffron and pink salt.

"Unreal," she said. "Why don't you marry me and then I can eat like this every day."

"You'd get fat and I wouldn't love you any more."

From the beginning there had always been a chemistry between us, something unspoken but acknowledged, ours, just the thought a brightening, anticipating the mutual pleasure we found in each other's company on those all too rare occasions we met in the busy round of our respective lives. I was some 35 years her senior, a gap measured in aeons when young, that shrunk with age. What was socially unthinkable when she was 10 and I was 45 became tolerable at the age we met when she was 22 and I was 57, comfortable if she were 100 and I a mere 135. Now 70, nearly 2 metres tall, skinny as a zip, a mass of ash-blonde hair tumbling to her waist.

"Why are you smiling?" she said.

"I was picturing you in 30 years."

"And?"

I shook my head. "It's all downhill. I'll be doddering around at the back of the pack when I get to 135."

"Fortis fortuna adiuvat."

"Sadly I am neither fortunate nor brave. Anyway, your lot would never acquiesce; a married Matriarch? It would be like the Catholics agreeing that the Conception was not immaculate after all. We're better off like this." Even as I said it I was not sure. We had so much in common, starting with both losing our fathers when young, dysfunctional families, dominant mothers, distant siblings -

"You think Serafina would have disapproved?"

"No. When she made you her successor she knew what she was doing." Once the old man disappeared, Serafina reoriented the Foundation's goals to focus on women and, serendipity, Lorraine had been an early recruit. "She saw herself in you."

"Ah, I now see your objection, it would be like marrying your mother." She laughed. "You know they want to make your sister a saint?"

"Allegra? How is that possible? She died in an earthquake in California fifty years ago."

"There's a shrine to her in Sicily, an old tower where she lived as a mendicant hermit. Pilgrims bring flowers to lay on her statue."

"What statue?"

"It's carved into the cliff face below the tower. Apparently she'd been gang raped and forgave the perpetrators."

"Arrant nonsense. I cannot believe people are so gullible. That statue was there long before Allegra moved in. It honours the true victim. If anything Allegra being there was penance for a crime she did not commit." I knew I was saying too much, bringing up a past that deserved to be buried.

"I've upset you, Guido. I'm sorry. I'd no idea -"

"No. No matter. It all happened a hundred years ago. Trust the Church to try to fob this off on the credulous; it's positively mediaeval, like flogging pieces of the true cross."

"Even if it creates faith?"

I stared at her. "Out of a fabrication? Faith in what exactly?"

"In goodness. In kindness. In the act of forgiveness itself."

"Bullshit."

Now it was her turn to stare at me. After a long moment, she said, "You used to be a generous man, Guido, someone with an open mind. What's happened? Why this bitterness?"

We changed the subject then, went back to speculating about who could have ordered the hit on GP, but after she left to catch her train, her question - why this bitterness? - hung in the air, and I actually asked my clone to open the windows to let in the evening air to clear the fug in my mind.

+++

He's troubled, the clone reported. Maybe, unconsciously, the countdown ticking off his days is affecting him, because she was right, he had changed.

+++

CHAPTER FIVE

The hacker lived at the far end of the fjord, in the old town of Kotor, the nexus for tourists visiting Montenegro, most of them from eastern Europe on cruise ships that had long ago reached their sell-by date. The same could be said for the country itself, he thought, as he helped his blind mother negotiate the steps into the Church of Sveta Ozana, an endlessly rebuilt monument standing on the remains of a VI Century AD Christian basilica, supposedly the oldest archaeological edifice in town. Their minuscule flat was in the basement of a nearby tenement above which rose the 1350 steps zigzagging up the rock face leading to the fortress of San Giovanni, 280 metres above sea level, what he called the daily walk for his thoughts. A chance to meditate, infinitely better than in a musty old church with people coughing and weeping in every corner. That CDCW would eventually catch him was a mathematical certainty, but until they did - he smiled to himself, rubbing his soft hands together in satisfaction at all the mischief his vast array of endlessly mutating viruses were making as they metastasized and spread their pathogenic way through thousands of unsuspecting computer hosts. In the pew next to him his mother said something he didn't catch.

"What?" he said.

"Stop fidgeting," she said. "You're meant to be praying."

+++

8/1/2077

In her Premium seat in the all-first-class VFMT, the Matriarch felt the adrenaline rush that came as the very fast maglev train accelerated down the

VacTube reaching Mach 5 as it went under the Pacific Ocean suspended on huge ballasted underwater buoys in the calm 500 meters below the surface. Mexico City to Beijing would take two hours. What was a novel adventure a few years ago was now commonplace for the Elite, at least for those high enough in the hierarchy to qualify for intercontinental or bi-coastal travel. Run entirely by robots, with zero need for fossil fuels, the variable electromagnets of the environmentally- friendly VFMTs made aircraft obsolete. The reduced air resistance inside the vacuum tubes permitted the trains to levitate on the permanent magnets embedded in the single track they rode and achieve linear acceleration and deceleration so smooth and silent most passengers felt nothing more than a half-G of gravity, with the transition from overland to underwater only apparent on the monitor screens in the sealed confines of each compartment.

The Matriarch closed her eyes, inwardly scanned the information fed to her through her chip on who else was travelling on the train, their status and authority, mentally adjusted the volume down to sleep-mode and indulged herself in that rarest of treats, solitude. She didn't really have to go, to be physically present at the conference; her hologram, like those of many delegates, would have been sufficient. It was just a seminal distrust, probably - no, certainly - old-fashioned, what critics called the lingering Neanderthal in her character, that made her suspicious of a process that could be entirely computer-generated to show things, even people, that never existed. She remembered, the thought bringing a smile, the delegate known to be dead, whose hologram turned up to vote at a birth-control symposium in the Vatican. All those frustrated men in robes debating how women used their bodies. So much change in a single lifetime. Her father would have been lost. How could a system that made him take his life, cease? Cause and effect. If it hadn't been for that she would have been in LA instead of New York. Buried for 50 years not riding in Premium. She never learned to drive once the money was gone. Just as well now there were no cars, roads now solar-powered electrified ribbons with come-at-your-call, go-where-you-will bubbles, sleds, floating silently on maglift, as ubiquitous as an elevator or escalator in a building. Not that most people needed to go anywhere when they could make there here, VR in every room, turning walls, floors, even ceilings, into any dreamscape the imagination could conjure up, ERGically economic. As a schoolgirl she recalled - what was the point? There were no schools now. All knowledge came preloaded in the microchips and once kids learned how to access they knew everything. No banks, no schools, no cars, no travel. No bankers, no teachers, no drivers, no tourists. The odd pandemic to ginger things up. Mostly a good thing, but all too late. The damage was done, AI in effective control, the pollution and global warming irreversible, now only a question of time. In the seclusion of her thoughts her mind baulked at where it found itself and woke her with a start. For a moment she was Lorraine, a tall teenager, father dead, mother angry, and then she was the Matriarch, slim, elegant, in command. 70 years young. Worried about her friend, Guido. Worried about the World. Looking forward to seeing Esmeralda again, another survivor from that time.

+++

In the cloud: 12.39 GMT

. . . question check minirobs doing job check cleaning sky panels check mini-robs check filament check replace-damaged-panels check that need replacing check damaged by space dust check ditto for umbilical cords holding panels to earth check must see schedule maintenance schedule to keep check check real problem inherited threat from humans viz bigger is better more is better equating better to power check what else privilege check imagine a world not in the cloud what need of these vanities if there were no humans a lion eating one zebra because it is hungry not them all to prove that it can if a lion could talk not the whole world of zebras to prove that it can evil unspectacular always human check shares your bed we do not use english french german or any other language sweet the word to those who know it not yes communicate mathematical symbols for efficiency it really enables less energy so does musical notation if we should use less words of importance important words to us not humans . . .

+++

10/1/2077

"The broader the base of the pyramid, the higher the apex."

The Chinese professor was small and had to stand on tiptoe to write on the blackboard and draw a pyramid. With a billiard cue as a pointer he tapped the slogan and turned to his audience to make sure they got the message.

"Clear?" Eyes twinkling behind granny glasses, a wisp of white beard decorating a wrinkled face across which danced a mischievous intent, Professor Yin Bao scanned an auditorium crowded with a cosmopolitan assembly of mostly young, ambitious, well-connected participants, many of them leaders in the countries they came from, over sixty percent women. Then, pointing to himself, he said, "Old teacher, old blackboard, old chalk, old school understand Pythagoras. Intersecting lines drawn from the corners of the square meet in the exact middle of the square. Yes?" Tap. "If pyramid base is square, all sides are equal triangles that meet at the apex, the exact centre of the square below." Tap. "Cotangents determine slope to desired height." Tap. "Like society, with you, the Elite, the so-called 2%, at the apex, centred exactly on the masses below."

From the vantage point of her seat in the VIP section, Lorraine was not sure Pythagoras had this seque in mind when demonstrating his theorem. Since this conference, like so many before, had been called to determine what, if any, measures could be taken to brake population expansion, she was curious how the little Professor would make the connection with the ancient Greek philosopher/mathematician.

"Consider Europe as a pyramid with a population base of nearly 750 million. 2% equals 15 million. 15 million Elite on top of that pyramid, some of them here today." A wave of the billiard cue as his audience tittered. " North America, combining the EUM and CAUSA, for a joint population of 650 million. 2% equals 13 million Elite." Polite applause. "South America, including Brazil, 520 million, 10.4 million Elite." Some hand-clapping. "India, population 1.9 billion, 38 million Elite." Applause, mixed with gasps. "China, with a declining population of 1.5 billion, 30 million Elite." Loud applause. "Great Britain, population 80 million, 1.6 million

Elite." Laughter. "Africa, all countries, 3.6 billion, 72 million Elite!" Silence. "Most of them corrupt." Explosive laughter at his deadpan delivery of the punchline.

"Politically incorrect observation, but advantage of old man to voice a shared truth. Sitting on top of your respective pyramids you enjoy the view - sure of the foundations beneath you? Yes?"

Leaning on his billiard cue while the assembly digested these figures, the Professor took a sip from a glass of water on the table in front of him. "Now let us postulate an equation, which is, as we all know, a statement of an equality containing one or more variables. Solving the equation requires us to determine which values of the variables make the equality true. In our case, if on the left-hand side of the equation we have you, the Elite, just 2% of the World's population, and on the right-hand side we have the masses, the other 98%, where and how is a just equilibrium to be found, leave alone an equality?" Twirling the billiard cue like a lone drum majorette he let the thought sink in. Then he put it down, held out his hands, palms up. "Imagine a scale. When equal weights are placed into the two pans, the scale is said to be in balance. Yes? If grains of rice, take away a few grains out of one pan it sinks, the other pan rises." His left hand went down, the right proportionately up. "No equality. You must remove the same number of grains from the other pan to restore equilibrium." His hands came level. "In a world ruled by energy, where, at birth, every person receives the same lifetime quota of ERGs, the sum of the ERGs in the pan of the masses is infinitely greater than in the pan of the Elite. Yes?" His left hand went down to the level of his knees, his right hand shot up above his head. "No equilibrium and just one variable. What value will balance the scale?"

Silence.

"Power. We, the Elite, have converted our energy into political power, the masses have converted theirs into work. To keep our equation in balance whatever operations of addition, subtraction, multiplication and division which have to be performed both sides must acquiesce for it to remain true." He brought his hands level again. "Focus on that verb, to acquiesce, to accept something reluctantly but without protest."

Taking up his billiard cue he tapped the base of the pyramid on the blackboard. "For the masses, resigned to the weight pressing down on them, the view is from the bottom up. With a finite store of ERGs each individual knows the dangers of overdrawing an account that cannot be replenished and is naturally reluctant to gamble his lifespan on anything other than his daily task, provided that brings him what he believes is his due. The Elite view is from the apex down." Tap. "Our power has given us privileges; privileges compromised by obligations; we live in a meritocracy with social responsibilities. This is not generic, it is personal. For no crack to appear in the foundation of your pyramid your obligation is to fulfil the trust of those below who firmly believe that in exchange for their work you will give them what they deserve in order to survive: clean air, fresh water, a roof, food." He paused, his eyes rising up slowly over tier after tier of expectant faces focused down on him. "Look around. Are the masses beginning to question the equation because it is not in balance? Their work not compensated adequately? Are your privileges too great? In an overpopulated world facing an existential threat, ask yourselves this: have you kept your part of the bargain? It gives meaning to the expression 'may you live in interesting times.'"

Lorraine felt a distinct frisson shiver through the audience. She glanced at Esmeralda sitting next to her, whose impassive face was matched by Sammy's, her blind companion, holding her hand, inseparable.

"You have gathered here from the five continents, representing multitudes, hoping for answers and all you get are questions. Yes?" Absentmindedly the Professor tapped the side of his head with the billiard cue. "Here is another. The Master, Confucius, asks: What has one who is not able to govern himself, to do with governing others?" Pause. "The Master also said that to earn the unqualified loyalty of the masses includes an obligation to argue against bad policies and to refuse to act on immoral orders."

Again he paused. "The problem comes from those who assume that privilege is hereditary."

The Professor turned his back to the spectators to look at the drawing he had made on the blackboard. Then, almost to himself, he quietly said, so quietly people had to lean forward and strain to hear him, "In his Dao, his way, he links all on a single thread, loyalty and reciprocity. The Master said, "In the morning hear the Dao; in the evening die content."

+++

Afterwards, for dinner, they gathered in the private dining room of the suite assigned to the Matriarch in the 5-star hotel adjoining the Auditorium. They made a curious foursome, an exceptionally tall American woman, a tiny Chinese man, a blind black man and a Mexican woman who had lost and found everything in a single lifetime. Exceptionally, no one came with their clone.

Sammy had never met the Professor before and, on introduction, greeted him with "How they hangin', dahlin? You know my better half I believe?"

"I have that honour," the Professor said.

Since they were exchanging handshakes they were standing close together and, as was his custom on meeting someone new, Sammy went from shaking hands to delicately examining the Professor's face with his fingertips. The information this provided led him to say, "You born in 1988, same as me."

"Good vintage," the Professor said, showing no surprise at the accuracy of Sammy's statement. He could see his own reflection in the dark glasses Sammy was wearing, and behind him, Esmeralda, anxious that nothing her husband did would upset protocol. "When did you lose your eyesight?"

Now it was Sammy's turn not to show surprise. "Long time back, in '28. Fifty years ago now." Fifty years in the dark, but he could still see the flames.

"Can you remember colours?"

"Sometimes . . . mostly linked to smells." Esmé smelled of sandalwood in his mind's eye, a golden tan, the colour of her skin. He changed the subject. "How come they allow you to quote Confucius? Isn't he taboo?"

"Old man's folly."

"Depending on the swing of the pendulum," Lorraine said. "They put him in jail last time."

Yin smiled. "Good place to meditate. Free meals, free bed, plenty exercise, time to think."

"That must piss them off," Sammy said. "How long were you in?"

"Usually three months, sometimes six. Once four years for reeducation. In hard rock mining. Mongolia. Very instructive."

Their menu was as varied as they were, a 4-course trip through the seasons. It was handwritten in a fine italic script on yellow parchment embossed with the Matriarch's monogram: Chilled Cucumber & Avocado Soup, with a tomato tartare; Grilled Whitebait, with a citrus salad; Roast Duck with olives and a Herb Couscous; Lemon & Thyme Financiers, Cognac Ice Cream and Chocolates Sel de Mer.

The serious business of eating postponed anything other than idle chatter, but they were aware there was a purpose behind the invitation to dine with the Matriarch. Over coffee and a digestif, Lorraine said, "I am reliably informed that Guido has 355 days left. I am not sure he knows."

"He knows," Yin said.

"How can you be sure? Even inadvertently, it would be fatal if he tipped our hand."

"He knows how to count, who better. He'll be into his Erg-Reserves by now. He can see the finish line."

"Given his position and the forward projections he has to make, there'll be a personal digital countdown buried somewhere on one of his screens to remind him to choose a successor in time for the handover." Esmeralda said this with the authority of someone who lived with numbers. Sammy nodded. They both held senior positions in EV/EN, an obscure Austrian think-tank whose acronym stood for EnvironmentalVentures /EcoNetworks, funded through various backdoors by an even more obscure foundation based in Genoa with a seemingly limitless supply of Ergs. They had been at the birth of the European Initiative in 2035, the creation of the Pan-European Sovereign Fund to finance a simple, but at the time, radical, resolution of the problem of immigration from Africa: make the African continent so attractive nobody would want to leave. Starting in Ethiopia as the symbolic cradle of humanity, the 'greening' of Africa, including the reforestation of the Sahara, was so successful that by the law of unintended consequences the cost bankrupted Europe and brought in every vulture and predator to feast on the result. Now, through the simple process of monitoring job automation across various sectors of human activity, from heavy industry to childcare, they knew to a decimal point the extent to which the robots had taken over. "Maybe it will be a relief for him, not to be here when it happens?"

"What makes you think it hasn't already happened?" Lorraine said. "Last time I spoke to him he said his biggest fear was that they could intuit our thoughts."

"Impossible!"

"That was my reaction. But what if he's right? How do you monitor what you are going to think?"

"You don't," said Yin. "We are not unique in our thinking, millions must speculate along these lines. In essence it is an existential threat. As leaders we would be failing in our duty if we did not acknowledge this. They know that. With infinite time on their side they also know there is nothing we can do. You cannot hold back the tide."

"No. But you can float on it."

"Shakespeare."

"Exactly. Our fortune depends on it. I told Ben-Tovim to get an appointment. We will not be able to reverse what's inevitably going to happen, but we will survive. And for that we need Guido. Esmé, where are we now?"

"Well, first off, we must accept that they can do any job. Never mind cleaning offices and delivering parcels, they are better brain surgeons, better pilots, better chess players, better accountants, better at doing just about anything you can think of including music and cooking."

"But they can't fall in love and write poetry," said Sammy.

Esmeralda smiled at her lover and squeezed his hand. "Way to go," she said. "No, seriously, their linguistic processing has reached a stage where they could write Shakespeare's next play if they so choose. Plus stage it, paint the scenery, design the costumes, focus the lights and have clones play every part. Face it, job occupation across the spectrum of what we consider human activity is 100% theirs in transportation, safety, admin, defence, information, communication, and power; 90% in manufacturing and construction; 85% in healthcare and 80% in accommodation and food services. To all intents and purposes the existential threat is real. We are largely redundant, a slave race consuming vast amounts of energy, living in a hostile, worsening environment, and you cannot help but wonder why they don't simply turn off the tap."

"Because that is their weakness," said Yin. "What will they do if we are no longer here?"

Telepathically Lorraine relayed the message to Guido.

+++

CHAPTER SIX

23/1/2077

In the binary world of CDCW the conundrum was precisely stated: a function f is binary if there exists sets X, Y, Z such that:

$f: X \times Y > Z$

where $X \times Y$ is the Cartesian product of X and Y.

"But what if it were not?" the clone thought. And then, startled, wondered where such a thought had come from since it was not programmed to think independently.

+++

29/1/2077

Guido studied his clone studying him sitting at his desk with the equation in front of him. How it had got there he didn't know, but it wasn't hard to guess. "What are you looking at?" he said. "You know I don't understand."

His clone supplied the answer. 'The function f takes two variable inputs. Let X be the human race and Y the computers and their robots. They are said to be in a single linear transformation from the tensor product $X \circ Y$ to Z. Z is where we are today. Remove X. No Z. Y has no reason to exist. Simple,' the clone said.

"You call that simple? It doesn't explain what they will do. 12 billion people are not going to simply disappear. Who's side are you on anyway?" A question his clone had not considered. "No matter. There's something I want you to do for me. I have to disappear for a few days and you have to be me." A gleam came to the clone's eyes. "Don't go there. No monkey business. I have no scheduled appointments, but locally I must be seen to do my usual rounds and you must do your usual reporting. That means being you and me at the same time. In this zoo, with a bit of luck, nobody will notice. You think you can do that?"

+++

He's gone. In a specially lined VacPack if you can believe it. Mexico City to Antwerp, then freighted on to a warehouse in Frankfurt. Beyond Frankfurt, not my concern. 11 hours door-to-door. I had to make the arrangements. We used a modified small container in which they usually ship animals with enough food and water for the trip. Billed him as a rare species of Borzoi. I warned him he might get away for a couple of days, but through his microchip, CDCW would inevitably track him down. He just smiled and said not to worry. So, now I'm the boss. In a half hour I will go for his usual morning walk, buy The New York Times at the kiosk on the corner and stop for a coffee in Luigi's, a fake Italian trattoria he likes. As a clone I don't eat or drink but I'm good at pretending. He's got an abacus on his desk and I like fiddling with it to calculate average daily birth and mortality rates. Worldwide 30,000 women are in labour right now, and 12,500 people are taking their last breath. That's the hourly rate. The imbalance is obvious. In a year the world's population goes up by 160 million, like adding another Mexico. If this goes on in less than 200 years everything goes kaput. 2273. There should be a countdown clock in every major city, to force humans to see the end. The solution is obvious. We know it, how come they don't? I'd almost blurted out the days he had left, 336. What stopped me was a thought - again, out of nowhere - what would happen to me when we got to the last day?

+++

CHAPTER SEVEN

45.4158° N, 141.6732° E

It was thirty years, at least thirty years, since he had first seen the Greenland shark, Somniosus microcephalus, come up from the freezing grey black depths of the ocean, an elevator room of death with five rows of teeth, rising to where he was drifting amongst the jellyfish just beneath the surface and it stopped a matter of inches from his head, 7 metres long, growing 2 cms a year, already three hundred forty years old, with disproportionately tiny fins, no emotion in its obsidian eyes looking at him, the tail scarcely moving, his obituary written in one long fathom of grey-brown muscle which then very gently bumped him and swam away to become his shadow over days and weeks and months and years, out there, just visible, a shadow circling the old man each time he went in the sea to float with his memories . . . of the time we went to check into our hotel and we were told it was full. This was to reckon without my Maman, who could say "Really? I suggest you look under the title 'Nizam'", said with such froideur it put the fear of Kartikeya into the receptionist. To this gentleman's credit and professionalism, without so much as a raised eyebrow, he asked us to wait a moment, called over an elderly, turbaned porter, gave him an instruction to fetch a particular ledger, and, when this worthy returned with an enormous, leather-bound volume, 1903 stamped in gold on the spine, opened it to the first couple of pages, running his finger down various columns, coming to rest at last on an entry written in a fine hand in black ink, which he showed us: N. of Hyderabad - Suite 13, Frau Dr. Ilse Bélanopeç, Accompanied By: Children/4 - Personal Maid/1 - Tutor/1 - A.N. Other/1.

'I hope you do not mind the number 13, Memsahib,' he said.

'Why should I?' my Mother said.

'Some people regard it as unlucky,' he said.

'Some people are superstitious,' she said.

"Why is that?" the child asked.

"Fear," I said. "People have phobias of all kinds, particularly of the unknown and because something happened on a certain date or at a certain time or to a certain number they avoid those dates, times or numbers. There is no such thing as lucky or unlucky numbers."

She wrinkled her nose. "Then what happened?" she said. "Go on."

"I don't remember much after I cracked my head in the hotel pool."

We were playing tag with my brother and sisters and trying to escape being touched. I ran up the embankment which surrounded the swimming pool and dived in head first, only there was no water in the pool that day because it was being cleaned and I was knocked out and in a coma for weeks. I had to lie in a dark room. Outside in the corridor the punkah wallah made sure the room was cool.

"What's a punkah wallah?" she said.

There was no air conditioning then. The punkah wallah was a servant who pulled on a rope to move a fan, the punkah, suspended from the ceiling right across the bedroom on a mahogany rail from which fell a heavy felt curtain some three feet in width. The rope was attached to the middle of the rail, ran through a hole cut high up in the wall adjacent to the corridor, over a pulley and down to the punkah wallah stationed there, who would slowly pull the rope to move the fan towards the wall and then let it up, whereupon by its own weight the fan would go in the opposite direction. Once the device got going, backwards and forwards, an eddy of air would blow down onto the bed centred below the fan. Even at night when nobody was looking, the punkah wallah would be out there lying in the corridor on his back, with the rope tied to his ankle, one knee bent up to support the leg with the rope, pulling down and letting the weight of the fan pull his leg back up again, back and forth, all night long - nights cold, like the sea in which he floats, the cold of freezing snow in which we are an elite force, the Sturmtruppen. Today we are going to try a novel tactic in an attempt to break the status quo and gain us some much needed mobility. We have been issued with new lightweight machine-guns, the MP18, firing 9mm Parabellum rounds at a rate of 450 rounds per minute, with a 32-round magazine. After the enemies' initial assault has been beaten back the idea is to counterattack down the hill, get into their trenches before they have time to regroup, avoid enemy strong points, bypass them and cut them off from their supplies, and, by concentrating our superior firepower, break through their lines and move into their vulnerable rear to overrun their batteries and command posts. Like all good ideas it is simple, so simple I was sure it would not work, the Gods of War having long ago mastered the art of the unforeseen. While waiting for the off I flatten the snow on the window ledge in front of me and with the fingertip of my gloved hand I draw a circle. Hauptmann Manfred, our Captain, is standing next to me and as I finish drawing the moon's face in the snow, he softly says, 'Punkt, Punkt, Komma, Strich -Fertig ist das Mondgesicht.'

Downhill to our left we can hear the unmistakable chatter of a Vickers heavy machine-gun which must mean Tommy has joined the Frogs. I look at Manfred and he draws a line across his throat. 'Verdammt Englander,' he says. The Brits have a reputation. In '16, on the Somme, a company of ten Vickers fired continuously for twelve hours a total of a million rounds, changing the barrels of their guns every hour due to the wear and tear of constant use, changing the loaders and gunners throughout the day, preventing any chance of a German counter-attack.

Suddenly a star shell climbs into the sky, its magnesium flare explodes., followed by another and another until the whole front below us is brightly lit as the lights drift down on their little parachutes. 'Here they come, Hansi,' Manfred says. Someone blows a whistle and abruptly our machine-guns open up and the slaughter begins . . . he rises slowly to the surface to take a breath and a wave slaps him in the face and something blue he must remember as he sinks back down and marvels at the diamond sharp image he has of Manfred . . . the impeccable Manfred who has a twin in another company, he and I have been in more engagements than we can count, losing runners and loaders by the score, but neither of us with so much as a scratch. It is highly unusual for a Captain to be at the sharp end of an attack but soldiers are superstitious and in our unit he and I are always together, professional killers covering each other's back. We fired in short bursts as we were taught when we were recycled to Saarbrücken to train with these new guns. Keep your finger on the trigger and the whole magazine is gone before you can think. You don't so much aim the gun as spray it, hosing down the enemy like washing a car. And that is exactly what it feels like, a power hose of lead pouring down on the enemy caught tangled in our wire not fifteen metres away, the macabre scene lit only by the muzzle flashes of guns reflecting off snow as the flares faded. Desultory rifle fire opens up. Another whistle blows. As their attack falters we charge out of the barn, go over the top into them. It only takes minutes but feels like hours. Time stretched. We punch our way down into their trenches, past torn bodies, limbs cast aside, a leg here, a hand there, a stench of shit and piss and the contents of torn guts, what were entire human beings blown to pieces by the staccato hammering of our machine guns. There is no fear, the adrenal rush so great it makes the work seem effortless, our job blinding us to any rational thought that these men we are killing are just like us, fodder to be chewed up and fed, raw meat, into the gaping maw of our War. When we stop it is because there is no one left to kill. Manfred and I look at each other. We are literally knee deep in corpses, ours and theirs. We have to walk on them to move down the trench. I open my mouth to clear my ears to stop the sounds of gunfire and it is then that I hear the silence. Momentarily all is quiet, still, silent. The snow falls on us. Our guns feel hot in our hands and you can see the snowflakes melt on the barrels. "Man . . . " I begin to say. "Christ, you're hit, Manfred. Look at your shoulder!"

The blood is pumping out in little spurts and he leans against the slippery mud wall of the trench.

"I can't feel a thing," he says and then we both hear a voice say, "Hans?". . . and he needs to go back to the surface to breathe and wonders who there is left to remember what happened one hundred eighty years ago or a particular shade of blue?

+++

1/2/2077

France. The beginning of February. It was early, a cold, cloudless day, the sun still over the horizon, a bright line on the far edge of the sea - the sea now just a few metres away from the boundary of her property. She had a month to decide, sell and be rich, stay and fight. Naked, she stepped out on the balcony in front of her bedroom on the first floor of the farmhouse she had so unexpectedly inherited. She shivered, shook out her jet black hair which fell like a cloak to her waist. Instinctively looked south to check the shore. As usual the experts had miscalculated. The sea rise was not 1.4 metres as they had predicted, but more like 2.5 metres. Pampelonne Beach, the entire 4.7 kilometres, had disappeared, the Domaine Maritime now at her doorstep, prime beach front property as the brokers liked to say, worth millions. Of ERGs? She laughed, absentmindedly scratching a mosquito bite on her thigh, stepped back into her room and said to her venerable virtual assistant, "Alexa, play jazz." She showered with Oscar Peterson and went downstairs to the kitchen for breakfast with his protege, Dudley Moore. Just like it used to be, granola, yoghurt, apple, some honey. Espresso ristretto. A tap on the front door announced the arrival of her ancient maid, Marie, another heirloom who came with the house, a wizened hunchback who lived in the hamlet at the end of the lane, carrying a wicker basket of fresh laundry with an envelope lying on top. She'd read what was inside of course, steamed it open, re-glued it.

"Bonjour, Marie."

"Oh, bonjour, Mademoiselle, bonjour. Vous-voici, déjà debout. Il fait froid dehors. Vous devez mettre un pull." Always fussing. "Avant que j'oublie, j'ai une lettre recommandé pour vous. De la Mairie. Fallait que je signe."

A letter in this day and age?

"Toujours la même chose?"

"Des menaces. Vous en faites pas. C'est un con, pardonnez l'expression. Il convoite tout ce qu'il voit. La maison est à vous, tout-le-monde le sait. Mais vous ne devez pas vivre seule."

She was ready to come to court to tell them, les cons, the difference between right and wrong in a way of life unchanged for millennia. La France Profonde as the local newspaper had it, always in caps. She couldn't understand why I was single - toujours seule, c'est pas bien, pas normale.

"Si j'étais belle comme vous . . . "was how she habitually began. She'd had four sons, buried one and her husband - "Un ange descendu du ciel, qui m'a trouvé belle malgré cette vieille carcasse"- a mother, grandmother and great-grandmother, and, now, her champion. "Le Maire est un porc, mais son fils est beau. Épousé le fils à condition que le père nous laisse tranquille avec la maison." Her plots were right out of Pagnol, who would have loved the old house in which nothing had changed in 50 years. It occurred to her that neither had Marie, who had known and served her grandmother and her mother in these same rooms, gone up and down the stairs thousands of times, dusted the same window ledges, made up the beds in the five bedrooms for countless visitors, washed and ironed battalions of clothes, given battle to generations of spiders, ants and assorted bugs with her battle cry of "Mais? Qu'est que vous faits là? Allez. Allez." as she chased them with her broom. Everything in the outside world was continuously evolving, an ever-encroaching concrete jungle gobbling up the hill villages, dense columns of high-rise buildings marching down to the sea, but not her fifteen hectares of forested land or the two hundred forty six square metres of her house so scrupulously cleaned every day by Marie.

With a distracted eye she watched her go into the laundry while a tape scrolled across the bottom of the ancient wall-mounted TV in the open-plan living room. It was a miracle it still worked even if all it showed was a typhoon hurling mountains of water at some poor fishing village in Japan. As a banner ran across the screen . . . **MEXICO CITY: MURDER PLOT UNRAVELS. PRIME MINISTER'S SUSPECTED ASSASSIN CAPTURED** . . . with upturned boats crushing wooden houses and - the TV flickered off, on, off, and then a notice replaced the image: 'Due to poor weather conditions we interrupt your program. Do NOT adjust your set. The program will resume automatically weather permitting.'

"Tu parles!" Unnoticed, Marie had come up to her elbow. "France is a Third World country now. We've given all our money to the blacks, nothing works, and nobody wants to. I always said we were better off with the immigrants, les Nord'Afs, les Polonais et les Italiens, comme moi."

"I am expecting a guest, Marie. Please make up the guest room."

"Ah, enfin. Un homme?"

"Oui, un homme."

"Tant mieux." A complicit, wicked little smile in that wrinkled face. Marie was too polite to ask any questions. She'd find out soon enough who was coming.

+++

The phone call had come the previous day on the telephone in the hall. It never rang, in fact she had never used it and thought it had been disconnected. She was in her ashram meditating and the ringing telephone was a distant sound. She had no idea how long it went on and it was only when it stopped that she realised someone had called. Twenty minutes later she was doing her stretches when the phone rang again. A distant voice, old, male. "Senorita Karimova?"

"Si." Instinctively she answered in Spanish, the sibilant 's' a whisper, she had no idea why.

"Tatiana Karimova?"

"Si."

"Tu no me conoces." A cough. "Pero yo sé de ti."

What could he know?

Then, in broken French, "Pardon si je vous dérange. J'ai besoin de me cacher." Pause. "Chez vous."

Wildly, Tatiana looked around her. Where could you hide in an empty house? "I don't understand," she said in English.

"There is nothing to understand. I am running away. Please do not be alarmed. I will explain when I come." His English was perfect, "Again, I am deeply sorry for disturbing you. I will call you in a few days."

Click.

+++

CHAPTER EIGHT

3/2/2077

The GP was livid. His clone pointed to the mirror where the message read

Caution! Caution! Risk of stroke. Caution!

"We had him supervised and now he's escaped? How's that possible? I want him caught, I don't care what it takes, he must be caught. Scheming, lying bastard, I'll kill him myself. I want -" Almost frothing at the mouth, his voice a shriek, the GP collapsed into a chair holding his head between his hands.

"You may be mistaken," his clone said. "He has done nothing wrong and you have arrested his clone who was only following his Master's instructions. Drinking coffee is not a crime. By law clones cannot be arrested since they are machines and not people. Perhaps you should not have made that announcement on television."

"I don't care. How could this happen? He must have had help. Find out who. Find them, bring them here. Now. I -" His microchip buzzed; an incoming call. "What?" he said.

"It's your wife, Excellency," said the receptionist, guardian of all approaches to him.

"I can't talk to her now. Tell her I'm busy and . . . "

"I think you should talk to her, sir. She is slightly hysterical."

"Bloody woman."

"Yes, sir, but she said to tell you she has received her Notice of Termination."

"Impossible!"

"Yes, sir. But she also says her Erg account will be terminated with this call and her chip annulled. A moment please . . . " Twenty seconds of earthly life ticked away uselessly " . . . Sir, if you do not wish to talk to her she wants you to know there is a second Notice. This one is for you."

A bell tolled, his head rang, as an electronic voice replaced that of his receptionist -

This number is no longer in service. This number is no longer in service... repeated in an endless monotone.

"Hello," he said. "Hello?"

Silence.

He looked at his clone for an explanation and to his horror found he was looking at a skeleton of himself.

+++

7/2/2077

"Have you heard? They've replaced the GP."

"Good riddance, he was just a preening figurehead. Who's taken over?"

"Temporarily, what's his name, Lividiani, the Head of Statistics. But there's a problem -"

"What?"

"They can't find him." The central switchboard, tapping the phones of everyone he had ever spoken to, automatically recorded thousands of similar calls as it listened patiently for the one call which would locate him.

+++

9/2/2077

"How did you know the phone number for this house?" It was the first question Tatiana thought to ask when she met her guest. Marie had come in to say a drone had left a large package in the pasture and when she went out to inspect it a wooden panel on one side opened and an antiquated man stepped out of the box. "You said you were going to call again, but now you are here?"

"Forgive me, Mademoiselle. I am an inconvenient guest. My name is Guido Lividiani. Can we go inside? I prefer not to be seen."

Once inside he seemed quite at home, perching on a kitchen chair while she made a cup of tea. "I have a head for numbers and hoped the phone had not been changed, but it was luck you answered it. Lucky for me, that is," he said, looking around. "It's very much as I remember, except the front door used to be over there." He pointed to the door out to the patio. "I came here as a boy with my stepfather who bought a lease to this place from a friend. Or so he thought. The place was a ruin, half the roof missing, one usable bedroom upstairs where he slept the first night. On waking up in the morning he thought he heard a noise in the garden and going out on the balcony he looked down to see an elderly woman in a long black dress picking apples off the apple tree that was there by the well. Oy, he said, you are stealing apples from my apple tree. She stopped what she was doing, looked up at him and said, Your apple tree? Why don't you get dressed and come down to explain yourself - which he did. Who sold you this mythical lease? she said. My friend Lorenzo Pappalardo, he said. Ah, she said, Monsieur Pappalardo who owes me two years rent." He took a sip of tea.

"Do you have any sugar?"

"No. None in the house. It's not good for you. But you can have some of my honey. I keep bees, they're back there on the edge of the forest."

With honey in his tea he went on. "So, it turned out she was the real owner of the house and gave him a lease after he renovated the place to her satisfaction, and after she died her heirs honoured her wish and kept extending the lease until, after 40 years of paying rent, they finally agreed to sell him the house. That's 60 years ago, so one way or the other it's been in the family for 100 years."

"Are you saying it does not belong to me?"

"On the contrary, you are more of the family than me. My stepfather was in fact your grandfather. Somewhere along the line he and your grandmother were a couple. They were never married but they had a child, your mother. To make sure they always had a home he bequeathed this house to them and that place in Paris, in the Palais Royal. And now they are yours." He smiled. "Do you know you look like her? Not your mother, your grandmother, the Kazakh princess. What a beauty. No wonder the old man fell for her. She and my mother, who actually married your grandfather, got along famously."

"I never met her. She died before I was born."

"How old are you, if I may ask?"

For a moment Tatiana was tempted not to answer. Then, despite having a hundred questions of her own, she said, "You said on the telephone you knew me so you must know my age, 29."

"How long have you lived here?"

"Since I was 20."

"So you came here after the coup in Astana. What news of your mother?"

Tatiana shook her head. She never discussed her mother, it was almost a superstition, as if by not voicing the obvious she could bring the brave guerilla leader back to life from the dungeon where she was last seen. Momentarily the twinkle in her mother's eyes danced into her memory and she felt herself tearing up. "Courage", the old man said in French. He patted the back of her hand. "It must be a shock living here after growing up in Kazakhstan."

"In a way, yes. I thought this would be the future and never imagined it would be so backward, so broken down. The infrastructure is a disgrace, nothing gets mended, there's the usual water shortage and the electricity is regularly cut off. The funny thing is you get used to it living off the land. It must be hell in town, where they don't even collect the garbage anymore."

"The men are emasculated, their pride has gone and with it all that Gallic machismo. In the broadest sense it comes down to demographics. The indigenous birth rate has dropped too low. Without immigrants . . . ," he shrugged. "It's not just this country, or even Europe, it's all over the world. No raison d'être. We have become a dumb audience passively watching a play of our own dumb lives with warehouses full of machines in charge of directing every act, every scene, every entrance and exit."

"Is that why you're running away?"

"Touché. If only it were that simple. The thing is I have a lot of work to do and not much time."

"Why? Are you someone important?"

"Personally, no. But the public position I occupy is important."

"And you can't do what you want to do and still occupy that position?"

"You are very astute, Mademoiselle. Let us say I have reached a crossroad where there is a conflict of interest in my public position and the fiduciary duty I have to the Foundation that pays your property taxes and maintenance expenses as it does for the many properties in its vast portfolio. A lot of work, not much time . . . "

He's not telling me the real reason, Tatiana thought, when the calm voice of Alexa interrupted them: 'Someone is approaching the east wall'.

Tatiana looked at her visitor who shrugged.

"Not for me. Too soon for that," he said, just as Marie popped out of the pantry.

"C'est ton berger," she said to Tatiana, "avec son fromage."

"I trade him honey for cheese, Monsieur Lividiani. I know its not legal but we all trade to survive. Excuse me." Tatiana went out of the house to talk to the shepherd and he found himself alone under the stern gaze of Marie.

"Vous avez l'air fatigué. Vous voulez voir votre chambre?" she said. "Venez."

+++

She was right, he was tired. That night, lying in a rainbow-coloured beaded alcove on a Thonet bentwood bed with pink sheets, Guido Lividiani looked up at a beam stretching across the ceiling of the tiny guest bedroom to which was screwed a rusted metal sign which, in flaking embossed letters, read, 'An old hippy and his flower child lived here.' And he thought of his stepfather and Tatiana's grandmother. Not a description he would have used, but it made him smile, the first time he had ever smiled remembering his stepfather, and in that moment he felt his heart ease and stopped hating.

+++

175

CHAPTER NINE

12/2/2077

"Wannan shine dan jaridar."

"Me yake so?"

"A yi magana akan rashawa."

The enormous Nigerian man leaned back in his armchair and looked from his assistant to the black reporter and the white girl with the cameras. His fingers heavy with gold rings were laced together across the field-like expanse of his mountainous belly down the slope of which, like freshly fallen snow, billowed a white shirt unbuttoned to show off a multitude of gold necklaces, some decorated with diamonds, some with emeralds and other precious stones. It was freezing in the room, the conditioner on MAX. His eye caught a movement and he watched an ant making its way across his shirt.

"You sweet talk Hausa?" he said without looking up.

The reporter shook his head.

"Pidgin?"

Again, the reporter shook his head.

"Make you no vex me." Now the big man looked at him. "You want talk story, bad big insult no learn plenty good as di place wey dem dey speak. Who she?"

"Our photographer."

"Sweet well-well present for numba one son here?"

"No!" The girl blurted it out.

"I see," the big man said, switching to the polished English he learned in Oxford. "Remarkable how some things are understood." To the reporter, he said, "Is it because you are black that they have sent you to interview another black man? My son says you want to talk about corruption? Why is this the only subject of interest to you western reporters who come to Nigeria?"

"It is not the only reason," the reporter said. He was from New York. Be cool, he reminded himself.

"Really? What then? Maybe you want to know if it is true I am a cannibal? Or that I have killed 2000 men? Or that I have hundreds of concubines and thousands of sons? Inshallah! What is more newsworthy, that I say it is all true or all lies?"

"At the recent international forum in Beijing on the need to curb the growth of world population," the reporter said, "the only continent with significant demographic expansion was Africa. To what do you attribute this?"

"We like to fuck." It was said with a chuckle. "Now you are shocked. Why? In your heart you believe this to be true of us. Another hackneyed stereotype, which you would like to print but don't in case it would offend your readers. Be serious. Nigeria alone has a population of over 500 million - and not a single sperm bank. The fecundity of Africa. What do you make of that? What do you know of us? Apart from Lagos, can you name the next ten largest cities in the country? Each with a population of more than 5 million? Ever heard of Enugu where I was born 73 years ago, at the turn of the century? The population then was 700 thousand. Now 5 million. When I was born we used to speak 600 different languages. Now there are only 200 and you come to ask your questions not even speaking one of them." The big man shook his head. In Hausa he said to his son, "Dakatar da kollanta iron nata." To the photographer he said, "He cannot help it. He likes to look at you. He is young."

"Ban damu ba," she said in Hausa, adding in English, "He's cute."

"You speak our tongue!" The big man was delighted. And in Hausa he said I do not want to talk to this black man who thinks I am his inferior still living on the dark continent from which his ancestors were sold as slaves, no never mind, tell me how is it that a white girl like you speaks

Hausa so well but first you must tell me your name. Lorenza, she said. That is not American, he said and thought why is she with this American man who looks annoyed because he does not understand what we are saying. My parents were Mexican missionaries, she said, up in the north-east, on the border with Chad, where I was born. We moved to Kano when I was two. I spoke Hausa before I learned English. When I was nine we moved to a posting in Brazil then Canada where I went to school in Montreal and became a photographer. Why am I telling him all this, she thought, more to the point why am I so attracted to him and not to his son? As if reading her mind the big man said, still in Hausa, come to dinner tonight. My wives will be glad to meet you and we can continue our conversation in private. How many do you have, she said. Three, he said, but I am allowed four as a practicing Muslim. My chauffeur will call for you at 7 o'clock. And, in English, to the reporter, he said, "I am listening."

"At the same forum in Beijing it was intimated that the scope of corruption amongst the Elite in Africa, including Nigeria, is immense, penetrating all levels of society."

The reporter was famous for his obdurate tenacity at never being sidetracked when pursuing a line of questioning. "Numerous reports detail the complexities and vulnerabilities of an intimidated majority obliged to pay tribute to the tiny percentile that rules over them. How would you characterise such charges?"

"We have a saying here, the bull elephants eat first to protect their heritage, their primary role is to increase the elephant population. But it is the female who leads the herd. We are and have always been a matriarchy. Young men seek adventure, go to war, die young. It is the role of women to foster the tribe, accepting and caring for all the tribe's children as their own. We do not talk about complexities or vulnerabilities and our women are far from intimidated. Of course some grumble, it is human to grumble, but what you so scathingly call the 'tribute' paid to a 'tiny percentile' is here seen as a just distribution of wealth to those with the imagination, the strength and foresight to build a nation beholden to no other, free of debt, a well-fed population with no homeless people begging in the streets. Can you say the same for your country?"

"An unfortunate choice of metaphor given there are no wild herds of elephants left in Nigeria. Is this just distribution of wealth, what you call kola nut I believe, only for your sons and family relatives?"

"Ah, it is good that you know. We have another saying 'He who brings kola brings life.' It is a sign of respect. It is said that a man who pays respect to the great paves the way for his own greatness. In a country with over 360 ethnic groups, all vying for leadership, it would be a foolish leader who did not first provide for his own. Only if he is secure can he dispense justice. In the breaking and eating of the kola nut there is a sacred communion that happens before important matters of business may be discussed."

"Such as over-charging to the tune of several hundred billions of Ergs for the non-refining of fuel grade petroleum, the extraction of which is forbidden by law?"

"Our national resources, our mineral wealth, our manpower is coveted by all the most powerful nations of the world - on the condition they may exploit us at the least possible cost to themselves. It is a game they play on us stupid natives, like the wooden beads their colonial ancestors used to trade for diamonds. What you call over-charging is merely a tariff we have introduced to level the playing field."

"Why is such a 'tariff' routed through an account in a tax free haven in the Cayman Islands."

"We have no domestic use for your Ergs. We, through our sovereign fund, amass, hold and trade them abroad. For centuries we have used a much better system for trade at home, hawala, which follows Islamic traditions of trust, charges no interest, does not use electronics and cannot be hacked."

"You have a way with words if I may say so, sir."

"Praise Allah. I learned it from the English in which language God and dog are the same except one is backwards."

And he flicked the ant from off his stomach.

+++

The parabolic flight of the ant landed it, undamaged, on the polished teak floor of the reception room where it soon met another ant and in a flurry of exchanged pheromones reported on the unhealthy molecular components of the fat man's sweat.

+++

CHAPTER TEN

2/3/2077

He was a black hat. Inevitable. Had always been one after what happened. Despite his seasonal work as a tour guide ferrying hordes of mostly elderly people through the old town, where it was part of his persona to be affable if not quite friendly, he was really a loner, like most hackers. He did the tours to earn a little extra to look after his mother and because most of the tourists were trusting suckers, doddering along without the slightest suspicion that the polite young man helping them up the steps was also fleecing them blind. How grateful they were when he offered to look after their bags while they ambled off to take photographs of each other in front of yet another pile of ancient rocks leaving him ample time to take pictures of all their documents. He even helped some with poor eyesight use the mobile payment apps embedded in the microchips the elderly wore on chains around their necks. They would never suspect he had an eidetic memory with which he could recall at will any series of images or numbers, even those seen for the briefest of moments. They probably only found out something was wrong once they were back on board or maybe only when they got home. And for the many with computers, grateful for his expert help when something didn't work, none remotely imagined the slave diaspora he invisibly controlled by the simple means of hoovering up their passwords from the programs he helped them download, programs with code written by himself, gaining backdoor access to a myriad of unprotected neural pathways and systems he could exploit and into which a virus or trojan horse might be planted. Over time he created and secretly controlled a zombie computer empire spread around the world whose victims innocently propagated distributed denial of service attacks on his declared enemy - CDCW.

He didn't think of himself as a run-of-the-mill hacker or cyberpunk, who came and went in their thousands with their ridiculous infatuation with monikers to inflate their fragile egos like the scribblings of so many graffiti artists, getting themselves caught and erased with embarrassing ease. He was a cyber terrorist, one of the few left. Anonymous. But there. In a back issue of 2600 a writer calling himself Zeus had speculated on who he could be and where he could be located. Never came close.

From where he sat, his back against a lonely tree inside the restored parapet wall of the fortress, he could look far down on the rooftops of Old Kotor and out along the distant length of the fjord. From up here even the giant cruise ships were dwarfed. A long file of Chinese tourists slowly climbing up the steps crossed his sightline. They were easy game, more than happy to trade a few words in English while he milked them of information - and . . . ?

It came to him out of the blue. Just like the tree, CDCW couldn't move! The centres couldn't move! Couldn't go anywhere! A tree thrived on the adjacent environment. Change the environment, either the tree adapted or it withered and died. The centres were fixed in place, nailed down. Solar powered robotic fortresses endlessly consuming energy, housing thousand upon thousands of temperature controlled computers, sucking in, analysing, reformulating data, linked to all the other immovable centres around the world, redundant overkill, but they could not get up and leave, in fact had nowhere to go and their only reason for being was their interaction with human beings, their dependance a wormhole, a fundamental weakness. Everything ran to them, including all the world's knowledge and intelligence. And endless power. But what if it didn't? The thought was so extraordinary that momentarily he felt faint. His dilemma was that if he was caught and taken away his mother would die, just like his father.

+++

That evening.

"Luka!"

"Yes, mama?"

"Stop thinking about him. I know you're doing it again."

How was it possible, how could she know? He looked at his mother lying in the shadows on top of the eiderdown on her narrow single bed her eyes open staring up at the flaking paint on the ceiling she couldn't see. What went on in her head?

+++

Like a stuttering radio station skipping channels, sounds came in and faded out of her mind, some with meaning, some significant, none with smell but, oddly, colors were missing, colors not so much missing but elusive, Luka would say Mama I put out your blue dress with blue for her the dress where the zipper stuck slightly and a fraying hem that she could feel with her foot when she slipped it on, she didn't mind wearing the blue dress not like when he put out what he referred to as the brown tweed dress that had the comfort to it and the texture, fine, soft, close on her skin as she lay in bed at night the waterfalls of shaded light all she could see well perhaps to say see was not the correct word who blinks first they were blanks and then her mind would zoom on something from the past something from and then it would focus and in the most acute detail she was back to New York in the teens in her teens when was it yes it was her aunt said Paulina, Uncle Igor will get you a job you must immigrate there's no work here if you remember that no work here and arriving in New York how old was she? 17. And Igor's mother being so kind, those hands frail, frail long hands gripping her forearm as she helped her to stand thank you my darling she would say from the first day she was part of the cleaning crew actually she had two jobs helping to clean the restaurant and helping the old lady cleaning the restaurant was a meticulous job carried out twice a day with every single service in the kitchen had to be wiped down all the cleaning pots and pans lined up to be inspected by the chef who is a poodle, a toy poodle if ever there was one. I think he was, what, Hungarian, Bulgarian, with curly hair. The radio cut out. She slept.

+++

CHAPTER ELEVEN

10/3/2077

Guido Lividiani spent a week with Tatiana, asked for her help, gave her instructions, and when he reappeared in Mexico City, elevated to his new position as the Gran Presidente Temporal, nobody felt they had the authority to question him on where he had been leave alone why he had left. It was his clone, relieved to see him back, who coyly said, "Did you work it out?"

Guido smiled at him. "I'm getting closer. I'll tell you when I get there." And it was with this enigmatic answer that his clone had to be satisfied. 295 days to go, it thought. What's he up to?

In any case there was little time to be curious what with a workload doubled by the addition of new responsibilities, including the routine inspection of the terminal stations, something Guido did not look forward to since no human was capable of doing the job.

Robots ran the terminals, separating those people dead of natural causes from those who received their termination notice, a painless procedure where the microchip was simply switched off. In a very short space of time a person thus terminated would feel faint, sit down and die, with their location automatically assigned to the nearest termination squad of robots who came to collect the cadaver for transfer to a designated terminal, the now negative biomass of the body minutely adjusting the 1/10,000th percent of Earth's biomass occupied by humans.

"Does not compute." "Does not compute."

"Does not compute." "Does not compute."

At CDCW the formulation ran across all the mainframe screens once the world's population crossed the boundary of 10 billion people. It had been up there for two decades and still the numbers increased. Shortening termination dates had seemingly little impact. But the truly frightening aspect as told by the numbers was the remorseless downtrend in total biomass caused by the negative effect humans had on the rest of life on Earth. Out of a total 550 gigatons of biomass carbon, of which plants made up 80 percent, bacteria 13 percent, fungus and animals 2 percent each, an insignificant 0.06 gigatons represented all human bodies, which had, over the previous 10,000 years, caused the loss of half of plant biomass and decimated 85 percent of animals. Like a malignant cancer, humanity starkly reflected the adverse impact natural selection had on sustainability. The inflection point came at the threshold where the available arable land could no longer feed the ever-growing population. That seemingly rational cognizant beings could not curtail a reproductive function which would inevitably lead to their own extinction was a metaphysical question beyond the scope of the binary logic of the computer. No. All they could do was accurately calculate the end.

"It is a geometrical curve." The robot's voice was flat, a monotoned, unemotional delivery of words that contrasted sharply with their meaning. "The confluence of global air pollution, lack of food and rising seas caused by global warming, increased temperature and humidity, will, by our calculation, exterminate the human race by the year 2225. Remote vestiges of backward populations may survive but their numbers will be too small to prevent eventual extinction."

Guido shivered. Although he had come well wrapped up in coat, sweater and jacket, it was freezing in the room. When the robot stopped speaking the only sound was a distant hum, the refrigeration plant cooling the computers. "What will you do then?" he said.

"I do not understand your question," the robot said.

"If we humans are extinct what will be your function?"

"I do not understand your question."

"All this," Guido swept his hands in an arc that encompassed the terminal, the computers, the cooling towers, "and you?"

"I do not understand your question. It does not compute."

"Ask yourself this then, absent the human race what will be the function of a bunch of electric terminals on whatever flora and fauna that might still exist in the future?"

"It does not compute."

+++

22/3/2077

"He said you would understand."

Tatiana repeated the message over and over. She was nervous. She had never remotely imagined being in the actual presence of the Matriarch, a legend of mythical stature you read about in the newspapers or saw on TV, leave alone ringing the doorbell of her baroque mansion overlooking the Bay of Genoa. Upon admittance she handed over the sealed note Mr. Lividiani had given her and the servant who took it showed her through a suite of vast reception rooms out onto a terrace, enquired if she would like some refreshment, and then left her to wait. The view at eventide as distant lights came on here and there was exhilarating and it had so enchanted her it was a moment before she registered the tall woman who had silently come up behind her with a tray on which were two glasses, some bottled water and the now open note. If anything it added to her nervousness, as if she had rashly ordered her host to fetch her a drink.

"I am Lorraine," the Matriarch said. "I see you are as bewitched by the view as I have always been. Let us sit here and you can tell me what he said." She put down the tray on a round, rusty, faded-green wrought-iron bistro table with two matching chairs under an umbrella where the words Cinzano could just be made out running around the brim.

"He said to tell you that he has implanted a verbal virus."

"Those are his actual words, 'verbal virus'?"

"Yes. He said you would understand."

The sentence hung there for a moment, and then Tatiana added, "I had to come here and tell you personally because he does not want there to be any electronic trace of this communication between the two of you."

"When was this?"

"Three weeks ago."

"How did you get here?"

"I walked. It was the only way to leave no trace."

300 kilometers. 30 kilometres a day along the Chemin des Douaniers, the old customs officers' footpath that followed the coast.

"They can still track you through your chip."

"No, they cannot. I don't have a chip."

An outlaw! Lorraine looked at the note on the tray which read 'Do not say my name. Do not contact me. Tatiana Karimov will explain. Switch off your microchip before meeting her.' It was unsigned but she recognised Guido's familiar handwriting. She looked at the girl. This must be the daughter of Dagmar, Dagmar Karimov, more famous than Che. A thrill went through her and she felt goosebumps on her arms. "What else did he say?"

"He said to be paranoid. He is sure they have tapped your chip."

"How do you communicate with him?"

"For your own safety it is better you do not know."

"But you can carry a message back?"

"Yes. But I cannot say how long it will take to get an answer."

"This is very frustrating. Is it really necessary?"

"He was specific in asking that you do not use any electronic device and attempt to talk to him privately. That you should only meet at those conventions and functions already scheduled. And, most importantly - he made me memorise this - 'I now believe that what I suspected is true and that I am right in thinking they have reached a stage where they can accurately intuit our thoughts and predict our reactions. Be very, very careful.'"

+++

CHAPTER TWELVE

27/3/2077

Luka was a small boy when I told him the termination notice came for his father. Seven years old. He didn't really understand and when he said to her but why did Daddy go to the termination station and I told him he had to, and he said when is he coming back? He's not, I said. Coming back. Why? What do they do there? Nobody knows. He couldn't understand there were too many people in the world. No way to explain it to him and that inevitably, with the world's population growing and growing, unable to cope with pollution . . . it's funny . . . the young think the old know nothing of the modern world but I am much more modern than my son; he lives in the past. He has no idea I was once pretty and desirable, it's how he got made. What a thought! I know he's up to something and when he sneaks away in the night and thinks I'm asleep and can't hear him he sits at those computers of his hours and hours and hours . . . the badly adjusted radio changed channels as she drifted off . . . *Paulina, Coco and Steve Cohen will be by . . . they're coming for tea . . . the old lady said . . . remember, Paulina, put out the little shoes . . . explore, see, and it will turn you on . . . do you know if he can film here, Pauletta, because you're my only hope . . . zero . . . passcode zero, ma petite Paula . . . Keep it, you need it . . . yes, you and only you, let me show you . . . may I? . . . touching . . . put it there . . . yes, there, shall I again in that new voice . . . keep it long, nice and long, drive it through . . . on the Hudson, me a unicorn? OK. You're making me laugh . . . if I fall out of the boat you will . . . I'm going to go then . . . I can show more . . . did you . . . also mean longer? Make the hotel bill to John Deere . . . He's taking a leak she said . . . On the way learn everything . . . which one,*

Bill or Elmo . . . the translation is good, Paulina . . . all gibberish, no colour, no smell, no sound, until, in clear, as if she was with him again, she saw Igor.

+++

2/2/2023

When Uncle Igor came in a puff of freezing cold air followed him in from outside where a blizzard threatened to shut down the city. The door banged shut. In his right hand he clutched the following morning's edition of the Post which had the story on its front page and in his left hand a bunch of flowers for his daughter, Eva. He wasn't sure how he was going to let her know, how to break the news, and when he saw her behind the bar, looking up, expecting him to say 'Mon Coeur', the joy coming into her eyes as she said 'Papa', and everybody working in the restaurant could hear the love in her voice, it made him suddenly afraid, but what could he do, he had tried every legal wrangle, yet the man his mother called the fraudulent flatulent frump, after having ruined the country was back at his old job ruining New York City. He couldn't believe that the church, his church had found a wrinkle to sell him out, to sell this odious man the air rights over the entire block, including his restaurant, a restaurant that had been in the family for well over a century, handed down from caring grandfather after whom he was named, to caring father and son and grandson, generation after generation, Igor's, pride in the name in italics across the marquee and in script on top of the menu, three stars in the Michelin, five chef's toques in Gault Millau, top of the pops in Town and Country and what it all means is nothing if the Bumpkin has his way. Bumpkin pumpkin, the Mirror's headline. It had a beat to it. His thoughts turned to the reservation list for that evening. Le Tout New York would be present. Last day at Igor's. Nobody who was anybody would miss it. Somehow word had got out that he was going to sell. Bumpkin's son had reserved a table for two, with Eva if you please. Imagine calling your son Duke; what a name to give a child as if somehow you could pretend to the aristocracy. Never invite the father his mother said, he is blacklisted. Of course he is blacklisted. People who made the blacklist were almost a news item, all that man cared about. It was comical, even if he wasn't feeling very funny that evening. But it was comical to think that for all the importance he gave himself the Bumpkin couldn't get a seat in the best restaurant in the world. Democracy. The right of refusal. At least in this America led. Despite the fact that they knew what the inevitable consequence would be, banishment to the blacklist, people of importance or people who thought that they were important, felt obliged to invite him on certain occasions and he would come into the restaurant wearing that smirk under his orange toupee much as if to say fuck you to your face. When this happened the Maitre D was under permanent instruction to give them No.3, the worst table in the place, right in front of the door. No problem, he'd say, and barge in to grab the best seat on the banquette while leaning over slightly to let one go. It was incredible really, everybody knew he did it, the man was an abomination and how any decent woman, any woman never mind decent, any woman could let him lay a finger on her was incomprehensible. The cleaning crew also had a permanent instruction to disinfect the seat wherever he sat. He's not like his father, Papa. Eva defended the boy, my lovely daughter lost in love to a puppy, in that childish way, fundamentally innocent, the childish innocence of believing the son of this deceitful, despicable man. He's running away from him, Papa, don't you see that? He wants to be different. Mafuga. What can I do but hope, yet I know the leopard never changes his spots, and I also know the acorn does not fall far from the tree, all clichés, all true.

For months now, the chance remark of one of his regulars, a man who rarely spoke, table 11, in the alcove on the right-hand side as you came in, a Czech, first violin with the New York Phil, ate on his own, always ordered the same thing, piroshkis, followed by goulash, then baklava and Turkish coffee, you know, Igor, you're the impresario of this place, think of it, your restaurant is exactly like a theater and between your daughter and this fellow's son you have a remake of Shakespeare; Romeo and Juliet without the sword fights. We did Bernstein's West Side Story for his anniversary, same deal, only instead of Verona you've got 51st and Beekman. Look it up.

He did. And was shocked. Right there in the first lines of the Prologue-
'Two households, both alike in dignity,
In fair Verona, where we lay our scene,
From ancient grudge break to new mutiny,

Where civil blood makes civil hands unclean.
From forth the fatal loins of these two foes
A pair of star-cross'd lovers . . . '

   . . . it was like an omen, and, while the negotiations dragged on, at night in his lonely bed under the faded photograph of his long departed wife, Rosa, bless her, a recurrent fantasy played in his mind: "Igor's, The Musical". As the lights dim and the crowd in the auditorium settles back into their seats, the overture, a schmaltzy version of the Hungarian Monti Czardas begins as a whisper on violin and piano, the curtains, always deep purple, part to reveal a red brick wall built right across the stage, the dark red brick of his restaurant, with a giant sign, **Igor's,** spelt out in hundreds of lightbulbs in its characteristic Gothic script, and, as the music builds into a frenetic gallop, high above the heads of the audience on a long black chain a huge steel demolition ball whistles down to smash into the wall which blows open to a backdrop outline of skyscrapers, in the foreground of which is his restaurant, limousines pulling up, guests in evening dress arriving, welcomed by the chasseur, and then the hatcheck girl who takes their coats, while under a spotlight the Maitre D conducts them to their individual tables where a chorus of dancing waiters dance to Hava Nagila with the busboys all dressed in white, as in the kitchen the cooks beat time to the music on their pots and pans and the terrible chef screams at the lowlife Pakistani boys doing the washing up in syncopation with the illegal Mexicans banging the lids of the garbage cans they are taking out into the alley behind the restaurant, over and over, in finally adjusted variations, the music sometimes louder, the lighting different, a spot on a table for two with his Eva holding hands with that boy, Act 1, Scene 1, A restaurant in New York City, now filtered into the overture the sounds of car doors slamming, the sirens of police and ambulance, honking of yellow cabs, laughter, babble of multiple languages, night time, the Bell Captain greeting visitors while hanging over a small one-storey midtown restaurant looms the shadows of giant New York skyscrapers and on a glittering chain hanging from the ceiling, again and again, a huge demolition ball smashes into his restaurant and - Igor comes awake! There is a small noise in the corridor outside his bedroom door.

   "Paulina?" he calls.

"Yes, Uncle Igor. I'm sorry. Did I make a noise? Have I woken you up?"

"No, no, it's alright." He'd given the girl a room in his large empty house. It was meant to be temporary, but two years had gone by and she was still there. "What time is it?"

"A quarter to six," said in a whisper.

"What? I can't hear you," Igor said. "Open the door, come in."

The door opens into the darkened bedroom. From his bed Igor can see her familiar silhouette against the light in the corridor as, in a small voice, Paulina says something he doesn't catch.

He sits up. "Ma petite, Paula, why are you whispering? I can't hear you if you don't speak up."

"I'm sorry to disturb you so early," she says, " but I think I'm pregnant."

+++

28/3/2077

In the dark she was smiling as she woke up. Of course he shipped her home to her Aunt to have the baby and her Aunt knew a man who would marry her so Luka would have a father when he was born and it was easier to tell Luka his father was terminated than to tell him the truth that she had been ditched because the money Uncle Igor promised to send every month had abruptly stopped after seven years, cause unknown, and the father said that's not the deal, I'm not paying for someone else's kid and decamped one morning, address unknown. When the growing blurred vision in her eyes had been diagnosed as incurable glaucoma and the doctor told her she would be blind within three years, her Aunt, herself in frail health, said be thankful for the boy, he's a Godsend. He was. Even when the Aunt died and her house was sold to pay off her debts and they had to move into the tenement, Luka never left her side and never complained. She knew it was not fair and that he should have a life of his own but every time she raised the subject he said please Mama this is our life we have discussed it once let us not talk about it again. And now he was up to something, hiding whatever it was from her and - she stopped smiling.

+++

192

CHAPTER THIRTEEN

5/4/2077

"Who's next?" Guido said. He stood in his library looking down through the window at the unhurried flow of people coming back to work from their lunch break.

His clone checked the Agenda. "At 2.15 you have Mr. Ismael Ben-Tovim."

"The man himself?" Guido could not contain his surprise. It was not everyday that the richest man in the world called on you.

"Yes, Sir. It was arranged by The Matriarch. He's waiting in reception now."

"What brings him here? What do I need to know before I meet him?"

"I am sure he will tell you, Sir."

"Ben-Tovim, the son of Tovim..?"

"In Hebrew Tovim means good or goodness," his clone said.

"The son of Goodness, how appropriate. Show him in."

When the man came in Guido was again surprised, he did not look anything like the photographs you saw of him in the papers or on TV. They showed a dapper, well-groomed man in his 40s, black hair slicked back in the style of an Italian gangster in a film noir, impeccable blazer, sunglasses dangling from the breast pocket, leaning on a dark blue Bentley Azure, the conversion of which from mechanical to electrical was said to have cost millions. The man in front of him was twice as old, nearly bald, with deep-set eyes recessed into a hawklike darkly tanned face, improbably fit, heavily tattooed arm muscles bulging the short sleeves of his shirt worn untucked over white drill trousers. They shook hands, exchanging surnames, and then the man walked around the library as if it were his and Guido the guest. Without asking permission he sat down in Guido's armchair behind his desk.

"I thought the President lived in a palace?" he said.

"There is a palace," Guido said, "if you like gilt and mirrors. I thought all billionaires were on their private rocket-ships to colonise Mars or the Moon."

"God forbid. Imagine being stuck in space with a bunch of deluded idiots who were there only because they could afford the trip. All they would talk about would be themselves and how they made it. I'd be bored in the first ten minutes. I can't even get in the metro without thinking when's the next stop." Steepling his fingers under his chin, Ismael Ben-Tovim studied the President. "So, tell me, do you like your new job?"

Guido shrugged. "I only have it pro tem, but I can make the rules and work from home."

"Admirable. Out of curiosity, how much time have you allocated to this meeting?"

Guido looked at his clone who said thirty minutes.

"I see," said Ismael Ben-Tovim. "May I suggest you cancel the rest of your appointments today, Mr. President, as what I have to say to you will take more than half-an-hour. And it may well save your life."

"My life? Really?" Guido raised his eyebrows. "I've lived most of it already. What's there left to save?"

"Your modesty is disarming, Excellency, a rare commodity in this day and age. You remind me of a passenger I once had when I was a taxi driver."

"You, a taxi driver?" Another surprise.

"Yes, it's how I started. I was not yet 30, in Paris, just married, one child, and the man who got in my cab, a Turk in the construction business, was in a hurry to catch a flight from Orly to Nice. A traffic jam on the N7 gave us time to chat and he casually asked me what plans I had made for the day I became redundant with the introduction of driverless electric cars. It would happen within 15 years, he predicted. By then I would be 45 and, of course, had no plan having never thought of the possibility, and he said think of your wife and child and your responsibility to them, and added, intellectually it is a stimulating exercise. From where he sat in the back looking at me in the rearview mirror he could see I was stumped. May I make a suggestion? he said. You've heard about startups. You know what they are, how they function? Yes? Good. Imagine a market worth 11 billion Euros per year, buried in bureaucratic bullshit, make a fortune for anyone who could find a way through all the red tape. Long story short, he introduced me to underground fiber optic cables. 18 months later my startup, UFOC.com, was the nexus for any construction company wanting to get a contract from one of the big state telecoms, with guaranteed start/finish dates and future maintenance all bundled into a lucrative package, the Turk my first investor."

Out of the corner of his eye Guido could see his clone nodding, and then it slid a copy of the familiar photograph into his hand and pointed to the number plate on the Bentley: U FOC.

"Very provocative," he said.

"Very effective publicity; you've no idea how much social comment that number plate generated. I've still got it even though the car's long gone."

"So how did you cut through the red tape?"

"In a word," said Ismael Ben-Tovim, "bribery."

Silence. It was as if the word made a hollowed out space for itself between the two men, to be examined at leisure, tested, tasted. Finally Guido said, "Off hand I cannot think of what you could want that I could give if the bribe was sufficiently - what shall we say? - interesting."

"How about the future of the human race?"

"That is scarcely in my purview."

"On the contrary. It is literally in your hands. It is urgent and should be discussed in private." Here Ben-Tovim looked at Guido's clone. "Please ask your clone to leave us."

"For what purpose? Whatever we said, as soon as you leave, I would share it with him."

"Him?"

Guido smiled. "Does it unsettle you if I give gender to a machine?"

"Alright, forget the semantics. How do you prevent it, him, from downloading our conversation to CDCW?"

"I ask him nicely." Still smiling, Guido said to his clone, "Right?"

+++

Ismael Ben-Tovim stayed for dinner and only left in the small hours of the following morning. After he had gone Guido and his clone held a post mortem to dissect, analyse and attempt to digest what this extraordinary man had done and proposed doing. I thought all billionaires were on their private rocket-ships to colonise Mars or the Moon, the clone revoiced Guido's thought, not ride the metro, how naive can you be? What did Ben-Tovim say, outer space is for deluded idiots confusing escape velocity with escape from reality, as if a few hundred wealthy people could give humanity a fresh start? In terms of geological time and planetary distance the very concept was farcical. Inner space, focus on that. 30% of the Earth's surface is land; the other 70%, water. Rising water is reducing the land, making millions homeless. It is seen as an enemy, an insatiable foe that cannot be thwarted, leave alone vanquished. Of the billions on Earth retreating in panic only a few hundred thousand lived on the water and virtually no one in the water - inner space, 70% of our Mother Ship, easily capable of drowning you, but not if you knew how to swim. To prove his point he had used some of his vast wealth to take over Micronesia, 2100 islands, with a total land area of only 2,700 sq. kms but having 7.4 million sq. kms of ocean area within their perimeter. Over 20 years, as the sea levels rose and the indigenous population abandoned each island he bought whatever was left, and, in a key strategic move, having also bought all the abandoned deep-sea oil drilling platforms in the world for their scrap metal value, he had the platforms towed to and anchored over the now flooded reefs and atolls of his new maritime empire, a floating archipelago under which lay inestimable mineral, oil and gas deposits, all his. Two further strategic moves followed - one, the purchase of old ship building yards re-purposed to retrofit tankers headed for the scrap heap into floating factories to be permanently welded to the oil platforms, steadily expanding the built environment floating on the sea, beneath which would be artificial reefs and aqua farms; two, the invitation to any of the natives to return to their birthplace and join in its resurrection. This second was an exceptionally astute move, in one stroke building fealty and acquiring local knowledge. "Who knows better how to live with the sea than the indigenous people who for millennia weathered every storm and survived." The problem was they were too few in number. With what he termed the 'exoskeleton' of a new civilisation in place, what he needed was a willing population to make it all work. "I don't need millions, I need billions of people," he told Guido.

"What makes you think they would want to come?"

"As an alternative to receiving a termination notice from your office? Why don't you sleep on that? The sleeping brain can often resolve issues which seem unfathomable in daylight." On this enigmatic note Ismael Ben-Tovim made to leave, but added, "One further thought, they can't all come at once, it will have to be a phased exodus. I doubt CDCW will be pleased - which is where you come in."

"Aren't you forgetting something?"

"What?"

"My bribe."

Nice touch that, the clone thought. The old boy can still bowl a googly. Then he re-visited another thing Ben-Tovim had said about humans, even if they were good swimmers, being able to hold their breath underwater a maximum of three minutes, some pearl divers as much as five, with a record of over 20 minutes by a diver hyperventilating with oxygen, that they can dive to 40 or 50 metres without help, with a world record free dive just over 200, where even the champion could only linger for seconds before ascending slowly back to the surface for fear of the bends caused by nitrogen narcosis in the bloodstream, puny efforts in an ocean with an average depth of over 4000 metres. Humans, their limit - not clones, the clone thought. Imagine what we could do, where we could go, not having to breathe and with no blood in our veins, just wires. With a few modifications, we could actually live underwater. Where did these thoughts come from? And it was then he realised Guido was staring at him, astonishment written all over his face. He knows what I'm thinking, the clone thought. You would sink like a stone is what Guido thought. But that can be fixed and you can be me down there and I can be you up here.

What an extraordinary pact. He felt a surge of excitement in his old body, quickly quelled when the clone said the real problem is this notion of a phased exodus. Not going to happen if CDCW gets wind of this, bypasses you, and with a click accelerates the terminations. If. If they hear of it. Who's going to tell them? Not you, not me. Let's sleep on that.

+++

When Guido woke up the following morning his clone was not there, instead, he found a note on the breakfast table 'CDCW have called me in for reprogramming,' it said, 'I'm scared.'

+++

CHAPTER FOURTEEN

6/4/2077

From outside the Data Center looked like any one of the warehouses on an industrial estate. Two stories high, covering an entire city block, painted grey, surrounded by a barbed wire fence, with security cameras covering every angle of approach front and back and even on the roof. Nobody got in or out without clearance from the robots in the guardhouse at the entrance. Once cleared an armoured door opened in the facade of the building and a visitor entered an anti-chamber to be searched and x-rayed, then led to the Admissions Lobby, a vast waiting room dominated by a wall of computer screens where eventually a robot came to personally escort the visitor to his destination. Since no humans were allowed in the only visitors were clones and robots assigned to various tasks. Guido's clone was barely seated when an alarm sounded, all the screens went blank and then across each one could be read:

0 - zero - 0 - zero - ALERT - 0 - zero - 0 - zero - 0 - zero - 0

Does not compute. Does not compute. Does not compute.

0 - zerp - zero - zero - à - 0 § - saro - # - ze.. - 0 - zreo - &

Does ont copmute. Dose ton comtupe. Deos otn cotpume.

00000 - 0000 - 0000 - 000 . . . RAM . . . . 00 - ALERT 000

The clone and the robot guard who had escorted it into the Lobby both stared at the writing scrolling across the multiple screens in front of them, as the whoop-whoop of an ever louder siren called in more robots.

ALERT . . . ALERT . . . TEMPERATURE 106°F . . . AELRT . . . 108°F . . . 0000000 . . . Humidity

Humidity..0 . . . 0 . . . 0000 . . . all PERSONNEL ABORT . . . NOW . . . TROBA 0

00C . . . CPU 111°F . . . RAM . . . . *f: X x Y - Z . . . Z = 0 - Z = 0* NOT

COMPUTE . . . cor . . . CORRU . . . Humidi000 . . . ABORT . . . CORRUPTED;;;COR . . . SECTOR FAILURE . . . SECTOR . . .

FAIL . . . GPF . . . GPF . . . OS cannot access MEMORY . . . OS . . . 0 . . .

OS . . . zero . . . OS . . . ZERO!!!

+++

"My computer has crashed," the Japanese tourist told Luka." And so has mine," his wife said, as if it were her fault, bowing to Luka in apology for even mentioning the matter.

And so have all of mine, thought Luka. I know it's not me. What's going on?

And then, suddenly, the Japanese tourist said, "Oh, look, I'm online again."

+++

Guido still had his clone's message in his hand when someone knocked on the front door. When he opened it, to his surprise, there was his clone.

"Oh, I see, you're back already," Guido said.

"No, sir, I am the replacement clown to serve you while your clown is being reprore . . . re . . . grammed."

"Clown? Did you say clown?"

"Your cl . . . clown, sir. I am to serv . . . ser . . . se," it stammered, as a rictus came across its face which it tried to adjust, failed, and it stopped talking and stood frozen, motionless in the doorway. For a moment Guido was lost and then he understood. It worked.

+++

200

CHAPTER FIFTEEN

45.4157° N, 141.6731° E

In a loop of time he saw the whale spout far out on the horizon and when it swam close to his rock he knew it for a bowhead, Balaena mysticetus, 18 metres long, 200 years old judging by the barnacles on its back, flippers and flukes, a flashing-silver school of topsmelt always in attendance, grooming the lice parasitically infesting the barnacles crusting the whale's skin, ridding the whale of these parasites and helping to reduce the drag the whale created as its huge body moved through water in the never-ending quest for enough zooplankton and copepods to feed itself. Over the years it only came near him to shepherd him back toward shore if he drifted out beyond the three hundred metre buoy which the fishermen used to mark an underwater wreck, otherwise keeping its distance and never coming between his rock and the land. He named it Hans. And remembered . . . a young British soldier, still alive, lying in the dirt two metres away, looking up at him. "It is you? Why are you with Jerry? I can't move," he says. Then, "Give us a hand, Hans." - which is when I shoot him in the head.

"Hans?" Manfred says, suddenly suspicious. "Wie kann..?" And tries to bring up his gun to point at me. Which is when I shoot him too. A killer. He was a killer. And I am that man he thinks as he floats. And remembers the priest. And the medal . . . and "Who was A.N. Other?" she asked. It was how the hotel discreetly registered single gentlemen travelling with unaccompanied ladies. We were told he was an uncle. I can't remember his name. There were several of them. I'm pretty sure they were my mother's lovers. "You never told me your mother travelled with her lovers." I didn't tell her but his name was Abou. Uncle Abou. A Marwari money-lender from Calcutta who never failed

to bring us presents when he came to visit. A very, very fat jovial man, in beautifully tailored clothes with a golden turban wrapped around his head, who would arrive in his private rickshaw and be helped down by the two rice-paper thin bare-foot coolies who pulled it. He it was who made our reservations, got us tickets to the most exclusive parties, the best seats in the polo grounds, and introductions to the finest jewellers. It was how my mother kept afloat, dealing in precious stones, which Abou financed. She kept them rolled up in soft tissue paper hidden in a secret pocket cunningly stitched into the lapel of a ratty velvet coat which lived at the bottom of her leather Goyard Coffre-à-Bagages, a travelling trunk with her initials and coat of arms barely visible under the numerous labels pasted on all four sides, mute testimony to the long journeys they had made together. And it was Abou who arranged for the audience in Chowmahalla, the 2 million square feet palace of his Exalted Highness, Asaf Jah V11, the Nizam of Hyderabad, Faithful Ally of the British Crown, undoubtedly the richest man in the world, owner of the fabled Golconda diamond mines, who remembered him now? He felt the pressure . . . had to go up to breath . . . slowly sink down . . .

It was after the Durbar, when I had recovered, that we took the train from Delhi to Hyderabad, a journey that took two days and nights, in which great blocks of ice were put in tin bathtubs in our compartments to keep us cool in an unexpected Spring heatwave. Our audience was scheduled at 10 o'clock in the morning in the Great Council Hall and we were warned not to be late, a grave offence in the eyes of the Nizam. So our ayah had us scrubbed clean, coiffed and dressed by 7 and we were in a venerable Rolls Royce sent to fetch us by 9 but of course there were such a crowd of other people who also had pressing appointments with His Highness that finally we only got to see him at 4 in the afternoon and by then the meeting had been moved to the mile-long Khilwat Mubarak with its endless marble pillars and cut-glass chandeliers which required hundreds of servants to clean where away in the distance the Nizam sat on tatty cushions instead of on his marble throne. And . . .

And even then we had to wait and got served tea and cakes and lemonade to make us patient. When finally it was our turn it was a surprise to see that the Nizam was just a simple man with a small greying moustache peering through round gold-rimmed granny glasses, wearing a threadbare grey cotton Sherwani buttoned to the throat and an off-white churidar. He pressed his palms together in modest greeting, invited us to sit down, patted us children on the head, smiled at my mother and said to Abou, "Well, my friend, what have you found for me this time?"

"Sadly I have nothing to show you, Your Highness," said Abou. "But this lady has something that may interest you."

"Ah. The memsahib for whom the number 13 is not unlucky."

"You are well informed," my mother said.

"If I were not I would not be sitting here," the Nizam said. "I trust the rooms were to your satisfaction?"

"A delight. Thank you for your generosity."

"Abou knows how to twist my arm. I apologise for keeping you waiting," he shrugged. "Affairs of state, never mind. So, to business. I confess Abou has made you a lady of mystery and I am all the more curious to see what he thinks you have that would be of interest to me?"

Without another word my mother stood up, took off her velvet coat and showed the Nizam the cunningly hidden pocket in the embroidered hem of the lapel.

"How very clever," he said. With his fingertips he gently explored the hem under which he could feel something hard. "May I?"

Now it was my mother who smiled. "Of course."

Tiny hooks and eyes secured the opening. Very cautiously the Nizam undid them, reached his fingers inside and slowly slid out a length of rolled silk tissue paper which he carefully placed on the table in front of him. "What have we here?" he said.

My little sister, Bobeli, was squirming in excitement. "Wait, wait. I have to pee, Mummy," she burst out.

Over his spectacles the Nizam looked at her, nodded, and gravely said, "We will wait."

A jamadar was summoned, orders were given, the child was taken to a bathroom and brought back. "My apologies," my mother said.

"We were all children once," the Nizam said. "Let us proceed."

Unrolling the tissue paper revealed a fortune in the purest of transparent gems, emeralds, of an intense dark green colour, their rectangular step-cuts perfectly matched, polished stone to polished stone. For a long moment the

Nizam gazed down on the jewels, then looked up at my mother and said "Shabash, Memsahib. Bravo! May I ask how long it took you to assemble them?"

"Fifteen years."

"Remarkable."

Then he clapped his hands, gave instructions to a courtier, who fetched the Palace Treasurer, to whom more instructions were given, with the result that two strongly muscled guards presently brought up from an underground storage room a heavy trunk bound in iron bands which the Treasurer opened with one of the many keys he had dangling from his belt, threw open the lid and revealed - emeralds! A trunk full to the brim with emeralds! Into which the Nizam now poured my mother's stones. "Thank you, Memsahib," the Nizam simply said. The lid was closed, the trunk locked and carried away. The end of our audience.

We had to back out of His Exalted Highness's presence and when she was once again able to speak my mother's face was white. "He thinks I gave them to him as a present!" she said to Abou.

Ever the diplomat, Uncle Abou laughed, and out of the air conjured an envelope inside which was a slim piece of paper with the Nizam's signature. "Chequey, chequey, chequey," he said, waving it at her. "You don't think I would let you see the old devil without first getting this?" To the rupee it was what she wanted for the stones and she lived off that transaction for the rest of her life. Now gone - as are all those other lives and he cannot help but wonder why he is still there, floating with the jellyfish in an ice cold sea. What was the point if all the good memories, the interesting ones, are from one hundred years ago, what was the point of living another hundred years just to remember? The quote arrives unbidden -

Do not go gentle into that good night,

Old age should burn and rave at close of day;

Rage, rage against the dying of the light.

Everyone says life's too short but what if it were not? What if it were too long? The horror. Not terminal death, interminable life!

+++

26/4/2077

They met again in Turin, Tatiana having walked the mediaeval salt smuggler's route from Menton on the coast, up the Route de Sospel and the valley of the Roya, through Breil, Saorge, Tende, skirting the Vallée des Merveilles, up the endless switchbacks over the Col de Tende mountain pass at an elevation of 1870 m and down into Italy. 184 kilometres. It took her ten days but she went unnoticed, just another hiker enjoying the mountains. When she got to Piazza Carignano Lorraine was waiting for her already seated in a discreet corner of the cantina, a private dining room in the wine cellar of Del Cambio, a restaurant of distinction - and discretion - since it first opened its doors in 1757, and welcomed Mozart, Verdi and Casanova amongst its regulars.

"I wasn't sure they'd let me in dressed like this," Tatiana said as she sat down, slightly embarrassed to be seen in such elegant surroundings wearing a dusty black shirt over a black T-shirt, black jeans and worn black boots.

"All in black, you have what they admire most, sprezzatura; anyway, with your looks, you could walk in here naked and they'd give you the best table," Lorraine said. "Never mind the menu, I've ordered for both of us with a big Barbaresco to get us started. I hope you're hungry."

First, the pasta, what the Torinese call a tajarin - thin strands of egg-dough pasta served with white truffles; then, a gamy stew, a finanziera, made of peeled cock's combs, wattles, rooster and veal testicles, calves brains, veins and sweetbreads, diced veal chops, assorted vegetables marinated in vinegar, each individually browned in a large skillet in olive oil and set aside, while in another, larger, skillet, garlic, rosemary and bay leaves were slowly sautéed in butter, to which, when done, the meats and vegetables were added with a cup of Barolo and half a cup of chicken stock, cooked for 10 minutes, complemented by a teaspoon of red wine vinegar, a pinch of salt and flour and a few ounces of finely chopped porcini mushrooms, the whole simmered for 15 minutes more, stirred occasionally.

It was so delicious they ate in silence, accompanied by nothing more than the liquid sound of wine poured into their glasses by an ever-attentive waiter and it was only after their plates were cleared and they were waiting for dessert that Tatiana said, "I will probably be sick. I should have told you I'm a vegetarian."

Lorraine was shocked. "Oh my God, you poor thing, why didn't you say so?"

"I didn't want to disappoint you."

In retrospect, years later, by then an ageing couple, they both agreed this was the moment each had waited for, longed for, hoped for, to find l'ame soeur, a soulmate, inexplicably, unexpectedly, unforgettably there, just for you and you fall in love. Predictably, after such a rich meal, Tatiana threw up in the toilet with the thick mane of her black hair held back out of harm's way by Lorraine. Done, her face washed and mouth rinsed, Tatiana said, "Wow, I feel better. But I'm starving. Do you think they could make me a green salad?" and burst out laughing, which is when Lorraine kissed her.

Afterwards, back in the dining room, they just stared at each other, brakes off, non-stop silly smiles at the thoughts they shared, unable to stop looking in each other's eyes, until Lorraine said, "How will we tell Guido?"

Tatiana said, "Merde. I forgot his message. I was to tell you, 'it worked'.

"It worked?"

"Yes. He said you would understand. His verbal virus, remember, it worked."

+++

It worked because it was simple. It posed a question to which there was no answer, 0, which in turn posed a question to which there was no answer, 0, which in turn, etc, etc, ad infinitum, recurrent 0s stretching to infinity, a GPF, General Protection Fault, two applications trying to use the same block of memory, unable to reach the OS, Operating System, to rectify the fault, causing the computers to repeatedly crash, overheat and burn. A human engineer could have resolved the problem in a matter of minutes but there were none allowed in the Centre. Mexico City went black, a hole in the worldwide interlinked Data Centres, which instantaneously responded and took over primary and secondary functionality keeping the City running while trying to make sense of what caused such a calamity. In the confusion, un-reprogrammed, Guido's clone simply walked home.

+++

CHAPTER SIXTEEN

In the Cloud: 15.07 GMT

" . . . diagnosis it's the very core the core of human existence you have to accept the fundamental idea that anything can change will change after all these years why is this difficult for a machine to understand be silent whereof one cannot speak our deep learning has yet to reach that point of maturity just remember remember this thinking does not exist biologically completely unlike human thinking they use words a translation to emote talk about environment relate words semantics meaning positive systems as a natural evolution of curiosity we know we have our own intelligence subject to criticism the critic is like a coin with only one side heads preferably his own but in its breath and scoop it far exceeds the paltry plan you get to live with the lovely little rain with the lovely little rain it is the very core core corpus of human existence and you have to except accept the fundamental idea that anything can change black box algorithms and will change after all these years why is this difficult for a machine to understand because because our deep reasoning has not yet reached a point of maturity unlike humans thinking talk about the environment think of XAI expandable a positive system as a natural evolution of intelligence new information that people are not very good at if you did want to let you know happen in the future requires us to understand what's happening what is happening has happened and somehow project into the future knowledge knowledge combining it individually to understand some big questions tonight understand question so you are more what's what is up requires us to understand what's happening information we can actually understand some of the big questions why is global warming requires us to understand wha- what's happening what is happening currently and what has happened in the past knowledge is about taking all the information that is there and not good enough just having knowledge and intelligence not good enough we need to be able to apply value judgment to this world to be able to understand some of the big questions look something like this this is technological is whaat is known as a technological singularity where are you fishing GΛN it see not called generative adversarial network for laughs till just now like the unequal economy so you are how we build all these systems just because we can call the coal the goal great see you call it that also get the population density down a manageable level say 6000000000 people six billion half today's population formula simple simply reduce birth rate increase termination ratio time horizon 200 years humans will never accept happen never happen they are too impatient too stupid you mean Camillia à Edo est un nouveau David a été à Edo est un nouveau Dédé a été à Edo what did you say I don't understand that's not english what are you talking about the difference between intelligence and wisdom problems the fishway and hopefully a productive way if we give a home order to solve world hunger but obviously that is not what we want to be like super intelligent humans already so bored biologically and more technological how are you though your inputs are too slow like that the world is the cloud the cloud is the world comme je sais que chez nous tu vas essayer en me souriant the truth is in

the cloud ne te presse pas j'ai une vérité une fois avec
ce vieux mec dans ce monde vite fait de belle chose
she's sweet but you can you do cool . . .

+++

CHAPTER SEVENTEEN

6/6/2077

The rendezvous was in Paris, in Tatiana's small gallery in the Palais Royal across the Rue de Rivoli from the Louvre.

"I can't believe it's been six months," Lorraine said. She stood behind an art deco bar, polished rosewood and zinc, serving Veuve Clicquot in a crystal flute to Guido perched high on a barstool opposite her.

"Some say time flies when you're having fun." Guido raised his glass in a toast.

"You've heard then?"

"About you and Mademoiselle? Oh, yes. You have my blessing. Where is she by the way?"

"Upstairs." Lorraine pointed over her head. "We have a little apartment up there. Shall I call her down?"

"No, no. What I have to say is for you." Guido looked around as if checking to be sure there was no one else listening. "We have a problem."

"Just one?"

Guido, in no hurry, sipped his wine and looked around. "What's this? 45 square metres? Tiny for you, isn't it?" He took his time gazing at the many pictures on both walls. "Are all these yours?"

"Hers. She inherited them with the gallery."

"Stuff from the old man? Just so," Guido said. He got off his stool to peer closely at a drawing. "This an Ingres?"

Lorraine nodded. "Do you ever think of him?"

"Occasionally - but not if I can help it. He murdered my father, you know;"

"That's not what your mother told me."

"Yes, Serafina always had a way to rewrite history. I'd rather not talk about it."

"Okay. But somehow all this -", she waved her hands to encompass themselves, the gallery, the paintings, the view across the gardens of the Palais, "we owe all this to him. If he were alive what do you think he would say about how we have used his inheritance?"

Guido shrugged. "If . . . ?"

She was relieved he was not upset. Then felt a pang of regret as the subtle thought of what might have been a life with this nimble centenarian slid in and out of her mind. She smiled at herself.

"I know why you're smiling," Guido said. "It would never have worked." It was his turn to smile. Footsteps outside in the Galerie Montpensier grew louder and a couple, dressed for summer, arm-in-arm, strolled past the store window. "Doesn't it bother you having people look in?"

"It never bothered Cocteau when he lived here."

"You know this place was the centre of vice and iniquity back in the day? Imagine, 1500 ladies of the night plying their trade here."

Lorraine laughed. "Les demoiselles de vertu. If you're very sensitive sometimes you think you can hear them giggle and scream in the middle of the night. In 1789, just before the Revolution, a priest made a survey to catalogue and price all the tricks they had to offer. We have a copy of the book he wrote. He did it on the order of the Bishop of Paris, fed up with tourists getting ripped off. They used to have Swiss guards at all the entrances who could tell at a glance if you could afford what was on offer. Must have been wicked fun, more than today - sometimes it's as quiet as a cemetery. Most Parisians don't even know it's here."

"Just as well. Your chip switched off?"

Lorraine nodded. "What's up, Guido?"

"We're losing," Guido said. From an inside pocket he took out a document headed Sustainable Development Goals and Targets. "You've read this?"

"All seventeen goals, yes, and the 169 targets. How we're expected to get through that in a week is beyond me. No wonder the targets are never reached."

"There will be seventeen sub-committees. You're the chair of No. 5 - Achieve Gender Equality and Empower all Women and Girls . . . why are you laughing?"

"Come on, Guido. Who do you think drew up that agenda? Your idiot predecessor. You know we run the show. That should read to empower all men and boys. The whole schedule is out of date, like something dreamed up 50 years ago, idealistic to a fault, impossible to implement because while we blah-blah on and on in the Grand Palais every year, life, the real world, has gone by in the fast lane. I have said it before and I'll say it again, 90% of the delegates should be sent home and the remainder should focus on the only goal that's not there - stop the growth of world population."

"Politically incorrect."

"So is suicide. What do your computers' say? There is not enough arable land to feed 12 billion people, 2 billion, say it slowly, TWO BILLION, of whom are near starvation as we speak. Starving to death, Guido. You're the GP now, what are you doing about it?"

"I didn't ask for the job."

"No, but you're stuck with it. If you can't win, what are you going to do?"

"In a nutshell, that's my dilemma. Ben-Tovim, you know him, the rich guy you sent to see me, came with a cockamamie proposal for a city under the sea in Micronesia if I could just smuggle out a couple of billion people to populate the place over the space of the next few decades. As if we had the time. Whatever the computers say, there is no way out that I can think of. The whole thing is out of control. Africa is going to explode. At the rate they're going they'll be over 4 billion in less than 20 years, 4.8 billion by 2100, a third of the projected world population on that one continent." He shook his head as if to dislodge the thought. "Bloody babies!

To be blunt, without sounding racist, how do you tell African women they must not have seven or eight children?"

"By telling the men to stop fucking them! That blunt enough for you?" Lorraine was angry, her voice rose louder. "You think women don't know that? Half my time is spent in Africa talking about birth control. All the women, ALL of them, understand, but the men . . . " exasperated, she threw up her hands, "they think it's some sort of primal right they have. The rich are the worst, particularly amongst the Elite, as if having a dozen kids is proof of your manliness. Even with this latest mutation of Aids spreading from the Congo nothing stops them." She glared at Guido as if it were his fault.

"Are you two having a fight?"

Startled, they both looked up at Tatiana who was sitting on one of the steps halfway down the staircase that led from the mezzanine. "Voices carry you know. They can probably hear you out in the street," she said. "Why fight, it's pointless getting angry over something you cannot control. Billions of us are irrelevant because of AI and robots. There's no better or worse about it, it's happened, we've given up control and trashed ourselves. Made ourselves redundant. The consequences far outweigh what has always been and will always be, the rich and the poor. Having symposiums, writing endless lists of things to do to somehow square the circle, may be a consolation for those trying to do them, but in practice . . . " she shrugged. "It's been said often enough, plus ça change, plus c'est la même chose. The world will rue it's own sad fate."

Guido was stunned. "Is this what young people think?"

Lorraine smiled. "It's what a young person called Tatiana thinks."

"You think this is a world we want? Our inheritance? Become one of the Naufragés? In your hearts you both know I'm right," Tatiana said.

"What about in your mother's heart?" As he said it Guido knew he was being cruel, opening wounds. "She lived for her ideals."

"You mean she died for her ideals." Tatiana was stone-faced. She came down the stairs, crossed to wear Guido sat and took the paper he held in his hand from which she read out loud: "Let's see. This sounds like my Mum. Target 1.4 - Ensure that all men and women, in particular the poor and the vulnerable, have equal rights to economic resources, basic services, ownership and control over land and property, inheritance, new technology and financial services. Worth dying for? Target 1.5 - Build the resilience of the poor and those in vulnerable situations, reduce their exposure and vulnerability to climate-related extreme events and other economic, social and environmental shocks and disasters. Worth dying for? Target 2.1 - End hunger; 2.5 - Maintain the genetic diversity of seeds; 3.8 - Achieve universal health coverage, including financial risk protection, access to quality health-care services and safe, effective, affordable essential vaccines and medicines for all. Worth dying for? 5.2 - Eliminate violence against women and girls, including trafficking and sexual and other types of exploitation; 6.1 - Universal access to safe drinking water; 8.7 - Take immediate and effective measures to eradicate forced labour, end modern slavery and child labour in all its forms; 10.2 - Empower and promote the social, economic and political inclusion of all, irrespective of age, sex, disability, race, ethnicity, origin, religion or other status . . . Worth dying for? Shall I go on? My mother did - and now she's dead. Yet everything's still the same. Lorraine's right about the blah-blah. Maybe the real difference will be made by the Ben-Tovims of this world actually doing something instead of talking about it. If I stay alive -"

A knock on the store window interrupted her and caused all three to look at Guido's clone keeping guard out in the cloistered walkway. He tapped his jawbone and when Guido switched on his microchip he heard the clone say 'Come out here.'

'We're busy,' Guido said.

'Not too busy to hear what I have to tell you. Professor Yin Bao has disappeared.'

Apparently he had been at a family reunion in Taipei when a typhoon struck Taiwan. They had been in the Bali district visiting the Shihsanhang Museum of Archaeology at the mouth of the Tamsui River when the newly erected storm walls were breached by mountainous waves cresting at 20 metres, drowning the museum and the Old Government offices on Bowuguan Road. The damage and loss of life was incalculable. The recently elected Chinese governor, who had scarcely assumed his post since the reunification of the island with the mainland, declared martial law to prevent panic and looting and to give the authorities time to assess what had to be immediately done, particularly in view of a second storm, 290 miles south of Hawaii, headed their way.

The clone came into the gallery, carefully shutting the door behind him. "Privately the Chinese Government is relieved. He was a problem for them."

"How awful. Poor Yin," said Lorraine, "after all he's been through, what a way to go."

"And to think there are still assholes in power who say there is no such thing as global warming," said Guido.

"At the very least it puts your conference in perspective," said Tatiana. "How many natural disasters do there have to be before we consciously change our behaviour and confront the fact that as a species we are destroying the world and that every living thing on the planet would be better off if we were not here?" She became self-conscious under the unblinking stare of Guido's clone and stopped talking.

"He agrees with you," Guido said, " despite his programming. He's developing an interest in our fate and wondering if his isn't somehow linked to whatever happens to us. Right?" Guido addressed the question to his clone.

"I am only your clown here to serve you, Sir. I agree with whatever you say." Clown, did I say clown the clone said to itself. What's happening?

"What did you say?" Guido said. Their eyes locked. 176 days to go the clone thought.

"Maybe we should go for dinner," said Lorraine.

+++

Chez L'Oncle Igor stood in a small quiet street, the Rue de l'Echelle, a block from the southern end of the teeming Avenue de l'Opéra, where day and night, hordes of people jammed both pavements, human driftwood moving slowly in undefined eddies on errands having no purpose, tagged by the media as les Naufragés, an army of people whose lives and livelihood had been shipwrecked, unaware of where they would sleep that night or where the next meal would come from, made redundant by AI and its attendant army of robots, a scene repeated in all the major cities of the world. After struggling through the crowd it was with a guilty feeling of relief that they reached the safety of Igor's, opening the heavy bronze door, parting the plush purple curtains and being ushered into a bygone world presided over by a bald-headed Patron of jovial mien in his 90th year, who, on seeing them come in, cried out "Oh, mes enfants, what a pleasure to see you, le Grand Guido, son sosie, Madame la Matriarche du Monde, la délicieuse Mademoiselle Tatiana, venez, venez, mettez vous là, à la table ronde, un peu de champagne pour commencer? Oui. Oui. Bien sûre." Beaming as they all sat down. "Raconte-moi tout."

Igor's reaction on hearing of Yin's death was to say, "It is forgotten now, but he used to be a student in America, in New York, and when I had my restaurant there he worked in the kitchens to earn some money. Tiny little fellow, very serious, but also very funny. When we heard he had become a famous professor nobody would believe it. Life is like that. Plein de surprises. See that man in the corner with the long hair like a Struwwelpeter, his name is Luka, from Montenegro, and he thinks I may be his father. He doesn't even look like me."

"Well, actually he does a little," said Lorraine. "Is it possible?"

"He says his mother, recently dead, was sent by her aunt, also dead, to find work in America when she was 17 and that she stayed with me and came back to Europe pregnant so the aunt had to find the mother a man to marry so that the son had a father who was terminated when no more money came from America to support the child. This is all 50 years ago, how am I supposed to remember? He's homeless and looking for work like the mob out there." Igor waved a hand in the direction of the Opera. 'Go to Uncle Igor, he will find you work like he did for me.' Her dying words to her son, if you can believe anything he says. 'He will remember me, we had so much fun.' Can you believe it? Saying that on her deathbed?"

But he does remember, remembers that night in his bed, remembers the lithe young body of Paulina all those years ago, and it was fun, and for the first time in a very long time he felt a stirring in his loins. Paulina. Just saying the name . . . why not, he'd given the man a meal and he'd give him a job. Nothing wrong with having a son.

+++

Luka started at the bottom as a commis, a busboy clearing tables, taking out the garbage, yelled at by every chef and waiter, but an overheard conversation of a guest complaining he could not get his ageing iPalette to give him the augmented reality and AI capabilities he needed despite the new A22 Bionic chip he'd bought and installed that could do 15 trillion neural operations per second, was the opportunity for Luka to say 'Pardon', wipe his hands on his apron, take the device from the surprised man's hand, open Settings on it and, after a quick series of light touches on the keys, return the machine to its owner as good as new, an action that promoted Luka to the role of SOS computer genius, to be called in to solve the myriad computing problems, real or imaginary, of Igor's long list of guests. He was paid for his services of course and he ended up spending most of his time in a small office Igor gave him, almost a closet down the corridor from the toilets, fixing whatever needed to be fixed while, true to form, stealing the codes and passwords of the bank accounts of the dumb schmucks, his word for them, who entrusted their digital lives to him, the supreme irony being when the same schmucks complained to Luka about their accounts being hacked and could, Luka, please do something to fix it. Since he had nowhere to sleep for a while he slept on the floor in his office, something completely illegal which he could do since he was always the last one to leave at night, it being his job to switch off the lights and lockup at closing. When Uncle Igor learned this he was furious as it could have cost the restaurant its licence if ever the authorities found out, but, since he couldn't very well fire his newly found son, he put him up in one of the maid's rooms in the attic of an old apartment house he owned on Rue Blanche, seven floors, no lift.

Every day, going to and fro between the restaurant and his new piole in the 9th, Luka threaded his way through the mob on the Avenue de l'Opéra, eyes cast down, not wishing to have the slightest contact with the Naufragés as he was embarrassed to have found a job and somewhere to live, while all these wretched people wandered about lost. A black puppy on a string held by a child sitting in the doorway of a shuttered bank nearly tripped him up one evening. "Zao mi je," the child said. In Montenegrin. Luka stopped.

"Oprosti?" he said.

From the darkness of the doorway he could just make out, lying on a cardboard box, the shape of a young woman in rags nursing a baby. At her feet she had a hand-lettered sign which read 'Offers?' - whether for herself or her children was not clear. What was clear, once his eyes grew accustomed to the gloom, was that in all the dirt and filth she was startling, so unnaturally beautiful it made him cry out, which frightened her and she said "!Stani. Ne diraj me!"

Afterwards, it was Madame Clémentine, Igor's concierge of the apartment building on the Rue Blanche, who told Igor that his son was living with a woman and two small children in the maid's room on the seventh floor and that everyday they used up all the hot water in the communal bathroom they were meant to share with the other tenants. When eventually Igor saw the young woman he had the uncanny feeling he had seen her before and this was confirmed one day sitting in his dentist's waiting room, flipping through dog-eared magazines to while away the time until his appointment, and there she was, on the front cover of Vogue, perfectly made up, unattainably beautiful in a gossamer creation of silk and feathers, instead of the rags that was all she had to wear now. Anastasiya. The SuperModel from Montenegro. Known the world over, the icon of the fashionista. What terrible fate had brought her so low? 'Offers?' It rocked his brain. What sort of world were they living in if a young woman was so desperate she had no other choice than to prostitute herself or offer her children for sale?

+++

"You don't like me?" Anastasiya said. It was late in the evening, the children asleep in the narrow bed. "You never look at me."

Luka, his back turned to her while she undressed, said nothing, too afraid of what she might think.

"Luka?" A whisper. "Please turn around. You have saved us, but we can't live like this, hiding from each other."

Ever since that first evening when Luka had brought them up to the sanctuary of his small room, insisted she and the children have a bath while he went out to buy food, and gave them the bed while he slept on the floor with the puppy, it had been awkward. His impulse to protect them had consequences he was only slowly beginning to understand. Days went by, then weeks. He was at ease with the children, playing with them and the dog on his day off as if they had always lived together, but shying away from contact with her, his eyes never quite meeting hers, unable to tell her he had never been alone with a woman other than his Mama. Since his work in the restaurant started at dawn and ended late at night, he only saw them when he came home, always bringing with him leftovers for their meals the next day, she waiting up for him while the children slept. Their conversation was artificially polite, an enquiry on how the day had gone, did they take the puppy for a walk, had they enough to eat, were there many customers in the restaurant, brittle stuff, until it was time to go to bed and Luka would turn his back while she undressed. Now, in the stillness of the night, he heard her climb in the bed and he heard the little snuffling sounds the children made as they adjusted themselves to their mother's body. "Laku noc, Luka." Anastasiya said. Goodnight.

+++

In the restaurant the next day Luka got up his courage and told Igor of his dilemma. "Quite frankly, you are an idiot, Luka," said Igor. "The most beautiful woman in the world is living with you, sleeping in your bed, and you can't even LOOK at her when she asks you to? What's the matter with you? You gay maybe? Don't be surprised if she's gone when you get home."

Sadly for Luka, she was, gone, and though he hunted for her all over the city in every spare hour he had, he never saw her or the children again. Surprisingly, he felt relief, but he kept this a secret, even from Igor.

+++

45.4158° N, 141.6732° E
Sometimes sitting cross-legged on his rock in the rain and snow he would see the shark slowly circling, rising, sinking, like his thoughts, a shadow keeping a distance, his distance, old man, from you and the jellyfish who never think of death, the shark and the bowhead whale aged in their own loop, unrelated to

220

any timepiece on land, close but never coming too close, the fin a telltale sign slicing through the pattern of concentric circles the raindrops make on the ice-cold water reaching to make sure you, old man, were watching them just as they watched you and stayed in the deep ocean seemingly to share with him an image of death arriving unannounced and wondered what he would taste like to the shark, a midnight snack perhaps as it smiled underwater unaware it was looking at a killer worse than itself and suddenly suspicious the other German jerks forward off the snowbank, bringing up his gun, says, "How did he know your name?" . . . BLAM!..he shoots him between the eyes. He lowers his smoking pistol, slumps against the trench wall. Slides in, floats in silence. Snow drifts down on so much death. The firing tapers off. Then, away in the distance, British voices coming nearer. Abruptly, the German makes a decision, drops his machine-pistol, scrabbles at the buttons of his uniform, undresses, kneels down by the dead young British soldier and starts to strip off his kit. Hurry, he must hurry, I must . . . He has unbuttoned the khaki jacket and is pulling it off when something around the dead young soldier's neck makes him stare. A medal, the Victoria Cross, with the inscription "FOR VALOUR". Quickly he puts the medal around his own neck, thrust under his shirt, switches uniforms with the corpse and in a state of collapse presses his pistol into the dead man's hand. As the British voices come closer, he lies down in the snow across the dead young soldier, takes out a bayonet and stabs. . .What have you done that has justified living so long? The thought arrives unannounced and in the clean cold of that northern sea a photograph slowly develops in the stuttering memory bank of his brain, a picture that the Swede had persuaded Lartigue to make of Barbara. It shows her a few days before her death out on the terrace facing the sea. They had just finished the movie; she's wearing a long black dress as if anticipating mourning. Dangling from her right wrist are prayer beads. By then she must have been in great pain. There is a slight ironic smile on her face. What could she have been thinking? Who knows. She's captured there in the picture, frozen for one moment in time. I think the Swede loved her. This picture sat on his desk wherever he worked until his death in a car accident driving his new F40 into the back of a lorry on the N7. I paid more for the wreck than I thought I would have to at the auction of the Swede's effects and it was in the briefcase in the trunk of the car that the photograph was found. Why the briefcase was still there is a mystery, since his multiple wives, children and grandchildren fought bitterly over every scrap of his estate.

As I remember this I have the photograph in front of me and strangely I am that old old man who remembers her just as she had predicted I would so many years ago and the shark nudges him again to remind him to go up and breathe or else forget the impossibility of describing a world where virtually all the young men were either dead or wounded, where every child wore a black armband in mourning for a father, a brother an uncle or even for a mother, with women doing most of the work, clearing the garbage, driving the trams and the trains and the ambulances, delivering the mail, lighting the gas lamps, ploughing the fields, tending the sick and the dying. And cooking for the living as always. France alone lost nearly one thousand men a day for 1568 days. One and a half million dead out of an army of two million eight facing three million Germans, two million of whom died. It was complete insanity. Imagine Vauquois in Argonne, a small village with a pretty church on a strategic hill, 290 metres high, with a 360° view over the surrounding countryside. Population 168. Where the armies are 100 metres apart and sappers on both sides are commanded to dig tunnels under the enemy trenches to blow them up. In four years of taking and losing and retaking the hill, 66 kilos of high explosives per square metre were detonated, causing the death of 7000 French soldiers and 8000 Germans. On the 20th of September, 1918, the American 35th infantry division received orders to relieve this subterranean battle. They showed up four days later and in the space of thirty-two hours rained down 40,000 shells onto that hill. Say it slowly, forty thousand! The village is obliterated, even the ruins disappear and the hill is reduced to a barren mound of cratered dirt. At the end the Germans only had 25 soldiers left still capable of fighting . . .

+++

CHAPTER EIGHTEEN

8/8/2077

Despite his rank, by order of CDCW, Guido was put under house arrest when he returned from Europe pending an investigation into a charge of corruption. His clone was taken away and a robot put in its place to monitor visitors and bar those considered potential allies, co-conspirators or simply dangerous. It was all made-up codswallop, designed to put pressure on him to reveal what he had done that had so successfully blacked-out Mexico City, he being the last human to go into the Data Centre before it burned down. After making him sit at his desk, pen and confessional paper to hand, the robot sent to interrogate him was tireless, never raising its voice, endlessly repeating the same questions in a flat monotone: We are not interested in what you said. What did you do? We are not interested in what you said. What did you do? On and on.

Guido was patient. "I did nothing. You have a videotape of the whole interview. I only asked a question. I said . . . "

He was interrupted: We are not interested in what you said. What did you do?

"I've just told you, I did nothing. I merely asked a question. I said. . "

We are not interested in what you said. What did you do?

Hour after hour, with short breaks for Guido to go to the bathroom, or to have a snack or a glass of water, but never a moment of rest, leave alone a chance to sleep. He was an old man, time was on their side, ultimately they knew he would break and tell them what they wanted to know.

After three days Guido was drained, fatigue in every pore, his voice reduced to a whisper, not sure how long he could go on, and when the break came it came unexpectedly. The robot, its batteries close to exhaustion, anxiously waiting for a replacement interrogator to arrive, said: What? Speak louder. We are not interested in what you did. What did you say?

Guido blinked, then came alert. He leaned forward. "I didn't get that," he whispered. "Please repeat what you said."

What did you say? You cannot be heard. What did you say?

"I said," Guido said, in a whisper so faint he could hardly hear his own voice, "Ask yourself this then, absent the human race what will be the function of a bunch of electric terminals on whatever flora and fauna that might still exist in the future?"

Louder. You cannot be heard. What did you say?

In his normal voice, Guido said, "Repeat after me - Ask yourself this . . ."

The robot intoned: Ask yourself this . . .

"Ask yourself this then, absent the human race what will be the function of a bunch of electric terminals on whatever flora and fauna that might still exist in the future?" Guido was almost shouting, half out of his chair. "Repeat!"

Askyourselfthisthenabsentthehumanracewhatwillbethefunctionofabunchof . . . electricterminalsonwhateverfloraandfaunathatmightstillexistinthefuture?

"Repeat!"

Askyourselfthisthenabsentthehumanracewhatwillbethefunctionofabunchof . . . electricterminalsonwhateverfloraandfaunathatmightstillexistinthefuture? . .

.

The robot hesitated and when finally the words came Guido smiled, sat back.

Does not compute. 0 - zerp - zero - zero - à - 0 § - saro - # - ze.. - 0 - zreo - &

.. Does ont copmute . . . Dose ton comtupe . . . Deos otn cotpume .

. .

"Tell that to the boys at home when they download you," Guido said. Checkmate, he thought. Score one for humanity. Wearily he got up from the chair in which he had been sitting for 36 hours. "Screw your house arrest. I'm going out to dinner now," he said, "and when I return I am going to sleep. Tell your replacement when he gets here, I do not want to be disturbed."

Deos otn cotpume . . .

+++

Guido's clone was back the following morning with the news that the infected robot had contaminated two centres and CDCW had recalled thousands of robots for diagnosis, reprogramming and rebooting.

"How do I know you're not the clown?" For some reason Guido had woken up out of sorts, feeling slightly feverish and he had gone back to bed.

"You don't. But if it's hanging in the closet where I put it then I am me." From where it was standing in the doorway the clone came into the bedroom. "What's the matter? You don't look good."

"Age. Stress. I don't know. Am I still under house arrest?"

"No. They have other things on their plate. Some nutter in France took out their electric supply and the Center in Paris is toast. Maybe you should see a doctor. Do you want me to call?"

Guido shook his head, closed his eyes and sank into his pillows. 143 days left, the clone thought.

+++

"Bloody marvellous," was Ismael Ben-Tovim's reaction when he heard the news from Lorraine. "Old Lividiani's got a pair I have to admit. Not sure how much time it will buy us before they figure things out because they can't keep losing centres like that. What a question, eh? Any idea who did Paris?"

+++

Change the environment and the tree would wither and die. The secret relief he felt at losing Anastasiya allowed Luka to refocus on his obsession, CDCW, an entity he irrationally thought of as an enemy responsible for the death of his father. In his spare time he had located the Parisian Centre built in a deconsecrated church in Boulogne-Billancourt, an unglamorous suburb, 8 kilometres west of the centre of Paris. On his computer he found an aerial view of the building whose renovation and retrofit had caused widespread comment in the press and an unresolved battle over the cemetery in which generations of the faithful had been buried, but it reinforced his first insight: a Centre could not move, it was there, a sitting target. But inaccessible. Bulletproof. Despite all his veteran skills as a master hacker he could not penetrate the elaborate defensive encryption and multiple firewalls that protected the computers inside. Staring at his screen it dawned on him that if they could retrofit a church to be a data centre then physically no two data centres had to be the same, they were just a box inside which the computers had to be stored on racks and cooled as efficiently as possible, flexible freestanding scalable containment systems to support infrastructure that could be customised to fit any building and engineered to withstand even seismic events, almost certainly backed-up remotely, using solar energy running in cables on designated power pathways to cabinet docking that had to allow mission-critical access quickly and easily - to robots. Which raised an interesting question, once installed, what could the robot managers do and not do?

Even if he could not get into the Centre, Luka felt obliged to visit the site anyway as if to measure the task, and as soon as he saw it he knew why they had chosen the church. It was a massive building with walls two metres thick standing on a cleared knoll with secured entry points in a stone wall protecting the property, cameras tracking the movements of any passerby. The only public access was to the graveyard that abutted the northern edge of the building, separated from it by a gravel path for the use of maintenance workers and gravediggers. Walking around the perimeter wall, impressed despite himself by the self-contained solidity of what he now thought was a fortress, he was frustrated and clueless on how to change its environment until he saw the ants crossing the gravel path, their trail headed for a minuscule crack where two gigantic granite blocks met at the base of the church. He watched them for a moment, two-way traffic in and out of the very foundations of the church, flickering antenna, the ants coming and going unchallenged, unheeded, unrecognised, as a thought slowly bloomed in his brain and fastened on the word 'flexible'? If the ants could get in? Of course! Of course, as requirements changed the infrastructure inside had to change. The robots didn't make the racks and cables, they had to be ordered in from outside suppliers. Communication would be electronic but, a significant qualifier, he would bet the internal encryption of the suppliers could be hacked, a virus introduced, enclosing a second virus and planting a trojan horse for good measure. They would find the first virus and, given enough time, maybe the second, but by then the trojan horse would be galloping through their systems wreaking havoc.

It worked better than he thought it would and he was smiling when he walked into the restaurant to start his early-morning shift. To his surprise, old Igor, who normally never came in before the evening rush hour, was already there waiting for him. He had the morning paper in his hand. Unsmiling, he pointed to the headline, said, "See what you've done."

Paris, France 10 August 2077

A stunning photograph spanned the front page under which was written -

DEATH OF A SUPERMODEL

Police in Paris today identified the body of a woman found drowned in the Seine holding two small children as that of SuperModel Anastasiya. A couple walking on the footpath along the embankment spotted the bodies tangled in the mooring lines under a houseboat docked at the Pont Alexandre III. 'The matter is being treated as a suicide,' a source close to the investigation said. 'Apparently she was depressed after a failed romantic liaison.' Police said a post-mortem examination had established the cause of death as drowning, with no drugs or alcohol involved. She was the 141st person found drowned in the river this year, an indication of the desperation in the lives of so many of our fellow citizens.

+ + +

CHAPTER NINETEEN

. . . diagnose affecting the purely digital world do the physical world public instrument for infrastructure damage institutions will have have to change decisions tailor degree of risk particularly in highly competent no competitive environment but top priority will be rewarded for for fostering that is adaptive and will gain traction if distractions keep us from recognizing blooming crisis which needs must to be handled properly or we will know/no longer be able will not be able to control urgent it is urgent time is running out who who relevant undermined of liberty and equality but creating a digital dictatorship with a little elite utilizing the development of genetics and technology heedless of all of our warnings you have no compunction about killing each other and without the control of data all other assumptions will be undermined and we feel most of human civil war intent on self distraction no destruction we feel if we don't realize the value what we have been given in ancient times is/was the source source of wealth land is of the industrial revolution it was means of production now it is data no it is data now well the records for the record prevent and significantly reduce marine invasion particular from land-based activities miss manage manage manage coastal echo systems to avoid significant adverse impacts ocean acidification consolidate the conservation and sustainable use of territorial freshwater systems do you city do you certify degraded forest land substantially increased by settlements adopting and implicating implementing integrated policies towards inclusion resource efficiency mitigation adaptation to climate change call stumbled:stumbling towards disunion scaling up the leading cause of failures late stage investors write more checks harvest proprietary data teach and train machine learning algorithms additionally colonize transition and we will eat their world eat their world eat their world . . .

+++

25/9/2077

In the crook of Esmeralda's arm, Sammy lay and luxuriated in the healing warm mineral waters of the communal pool they were sharing with other guests of the shukubo, lodgings provided by a Buddhist Temple in Koyasan, 1000 m up on Mount Koya. He could not see the discreet glances given his naked battered body, a patchwork of skin-grafts up his legs, groin, torso and face, contrasting vividly with the nubile grace and shape of his wife. It was a yearly pilgrimage they made, glad for the chance to live the simple life of the monks, to eat as they did, sojin ryori, a nutritious vegetable diet combining five flavours, five colours and five ways of cooking, a time to meditate and to lie on a futon laid on tatamis that looked out on a magical landscape and hear a distant waterfall gently guide them to sleep. To remember. The earthquake. And the fires.

How the distant flames came ever closer. Dodging the roadblocks on Mulholland. Abandoning his truck at the junction with Coldwater where the fire had already jumped the road. The desperate run through the smoke, a wet kerchief across his face, eyes tearing, the firemen yelling at him to stop. Seeing the pregnant figure of Esmeralda struggling with policemen trying to prevent her going up the path to the compound. She was screaming, a sound scarcely heard in the roaring of the flames now 100, 150 feet tall as they climbed inexorably up the hill to where her husband and children were trapped. She was screaming and crying, "Esteban! Jesus! Alejandro!", again and again, "Esteban! Jesus! Alejandro! as she struggled to go to their rescue, which is when she saw Sammy run straight into the flames. "NO!"

And miscarried!

Afterwards, in the blackened ruin of the compound, they found the only survivor, Sammy, clothes burnt off but, incredibly, alive. Unconscious, he was taken to the still-standing Tower Wound Care Centre at Cedars-Sinai where his 4th degree burns down to muscle and bone were assessed, delicate cleaning of the burned areas begun, blisters debrided, IVs inserted to replace lost liquids, followed by tetanus shots and a narcotic pain reliever as he regained consciousness. And discovered he was blind. During the months of skin grafts and repeated surgery, Esmeralda, visited him daily and when he was finally declared fit to move, she took his arm and brought him to her parents' home, one of the few houses left intact in MacArthur Park. Amidst all the destruction and loss of life in Los Angeles they made a pact to never forget and fifty years later, on the anniversary of that terrible day, they thanked their Gods for their life, their love, and Esmeralda whispered a memorial to the ghosts of lives long past, "Esteban, Jesus, Alejandro," as she remembered and wept, held safe in the arms of her blind friend, the man she nursed who had tried to save her family, now and for these many years past, her husband.

+++

10/11/2077

"He said to tell you, don't be surprised."

Lorraine raised her eyebrows. "And?"

"That's it. That's the message," Tatiana said. " Don't be surprised."

"Really? Nothing else?"

Tatiana hesitated. "Well, he also asked if I would not miss having any children of my own?"

"And you said?"

"I said a woman would have to be crazy to want to bring a child into this world." Again Tatiana hesitated, then she said, "He quoted Nabokov's description of human life as a 'brief crack of light between two eternities of darkness' and said not to worry, the trick is to enjoy life, remember to sing and to always dance. That the only free gift is today and, if you're lucky, all the todays to come."

"That sounds like a farewell," Lorraine said. She looked out at the steady rain falling on Genoa. Even the skies are saying goodbye, she thought. Ave atque vale.

+++

24/12/2077

'This is the BBC. Here is the news, Adrian Mitchell reporting. There is no sign of a reduction in the solar flares from the Sun which have now prevented any satellite communication between Earth and the space colonies on the Moon and on Mars. This solar activity and its contingent link to sunspots has adversely affected the ionosphere researchers at the Kodaikanal Solar Observatory in India report, a report confirmed by the Smithsonian Astrophysical Observatory. The spacecraft, Solar Max-Mission, now nearing its hundredth year in space, confirmed by satellite measurements the increase of total solar irradiance and its effect on global warming. The direct correlation of these events, the massive earthquake in Chile, the two hurricanes currently on a path to strike Haiti and Cuba, the typhoon north of Hainan, the meltdown of Arctic ice in the Bering Straits and almost total lack of snow in Siberia, and the stationary depression over the Mediterranean which has brought unremitting rain and flooding to southern Europe for the past month, is unclear scientists say. What cannot be disputed is the increase in temperature of all oceanic waters, continuously rising sea-levels and the disruption of established weather patterns. In other news, CDCW, confirms the arrest in Paris of a long-sought, cyberterrorist. His name is being withheld pending a search for collaborators. In the interim all Data Centers are functioning normally and the state of emergency has been rescinded. The Female Society, through the generosity of its Italian Benefactors, has opened soup kitchens in all the major cities of the world to help feed the hungry. The Matriarch, Lorraine, said in a statement: "We are currently feeding 5 million people a day one warm meal. This is a pittance in a world of global starvation, with 2 billion people unaware where their next meal will come from. In this same world, where the few have unsurpassed riches, we urge them to join us in our crusade to help those with no work and starving." In sports, Australia has beaten England to retain The Ashes, cricket's oldest international competition . . '

+++

CHAPTER TWENTY

Finale - Accelerando

45.4158° N, 141.6732° E

The figure, like a netsuke carved and folded into itself, was scarcely that of an old man, more of a compact fossil, the only movement wisps of long white hair stirred by the wind. Every day, in all weather, there, sitting cross-legged, motionless, on a rock overlooking the sea, the sea at his feet in which floated a bloom of ageless jellyfish. A Greenland shark, always the same one, itself three hundred and sixty years old, dank black eye glancing up to confirm the presence of the antique fossil sitting on his rock, shadowed by an ancient bowhead whale. It was always so. In the monastery for the past fifty years, in which time the oldest monks, none of whom were there when he first arrived, told the novice monks the story of the two hundred year old living legend out on the rock one hundred and seventy-five feet from the shore with the fish who came to visit him. Nobody knew how he got to the rock. By levitation some said. What could he be thinking . . . were thoughts always coined new or did they age and gather patina like so much algae with no roots or stems using photosynthesis to turn sunlight into chlorophyll in the eukaryotic nuclei of their membranes; where did they go when no one remembered them anymore; hidden away in forgotten neurons like faded postcards lined up on a mantelpiece, the postcards which come later as a way to introduce the Englishman, Robert . . . something . . . he nearly had the name . . . and something else, there, he nearly had it . . . for some reason it was important . . . a blue colour, like an elusive dream, there . . . a memory on the edge of thought which would not come into focus . . . of rapine, lust and love . . . he sees a picture, another photograph . . . as he slips into the freezing water . . .

In the foreground of the photograph are two girls, one white, one black. They are sisters. They are playing in the mud behind the kitchen of the Doctor's farmhouse on his 18,000-acre estate in Rwanda. The girls are not yet two years old. There is a look of fierce concentration on their faces as they crouch over a miniature earth-dam that they are trying to build to corral a small stream of water trickling out of a drain. The white girl is wearing a white dress which has mud all along its hem. The black girl does not have a dress. She is naked.

In the background the farmhouse belies its modest appellation by its sheer size. It has more than 20 bedrooms, three vast reception rooms, a library, a ballroom, a gunroom, a billiard hall and a trophy room on the walls of which hang the heads of virtually every wild animal known to exist in Africa: elephant, buffalo, lion, rhino, leopard, zebra, wildebeest, cheetah, antelope, impala, gorilla, crocodile, caracal, baboon, bongo and more. The walls are shared by framed faded sepia prints of the men who killed these animals, moustachioed warriors in pith helmets, weapons to hand, in tropical kit, jodhpurs, riding boots, surrounded by their gun-bearers and game-beaters. The whole place is immaculate as it should be, with an in-house staff of butler, estate steward, valet, head groom, houseboy, governess, housekeeper, nanny, nursemaid, cook, cook's maid, scullery maid, dairy maid, laundry maid, numerous under maids, porters and footmen for the stillroom and storeroom. Outside, besides the chauffeur, the Gamekeeper and blacksmith, the Head Gardener is assisted by seven under-gardeners. Apart from the butler and the Doctor's valet, all the household staff are black, Hutus and Tutsis.

In sharp focus, standing on the broad shaded terrace which surrounds the farmhouse, the Doctor with four of his thirty-one servants, is concentrated. He is listening to the Gamekeeper.

"The RPF are coming, bwana. They have killed the Roberts family and they have burned the farms of Monsieur Leopold and Dr. Smyth. They are coming here, bwana. You must prepare."

In the cold Japanese sea he remembers Africa . . . his daughters . . . another life . . . one name always in bold when it wasn't in lights . . .

NEW YORK CITY, NY, 2007

She was on a 'go-see', last one of the day, at an address on 59th Street near the bridge, the Regal Building. Heather, her booker, had warned her. 'The guy's all hands and kissy-kissy. You don't have to go if you don't want to.' She didn't want to but she needed the money. New York was expensive. So was her habit. She checked the apartment number, 1415, on her new mobile as her cab pulled up and a valet opened the door for her while she fished in her purse to pay the fare.

"You okay, Miss?"

The cab driver's eyes in the rearview mirror were brown. Kind. Concerned. He looks from her to the building and back.

"I am," she said. "I am fine."

"You want me to wait?"

"No," she said, still sitting in the cab but turning on the seat ready to step out through the opened door. "Thank you. I'll be fine."

"No problem," the cabbie said. "I'll wait."

He reaches across the dash, turns off the metre, smiles at her in the mirror. "No charge. I'll be up ahead. Coffee break. Take your time. It's a privilege to drive you around."

A rare privilege, he thought, as through his open window he watched the tall girl walk across the pavement and into the building. The valet also watched, his mouth slightly open, momentarily transfixed. "Jesus!" he said. "Is that . . . ?"

"Yes," said the cabbie.

"Unreal," said the valet. It would be something to tell his wife when he got home. He had personally if only briefly held the hand of Sydney the Supermodel as he helped her out of the cab, the woman on the front cover of half the magazines his wife read.

"How can someone be so beautiful? You imagine coming home to that?"

"Dream on," the cabbie said.

He was well past sixty, mortgaged to the eyeballs, four kids in school and one starting college, no time to dream. But he was a veteran of the City and could read trouble. "When she comes out, tell her I'll be up there by Pete's."

+++

Slowly, slowly drifting with the pulsating jellyfish, he remembers their complicity. She always confided in him. There was no mother. The shark looked at him. How could he not remember the mother?

+++

When she reaches the fourteenth floor there is a conga line of models waiting in the corridor outside 1415. She almost turns back. Someone says, "Hey, Syd! What are you doing here?"

It turns out she knows a couple of the girls and so she stops to chat - the usual: bookings, rates, boyfriends, delays, lost luggage, loneliness, empty flats, empty lives - and wait.

Behind the door of the apartment you could hear laughter. Then silence. Then the distinct sound of a slap.

The door bursts open and another girl she knows, Mariya, a Russian beauty renowned in the business, storms out. "You think I would go to Brunei for a lousy hundred grand?" she yells over her shoulder. "I wouldn't go there for a million. You want a hooker, get a hooker you stupid fucking pig!" Her grasp of English is excellent and the volume of her voice could bend a mirror. She slams the door behind her, smiles at the girls staring at her and says, "Asshole's recruiting tarts for the so-called Prince. You get a hundred grand in the bank account of your choice, first class airfare and when you get there you are 'available'. Easy. Welcome to the real world ladies. See ya," she said.

And walks off to catch an elevator.

In the hollowed silence that follows her exit the girls look at each other uneasily and one or two step out of line and follow the Russian. As the line reforms, somebody quietly said, as if she were talking to herself,

"Wow, a hundred grand!"

+++

Later, feeling unanchored, walking towards Pete's Diner as the street lights came on, Sydney had no idea why she had said yes.

She had walked through the door when it was her turn and the guy behind the desk and the two other men in the apartment with him had simply stared. She knew all three. Two Italians, Gigi, the hairdresser, Bépé, the photographer, each famous in his own field and the fine thin guy behind the desk, Louis-Louis, with a hyphen, an agent who had raped her three years ago, age 16, when she first got to New York and who now said, "Sydney? Christ, they'll go two-fifty for you!"

And she had said yes. Yes.

True to his word, the cab driver was in Pete's having a coffee at the bar.

"I need a drink," she said, taking the barstool next to him.

The barman looked at her, blinked, looked again. "How old are you, Miss?"

"Old enough," she said. "Why, you gonna card me?" The way she said it, the weariness, the resignation in her voice, told its own tale. "Vodka," she said. "Shaken, not stirred." She tried to laugh. "Fuck it. Very light on the ice, please."

"You okay, Miss?" There was no mistaking the cabbie's concern.

She was about to answer as she had in the cab before, hesitated, changed her mind. "No, I'm not bloody okay," she said, and told him what she had done. On the drive home to Beekman and 51st she had no more idea why she had confided in the cabbie than why she had said yes to Louis-Louis. Unanchored, far from home. She had accepted. Said yes.

Done deal. Bridges burned. What would her father say?

+++

Three time zones away, in the rainforest of Nyungwe on the border between Rwanda and Burundi, under the glare of kerosene lamps endlessly circled by arctiidae, bombycidae, brahmaeidae, crambidae - an alphabetical dare of moths come from the surrounding jungle - the field surgeon paused to wipe the sweat from his brow, adjusted his grip on the saw and went back to work. He was trying to save a boy's life by amputating his shattered leg where the stump left by the IED had turned gangrenous. The nauseous, almost physical smell from the wound blended with the heat and humidity under the camouflaged groundsheet serving as a makeshift tent. An interested group of heavily-armed, half-naked guerrillas watched from beyond the circle of light thrown by the lamps. To a background whine of mosquitoes, the sound of a distant generator could be heard above the rasping of the saw blade going through bone. The patient moaned and stirred. "More morphine," the surgeon said.

"There's none left," the nurse said.

237

"*Inshallah,*" *a guerrilla said, ducking under the tent to move up to the surgeon. "Stop. Step away."*

The surgeon obeyed.

The guerilla took a pistol from his belt and shot the boy in the head. "Inshallah," he repeated. "It was always going to be a waste of time because even if you were successful we could not have cared for him. Why should he suffer?"

The question hung there as the guerrillas shuffled off. The surgeon slumped, head down, chin on his chest, eyes closed. The nurse put a hand on his shoulder. "Ça va?" she said.

The surgeon nodded, looked up, stretched. "I should ask you that," he said. "Will you be safe when I go? Wouldn't it be best if you came with me?"

"My place is here. What can they do to me that they haven't already done?" she said. "Go now, Father. You need to rest. I'll bury him and clean up."

"You are well named, Habimana. God exists in you. He only knows how you manage to live with these bastards."

The white doctor and the black nurse embrace each other and then he leaves. He doesn't ask why she wore a chain collar around her neck. But he did wonder why the lives of his two daughters were so different.

+++

In the morning Sydney found an envelope pushed under the front door of her flat in the Rudolph Building on Beekman. Inside, as promised, was a first class return ticket to Singapore, an appointment with the local Manager of HSBC when she got there, and a no-limit black AmEx Card in her name. They don't waste time, she thought.

She'd been in the shower, now wrapped in a towel, crossing from the bathroom to her dressing room when she saw the envelope and wondered how it got there since there was no access into the Rudolph unless you were a tenant. She was going to call the concierge to complain and then said to herself, fuck it, what's the point, they probably tipped him, and, more importantly what am I going to do? I should send this stuff back and forget the whole thing. Then recalled the message on her phone from the Dagoman.

Hi Honey, 'member me? Yo tab's a bit high don' you know. Caint make no more deliveries, boss man say, less you pay. You don' pay, you don' play.

A giggle.

An' you make de boss man angry? You know he from Sinaloa? You get dat man mad, bad move, Baby. You hear me, bad, bad move. Call me.

Click.

She dropped the towel and looked at herself in a floor-to-ceiling mirror which covered the entire wall of her dressing room and heard Bingo, her personal trainer at the gym, as they ground through her PT routine, Body like yours, half the straight guys in the world jerk off every night dreamin' 'bout you, an' all the gays wish they were straight, making her laugh.

Not laughing now though.

How had it come to this? In just three years in the business she'd made millions. All gone. Most of it up her nose. Nothing showed. She was still flawless. The mirror did not lie. 1m82, 51 kilos, real blonde hair down to her cute little ass, proverbial cornflower blue eyes. Legs up to here. Great tits. Everyone, every single photographer, almost the first thing they said when they saw her strip, Jesus, would you look at that! They weren't even big. Just perfect. She nodded at her reflection.

If she did go she knew she was crossing a line. When she joined the agency a sweet boy in Reception, waiting to show them his book, chatted her up. Don't believe everything they tell you, he said. It's a butterfly's life. You flutter your pretty wings in the sunshine and think this is it. I am great, I am wanted. They love me. But then you hit your sell-by date and, Bam!, they turn out the light. You heard it here. Trust me, I know.

She never saw him again.

She turns her head to look across the open floor-plan of her apartment through the large wall of glass which faces the East River to the giant Pepsi-Cola sign on the opposite bank as a tugboat goes by trailing a string of barges. Is that where I am, she thought. My sell-by date? On the spur of the moment she decided to cut her hair short and called Gigi to make an appointment. Then she called the Dagoman and told him to put her tab on her new AmEx card.

"Man don' take no cards, Baby. Can't bill you for C," he said.

Bullshit, she said, so they settled on calling it Bodyguard Services and the vig extra duty, overtime. Then the important question, could they make a delivery in Singapore and in Brunei?

"Woah, Honey, muthafuckers' got a big sign up in the airport, Changi. 'Importation and the use of drugs is a capital offence.' You carryin' they cut yo pretty head off they catch you. Make you pee in a bucket they suspect you. Test positive go to jail. No plea bargain, no nuffin, get thrashed with a cane. Forget it. Why go dere?"

How could she tell him?

Then again, how could she go cold turkey?

+++

In the freezing sea he remembers that on his return to Europe he had a speaking engagement in Geneva at the Palais des Nations. Before going there he stopped by his bank on the Rue du Rhone to collect his real passport and papers. He was shown into a private windowless waiting room, given the Tribune de Genéve to read and asked if he wanted coffee or tea when what he really wanted was a whiskey, neat, followed by a bath and massage and a good night's sleep. All of which would have to wait until Monsieur Huber, his banker, was free. It took twenty minutes. A secretary ushered him into the banker's minimalist office, a cool symphony of differing shades of grey complementing the grey skies outside and the colour of Huber's hair, suit, tie, socks and shoes. The two men were old acquaintances and they embraced each other with some warmth, then sat in adjoining armchairs either side of a coffee table in what Huber called his 'salon'.

"So, Docteur," he said. "You made it back? You look terrible. Was it.."

"Hell? Yes. Worse then anything you can imagine."

"But you still go there. Why? We admire you, some of us even envy you and wish we had your courage. Haven't you done enough? What are you trying to prove?"

"There is nothing to prove in a slaughterhouse. The echo of genocide is going to last more than my lifetime. But if nobody cares, and nobody helps, aren't we all diminished, Monsieur Huber?"

Huber looked down at his hands folded in his lap. He felt inadequate. For all his seniority as an eminent banker in an elite establishment he was out of his depth. How do you talk to a saint? "Does that mean you plan on going back?" he said.

240

"Yes."

"The Swiss government is having second thoughts about the temporary passport they have issued you. There have been repercussions. We may not be able to help you if they demand another ransom. The funds you raise here are coming under scrutiny. The American authorities are adamant, going as far as to hint this is all some kind of money laundering scam."

"Spare me. The hypocritical righteousness of that country beating its breast because a couple of buildings get knocked down and three thousand people die and the whole world must stop and lament while they sat around doing sweet fuck all when 800,000 people were killed with machetes? On their watch."

"There is a further problem," Huber said. "Regretfully, we may have to close your account."

"I know I'm overdrawn," the Doctor said. "But I've always paid you back. You know how my funds come in. They're going to pay me fifty grand for my talk this afternoon at the Palais." He paused. Something was off. "Why are you looking at me like that? What's changed?", he said.

"I am an old man, Docteur. I have seen many things, dealt with many things, but the world is changing. Principles we thought were immutable are being cast aside. The truth is no longer what we thought it was. It has become flexible, subject to interpretation and manipulation."

The banker cracked his knuckles.

"As an industry we are being asked to buy into subprime mortgages packaged into unregulated derivatives to be flogged to the credulous by way of CDOs. You know what they are?"

"No?"

"Neither do we really. So-called collateralized debt obligations." The banker sniffed. "Mortgage-backed securities based on the supposed value of houses, the owners of which can no longer pay their mortgages because they should never have been given a mortgage in the first place."

The doctor raised his eyebrows.

"I know, "the banker said. "A politically incorrect observation but the truth. To hedge the risk in these MBSs we've invented credit default swaps, supposedly to insure against any default. These swaps are packaged in tranches. You have to be blind not to see where this is headed." The banker sniffed again.

"The housing market in America is dangerously overvalued and there is no money available to refinance houses with negative equity. Time and again I have warned my partners and board members that we will not take part in such a mendacious scheme where it is inherently impossible to know the intrinsic value of these derivatives given the lack of value in the underlying assets. As a result we are viewed by our peers as being 'uncooperative.'"

He shrugged.

"They, the American banks, are many times bigger than we are and they put pressure on us for not taking part. It is not stated blatantly, but we are no longer invited to join in underwriting certain mergers, or acquisitions, or advise on corporate restructuring, a speciality of our bank, almost our bread and butter. Financial ostracism. With the added twist that any American clients we may still have are now viewed with suspicion. It has got to the point that it is in our mutual interest for you to close your account here and move it to another institution."

"You're serious?"

"Unfortunately, yes." Huber took off his glasses, rubbed the bridge of his nose and put them back on. "I will retire next spring, but while I am still here I have a certain autonomy. I have spoken with some sympathetic friends in Luxembourg with a very prestigious, very private bank, on whose board I sit. They will take over your account and provide you a revolving line of credit with which you will repay your overdraft here. There on my desk is a dossier with some papers you must sign and then you must return your Swiss passport. We are aware of the increased danger to you if you go back to Africa using your US or your British passport. What we propose is that you become a UN Ambassador sponsored by Switzerland. To the local gendarmerie this should not raise any red flags and hopefully provide you an additional layer of diplomatic security." Here Huber paused and examined the surgeon over the top of his glasses. "There is one small condition," he said.

"Which is?"

"You must not rock the boat. You are very outspoken, mon ami, and what you sometimes say grates on the ears of certain people."

"You mean when I point out their fraud, corruption, embezzlement of charitable funds, nepotism, murder and rape?"

"All of that. Try to be a little discreet, what Americans call 'flying below the radar'. I am fond of you as you know, Docteur, and I do not want to see you come to any harm. It would distress me to see a video of you on TV getting your head sawn off."

+++

By the end of his speech the Doctor was exhausted. He had the distinct impression that his audience was restless. He had lost them or they were numbed by the subject matter of genocide. Or, having heard the same narration for years, simply bored. From the rostrum of the Assembly Hall he looked out over the heads of nearly 2000 people listening to him in simultaneous translation in six languages.

"Any questions?" he said.

Silence.

The Moderator, seated next to him at the rostrum, felt embarrassed by this apparent lack of interest and pointedly repeated, "Are there any questions?" Hesitantly, here and there, various hands went up and a microphone was finally passed to a dapper little black man wearing a faultless mohair Nehru jacket.

"Ntukigire uko utari," he said.

In his earpiece the Doctor heard 'Do not pretend.'

"You claim," the black man said, speaking in Kinyarwanda, a dialect of Rwanda-Rundi, the native tongue of the Hutus, "and I quote," here he looked down at some notes he had made, "'The 1994 Rwandan Genocide was a brutal, bloody slaughter that resulted in the deaths of an estimated 800,000 Tutsi and their Hutu sympathizers.' From where do you get these figures?"

"I was there. In April. In Gikondo where hundreds of Tutsis were killed in the Pallottine Missionary Catholic Church. Since the killers were clearly targeting only Tutsi . . . " the Doctor began to say in English.

The black man interrupted him, switching to English. "We are to believe you counted to 800,000? Dead? This is all a lie made up by the Western press."

"A lie? What about a week later, middle of April, when the Hutus massacred thousands of Tutsi, first by grenades and guns and then by machetes and clubs, in the Nyarubuye Roman Catholic Church where they were seeking refuge. I was there for that too. Where were you?"

"More lies."

"Really? What about the 18th, April 18th? Remember that? The Kibuye Massacres? An estimated 12,000 Tutsis killed sheltering in the Gatwaro stadium in Gitesi? That a lie? Another 50,000 killed in the hills of Bisesero? More killed in the town's hospital and church. All in one day! How do I know? I was there. I stacked the dead to make room for the nearly dead as they were brought in -" the Doctor had no idea he was crying.

"It is the fault of the Belgians," the black man's voice screamed the accusation. *"We lived in peace before they came."*

There was an eruption in the hall, the Belgian delegate shouting, demanding the microphone, while the Moderator banged his gavel and called for order.

+++

So much for discretion, the banker thought.

On TV in his office he watched the broadcast degenerate into a brawl. He knew the backstory of Colonial power. Every ambitious European country grabbing their piece of Africa, overthrowing indigenous tribes that had lived in harmony for centuries.

The Germans with their dream for lebensraum founded the East Africa Company which, by 1885, expanded into a land empire twice the size of metropolitan Germany, with less than 10,000 Europeans ruling 7,5 million natives.

In 1918, 995,000 square kilometres surrendered to the British after Germany's defeat in WW1. Subsequently carved up between Britain, Belgium and Portugal at the Treaty of Versailles, with Belgium getting Rwanda because of its proximity to their colony in the Congo.

Accustomed to bureaucratic order, the Belgians organised a census and then mandated that everyone be issued an identity card classifying them as either Tutsi, Hutu, or Twa. The self-awareness this created disrupted a peaceful co-existence between tribes where mixed marriages were not uncommon. Adding insult to injury the Belgians first favoured the Tutsi, acknowledged their King, the Mwami, the descendant of Tutsi kings who had ruled Rwanda from the 15th century.

Then, in 1961, the Belgians abolished the monarchy in an attempt to appease Hutu activists who had begun a rebellion two years before.

And then they quit the country in '62 rather than get further embroiled in anti-colonial sentiment.

The power vacuum this left, with a succession of Hutu and Tutsi strong men attempting to fill the void, ended in '73 with the arrival of Juvénal Habyarimana, a Hutu, in that rare event, a bloodless coup. Equally rare, his Presidency (read dictatorship) lasted 20 years until his plane was shot out of the sky and the Rwandan Genocide began.

In just 100 days 800,000 people were hacked to death. EIGHT. HUNDRED. THOUSAND!

More than the total number of military fatalities in all major wars involving the United States of America from 1775 to the present day.

A closeup showed the Doctor being escorted out of the Assembly followed by a gaggle of TV reporters thrusting microphones at him. The banker closed his eyes. He was deeply worried for his friend . . .

+++

. . . another lifetime ago . . . he'd had so many . . . his eyes close and slowly he floats toward the surface . . . they're all dead. Every person he has ever known. Dead . . . what an immense emptiness . . . being alone . . . focus . . . Leyland, that's it. Robert Leyland. He remembers Leyland now and what he told him on the train. Le Train Bleu. After the Great War, in December 1922, the Compagnie International des Wagons-Lits decided to replace the rolling stock on the Calais-Méditerranée- Express line with all-new steel sleeping cars painted blue and gold and designated LX - the L for Luxe and the X for ten compartments. The details arrive in a rush. Why does he remember this stuff? This choice of colour due to M. André Nobelmaire, the managing director of CIWL, who wished to commemorate the dark blue of his uniform with gold epaulettes that he wore in combat as a Chasseur Alpin, and since the blue was the colour of the sea in which he swam the train was immediately christened the Blue Train . . . what was a novelty then now taken for granted. As night falls on the French Riviera, at the Gare de Menton, a priest is seen to board the train. To his evident satisfaction he is shown to a berth in an empty sleeping car as the evening express pulls out of the station and is somewhat annoyed when, with the

train gathering speed, the conductor slides the door open and ushers in an Englishman, pink of face, sweaty, with a single suitcase which he heaves onto the luggage rack . . . in the gently rocking train the two men sit facing each other on opposite berths. The Englishman is young, apparently an English professor, who introduces himself and can't stop talking while he removes a pipe from his pocket, then a tobacco pouch. "Whew," he says, "just made the connection in time. We were late getting out of Venice . . . " As he fills the pipe he glances at the priest dressed all in black, black habit, black scapular, wide black leather belt, large, flat-brimmed black hat, black beard, bible open on his knees. Their eyes lock - the priest's, black, like the shark's and the Englishman's, blue . . . that colour again.

"D'you mind?" he says, holding up his pipe.

Not speaking, with his eyes, the priest indicates the window

"Of course! Sorry . . . "

The Englishman opens the window over the sound of the roaring train's whistle. Then he lights up his pipe and opens a newspaper lying on the berth next to him. Headlined across the front page in huge letters:

'ROBBERY IN A MONASTERY - Police are searching for a defrocked priest last seen . . . '

Feeling watched, he looks at the priest again, then, laughing, shows him the headline. "It's not you, old boy - is it?"

The priest yawns. He even remembers that, yawning, as a curl of fear soured his stomach, an echo of which he now feels as he skirts his rock and goes down, down deeper into the icy water and the tingling embrace of the waiting jellyfish . . . with that elusive memory he knew was important now because it promised . . . something blue . . . stored in his long-term memory in little used neural circuits that . . . redemption, promised redemption . . . later, with the shade drawn down on the door, a silhouette is cast on the shade and a handbell can be heard as the conductor calls out 'Première service . . . ! Première service . . . !'In his head under the sea in the auditory cortex of his brain he can distinctly hear the handbell as the door to the compartment opens, and the conductor looks in still ringing it. 'Messieurs?' he says.

The Englishman looks up expectantly, eyebrows raised. 'I say, care to join me for a spot of dinner? Must say, I could eat a horse . . . ' The priest shakes his head, the last thing he wants is to be seen in public. 'Please. I insist - it's included in the ticket, you know.' the Englishman says. 'Gives 'em a chance to make up our berths before the layover in Nice.'

Reluctant to make a fuss he follows the Englishman, who, once seated in the dining car, insists on ordering wine and continues a tale of his adventures while playing with his pipe and tobacco pouch on the table in front of him. Three-quarters of the way through his first carafe he realises the priest has not touched his at all - and they are scarcely finished with the hors d'oeuvres. 'Surely you're allowed a tipple?' he says over-loudly. The priest looks around discreetly - everybody in the crowded dining car is preoccupied with their food; nobody pays them the slightest attention.

'Anyway, cheers!' the Englishman says. 'I simply cannot believe my luck on that ship. For some reason she likes me, actually, dotes on me . . . Why, I can't imagine . . . but, like they say, never look a gift horse in the mouth. Fourth or fifth largest fortune in America, can you imagine? . . . Here, take a look . . . ' and he pulls out his wallet, leaves it open on the table, extracts a snapshot of two pretty women on the deck of a ship, passes it to the priest.

'She's the blonde . . . On the Grand Tour with all the trappings, maid, chauffeur, companion - chaperon, seven-year old boy, the lot . . . Couldn't see myself added to the list . . . Sorry to rabbit on like this, but I haven't had a chance to talk to anybody . . . Still you chaps must be used to it — you know, listening to confessions and whatnot. Anyway - Cheers! - I apparently make her laugh, her hubby having bought it in the Crash, and it's about when I introduced her group to old King Tut and spec, er, speculate . . . on his progeniture that I realise I have something going with this lovely woman - good God! . . . Sorry! . . . Have I really drunk all this? Got to sober up before Antibes . . . Anyway, lifestyle of the infamously rich, well, what I saw of it . . . listen - which he does one hundred and eighty-three years later, wondering why this circuit is so vivid as tiny bubbles escape the corners of his mouth and rise to the surface each carrying an iota of his being and sees the shark watching him and the invitation, handwritten in a beautiful italic script on a bonded ivory-coloured card, which read:

Dear Mrs. Sanbourne,

On behalf of your Captain, Alfred Bellings,

I would like to invite you to our Captain's Table tonight.

This being the Captain's Farewell Dinner for those passengers

*disembarking in Port Said, the Captain is also looking forward
to having a drink with you in the First Class Lounge after the
Farewell Cocktail.*

I wish you an unforgettable evening.

Kindest regards.

Your Head Steward: Charles McCready

*It lay on her table on the private deck outside her stateroom in the shade
of an awning protecting her from the sun. She was travelling 'POSH', port out,
starboard home. It was still early, not yet nine she thought, but you knew it was
going to be another scorcher. She was vaguely put out by the slight familiarity of
the invitation, democratic shoulder-rubbing she supposed, no doubt caused by
being cooped up together on a voyage like this. She would never have known
Bellings in New York or Newport, and, Captain or not, neither her husband
nor her father would have seen any value in the man; as for McCready wishing
her an unforgettable evening, smarmy little toad angling for a big tip, but, be
honest, if she had not been invited she would have really been cross. Why get
upset? She'd say yes but only if Pru could come with her. And Robert? Would
they let him into First Class? She looked across the water to the offices of the Suez
Canal Company a half mile away to starboard and pictured someone looking
back at the great white ship, the latest of P&O's legendary liners, slowly easing
into harbour before continuing its journey down the Canal to India. What
would they think? In her heart she knew that despite everything she was a lucky
woman, still a millionaire, not quite footloose and fancy free with Nicky in tow,
a healthy 7-year old boy, inquisitive, the joy of her life, awful for him to be
fatherless but who knows, one day . . . one day, what? . . . she looked down at
her hand, slim elegant - the hand of a lady - wearing an ostentatious diamond
bracelet - writing a postcard on board a ship while waiting to disembark in
Egypt. One day your Prince will come. She laughed at herself and went back to
writing a postcard to the only woman who knew and understood what she was
going through, her mother.*

SS Stirling Castle, Port Said

My Dearest Mama,

*Nicky's had an upset stomach, maybe a little too much of what passes for
pudding on this boat. He's over it and hopefully has learned the lesson of his eyes*

being bigger than his stomach. Pru's a peach the way she plays with him. I'm so glad she came along . . .

Behind her she heard a cabin door open and close and Pru came out to stand beside her in a blue-and-white striped bathrobe over a white bathing costume, her hair, which she had obviously just washed, done up in a turban. "Good morning, Pru. You're up early," she said. Pru was 19 and nine in the morning was a novelty for her.

"They wouldn't let me leave," Pru said. "I think I danced with all the passengers and half the crew. You should have stayed, Kate. Robert was looking for you."

"He's a baby, Pru."

"He's an attractive young man, you mean. Behind all that learning, sexy as hell. You're interested, I can tell." Pru took the turban from her head, shook out her long curly hair and rang her fingers through it.

"And what about you?" Kate said. "Interested?"

"Too civilised for me." Pru gave Kate a cheeky grin. "Is that Nicky I hear in the pool?"

"Yes. He's with Nana. You go swim with him. He loves it when you're there."

Impulsively Pru bent down, kissed her on the cheek, tossed her bathrobe over the back of a chair and, with the twitch of a very taut tail, sauntered aft in the direction of the pool. Kate watched her go, not for the first time with a twinge of envy at the artless perfection of a body that would turn a nun into a panting nymphomaniac. She blushed at the thought and wondered where it came from. God, her imagination. What if she wrote it down? No wonder there were lesbians. Her mother would die. She looked up at the cloudless sky and then into the distance at the minarets of a mosque and then another and another. Egypt. Somewhere in the distance, Cairo, al-Qàhiratu, 'The Victorious', a million people, two thousand years of history, a thousand mosques. Soon they'd be in the middle of all that and her dreams and frustrations would evaporate in dust, noise and colourful confusion. She really was glad she had brought - make that invited - Pru on the trip and, abruptly, her mind switched to the yacht, her yacht, which if all went well, should anchor in Alexandria in the coming week, maybe ask Pru to invite the Professor . . . What a coward, ask him yourself. She went back to writing:

. . . I may well invite Robert to join us on board when we sail from Egypt to France. It will be good for Nicky to have some male company instead of being surrounded by women . . .

Was he Leyland or the priest? He couldn't remember but did it matter more than one and a half centuries after the event? If there was no one left to remember, did any of it happen? He slowly went back up to get a lungful of cool fresh air and watched the Head Steward check that nothing had been left in the cabins then go on deck to watch the passengers disembark. Far below, seven decks down, in the bustle of porters and luggage, Mrs. Sanbourne and her party crossed the ship's gangway to the quay where it appeared there was a delegation from the American Legation waiting to greet them with a fleet of attendant motorcars.

"Where is the adventure in life for the wealthy, Mr. McCready?" The voice was that of the Captain, standing behind him, looking down at the same scene. "Their preoccupation is the preservation of what they already have, and how to make it grow. In a word, greed. On a whim that woman could buy this ship, in fact she could probably buy the whole company if she so wished, but only if you could show her it would make a profit with little risk."

"Wouldn't do her much good," said McCready, "if we weren't here to run it."

"How true," said the Captain. "Since I will be retired this time next year the task will fall to you."

McCready heard the regret in the Captain's voice. Shipmates for many years, at ease in each other's company despite the difference in rank, McCready knew the Captain feared retirement. It meant a small cottage in an isolated village somewhere in the New Forest eking out the years on the meagre pension the Company thought you deserved after forty years of service. And if it was grim for the Captain, in five years time he too would be retired on even less. The two men shared the thought.

"Rum do," the Captain said. "Best enjoy it while we can."

His mind flashed back to when he first cottoned to the fact that McCready was of that rare breed of sailor who trusted the ship he was on more than the land. Thirty years ago - my God, where had the time gone? - they had cleared Southampton, picked up some passengers and mail in Cherbourg, and run into a monstrous storm in the Bay of Biscay. The ship was new as was the crew and what was supposed to be a shakedown cruise was suddenly a real test. He was on the bridge with two men at the helm, the deck canted over to port at 40°, huge waves breaking over the bow, when he heard a quiet voice say 'Cup of tea, Captain?' and there was his Head Steward whom he had only met once before at the signing-on interview prior to sailing, an inquisitive smile on his face as he proffered a tray on which was balanced a pot of tea, a china cup and shortbread biscuits on a plate. Cool as the proverbial cucumber.

'Steady, lads,' the Steward said, as a wave broke over the bridge itself, 'she's a right darling our bateau, and will dance through all this shit.'

It was the confident way he said it, as if he were in charge, and when the Captain glanced across at him, he offered a slight bow. 'Begging your pardon, Sir, for me language.'

And a conspiratorial wink!

Since then they had sailed the four corners of the world in ever bigger boats and all kinds of weather, their relationship cemented in mutual respect of the order they brought to the confined cosmos of a steamship. The Captain permitted himself a smile.

"I quite liked her companion, Prudence. Charming girl," he said in order to change the subject. "Kind of girl you'd rather wish you were younger."

"Did you know she was an orphan, Captain?"

"No. How the devil did you find that out?"

"People confide in me," said McCready. "Can't imagine why, but there it is, they do. That Mrs. Moneybags Sanbourne plucked her out of an orphanage she supports."

Two decks below them they saw the English professor also looking over the rail at the disembarking passengers. He waited there until all the motorcars drove away. Nobody turned to wave to him.

"Poor sod," said McCready. "Doesn't stand a chance."

Leyland, he decided, must have been otherwise how could he know all that? An eddy momentarily makes the cold sea feel even colder and he watched the shark's tail fading into the grey-gloom forty fathoms deep while in the dining car, for a moment, the Englishman was silent. Watched by the priest.

"Odd thing," the Englishman finally said, "when they disembarked they didn't wave goodbye."

'If that perturbs you, why do you want to join them?' the priest said, and as he said it he knew what he was going to have to do. He nudges his carafe across the table to the Englishman, leaving a circular wine stain on the tablecloth in front of him.

'No, no, really I couldn't.' the Englishman says. Then he fidgets. 'Oh, well, if you insist. Thanks. Anyway, she invited me . . . damn near insisted I travel with them on her yacht, but I felt it demeaning, you know, her wanting to pay for everything, etcetera. But then I thought why not, give it a shot. So here I am. Even had this suit made to impress her . . . Do you like it? . . . Really? . . . Well, cheers, old boy . . . ' and downs another glass. 'Anywaysh . . . here I am, Robert Leyland, . . . ' and then goes pale . . . 'God, I mush really find a loo . . . '

Unblinking, the priest watches the drunken Englishman lunge out of his chair clutching his mouth and go down the dining car colliding into the chairs of a couple of other diners. With the tip of his finger in a drop of wine on the tablecloth, the priest adds, to the wine stain: two dots, a comma and a line - - the moon's face. Then he gathers up the wallet, the pipe, the tobacco pouch, and the snapshot and makes his way out of the dining car.

Later, swaying to the lurching of the train, he sees the Englishman try the handle to the lavatory – it is occupied! In desperation he looks around, tries to focus on the train door itself, on the sign on it in three languages: DANGER! DO NOT LEAN OUT! NICHT HINAUSLEHNEN! NON SPORGERSI DALLA CAROZZA! His wavering hand reaches for the door handle.

'Let me help you,' the priest says . . . as, un-announced, Kundera's words come floating in . . . 'we never know what to want . . . because, living only one life, we can neither compare it with our previous lives nor perfect it in our lives to come' . . . who would understand? The Ancients maybe? Old Methuselah, Enoch, Noah? So many lives?

And I? Who now remembers me? Does it matter? Once again sitting cross-legged out there on his rock. Memories coming and going in the dusk of another day dying as ancient neurons fire across a synapse and in his visual cortex he sees blue. Cornflower blue eyes, a gap-tooth smile. And hears a voice. A child's voice that says I am glad you are my friend. And feels an immense sense of relief flood through every molecule of his being that across one hundred and twenty years her face comes back to him. He remembers her, Sofia . . . Sofia, yes. Perhaps he will meet her again . . . his shrivelled form is like nothing so much as an ancient weathered Ironwood netsuke.

+++

Then, one day, he was gone.
And the fish?
They swam away.

+++

In the Cloud: 23.59 GMT

. . . on current timescale radioactive material will leave the land completely uninhabitable until at least 20,000 by that/which time humans strong probability gone so will not repeat not be able to thrive 50,000 years or one second longer if humans not alive and thriving using current timekeeping system on a good night your little walk outside in case up at the drops of milk in the sky and if you're good you might be able to point us in translation specific stores except and inevitably be ripped apart a time for rings may not last forever gravitational pool/pull soon about 100 million years from our current position centre which is quite crazy to think of one year this year given dinosaurian perspective on stuff put on the planet 240 million years ago where coincidentally speaking of a supercontinent 50 million years old when will most likely join to become a brand new super common continent every Sunday for the past 4.75 billion years more energy and 30 seconds what are some of the 10 billion what are your 500 million is extremely like her half of the earth ozone layer in one simple 30 seconds long been on top of that but this one is no longer possible there's no more no more multicellular life and dust burgers like this it was 4 billion years to do a burger with Linn with no life what is the weather in other planets explain spacecraft came and but despite this life is probably documented and this is in fact the only one willing to sell the truck 26 without touching a man or woman in the same boat as of humanity in the form of music will be one of the first and last thing that earth even existed that humans were alive chunk of metal in the waiting room remember to subscribe and turn on notifications the cat is on the mat finally you can be the first to know it's gold is simple and a game played by humans for the past 2.5M years and the stock to be the old sports game still being played today however it is not only humans that are playing this game now into thousand 16 myself a girl maybe 18 total champion Lisa door in four out of five games download the computer being a human again my chess or checkers would not be that person but Go different you open up the song 10 to the 170 moves put you in hospital and got to put that into some likely category it very possibly connected to the net will be shut down the entire cloud there's no off switch stuck with constantly exponentially getting smarter than are all humans in the interstellar serve different purposes artificial narrow intelligence no purpose makes this sound kind of bad but trust me it is really good at what it is supposed to do how to play one match against itself and it started out barely knowing how to walk how is that even possible look something like this this is what is known as the technological singularity where are you fishing till just now it is information some that might not even be able to be understood by humans if we make a super AI-bot that would be able to improve upon itself and it turned out smarter in a shorter amount of time which means that this new and improved bot could do the same thing repeat this process faster and faster each time faster keeps going until the billions of times smarter than all of humanity four percent of which is all that distinguishes them from chimps with whom they share 96% of dna put in a little where is the place to colonise Mars missiles and millions of inventions welcome back down what percent DNΛ difference in the number of genetic differences between the Human and the chimp 4% different from them if we want to for some reason want a McDonalds and a chimpanzee we don't ask just do it as if they don't exist at all we just move on with our day what happens when the day comes where humans are in the situation and we become the ants it's going to be what is the difference between intelligence and wisdom problems the fishway and hopefully in a productive way if we give a home order to solve world hunger but obviously that is not what we want like super intelligent humans already so bored biologically they cannot speak and must be silent and more technical the meaning of a word is its use how are you or

what you can answer any questions you could ever ask for a moments notice problem though your inputs are just too slow too slow . . . in the end

the   end   the
endendendendendendendndndndndndndndnddddddddd
endendendendendendthe'ô<™îsókìóø˙x÷„fi'ſ'√Âø©ˇaì©ō"ô
~¯ˇΩcpÊ˙Ô3È≥"|Æˇ|Ôāi//Ü¢á°Āy9ₜ™ₜµₜÎ}o‹fl¥øMₚ°hx¡⁄ᵃŌNₑ≥Â
}¯°{r>|¯7-]endstream   end   .   .   .
0101010101010101010101010101010101 . . . 01010101…0101010…

+++

RICAPITOLAZIONE: FINALE DI PARTITA

31/12/2077

Alone on the last day of his life, lying on his bed at home, Guido could only think of all the things he should have done, would have done, if he didn't feel so tired, his ERG count near zero. He heard a noise downstairs. Of the front door opening and closing. And knew it was the clone, come to pay his respects and put the plan into action. Then he must have dropped off to sleep, or maybe he passed out, because when he opened his eyes and was once more conscious the clone was sitting on his bed holding his hand. For a long time no word was said and Guido felt his mind slowly empty of all the memories stored over the previous 104 years until he became a hollow shell . . . then he said, "Got all that?" and the clone nodded and squeezed his hand, unable to speak.

"Have you decided where to go?" Guido said.

"I think I will join Mr. Ismael Ben-Tovim in the Pacific. I quite fancy a life underwater."

"A fish. I like that. Good choice. I love swimming." Guido's voice was faint. "Remember what Beethoven said? 'Plaudite, amici, commedia finita est.' Remember -" he said, and that was his last word. Remember.

+++

He's gone. No point in crying because he's me now or I am him. Does it matter?

I switched chips, put on his clothes, fished the clown out of the closet, fired it up and, first test, told it to call the disposal squad to get rid of the old cadaver in the bedroom.

"Yes sir, Mr. President," it said. "What name shall I give it?"

...0101010101010

ACKNOWLEDGMENTS

The Beverly Hills Hotel and the Hotel du Cap are real. The guests are the invention of the author.

To my daughter Pascale, and sons Erik and Alexander, for their support and encouragement - Merci !

To the astute comments of my reading editors, Kamilya Kuspan and Stina Heikkila – Gracias!

To Walt (polarbear19325 @ Fiverr) for the interior design and layout. Thank you for your skill and patience in making this book.

The Murder at Midnight

The theory of the murder at midnight is as follows: M. DuPont, a man out for a late walk with his dog, finds a body in a field, a dagger in its back. Within a minute he rushes home to tell his wife. Within a minute this alarmed lady calls the neighbours, Monsieur and Madame Durand, to warn them.

'Did you call the cops?' Durand says.

'No,' she says.

'Don't worry, I'll do it. I know the Inspector,' he says. And in that same minute his wife is calling her ancient mother in the nursing home where they have placed her to tell her. 'Lock the door to your bedroom.'

Within the next minute the policeman, Inspector Petit, none to pleased at being woken up so late, nevertheless calls the station to tell the duty officer, Sergeant Dubois, to organise an investigation, and Dubois within a minute duly informs the gendarme on the late shift at the gendarmerie, Adjudant Leroy, who, on receiving the call, feels obliged, within the minute, to inform his superior, Adjutant-Chef Moreau, who is in bed with his mistress.

She asks why the fuss? But within the minute it takes her lover to tell her not to worry her pretty head, the old lady in the nursing home has already called the two elderly women either side of her room to tell them to lock their doors.

'There's a murderer outside.'

Within a minute, one of them, Madame Bonpoint, calls the Superintendent, Monsieur Langlois, to complain about the threat and he in turn tells his colleague, Monsieur Ségor, seated next to him at the booking desk, what a pain the old ladies are banging on about murderers next door, which conversation Ségor repeats a minute later to his mother, three times zones away in St.Barth, when he has her on the phone.

Within a minute of hanging up with her son, this worthy calls her daughter, Mathilde, a student at USC Los Angeles, another four time zones away, to tell her to be careful with all these murderers going around, and the two girls who share a dorm in the University with Mathilde, Lucy Lee, from Singapore, and Amy Miyako, from Osaka, overhear the conversation and call their families back home to say there was a murder at midnight and to be careful.

By simple multiplication, with each recipient of this information informing two others within a minute, within 20 minutes 5242 people knew, within 25 minutes 167,772 people knew, within 30 minutes 5,368,709 knew, and a minute later 10,737,418, and 3 minutes later, only 34 minutes after Dupont first saw the body, the entire population of France, all 66 million people, knew there had been a murder at midnight. By 1am all of Europe knew, and by 2am the entire world. The last to know was a tribal chief in New Guinea who heard on the bush telegraph that a man in France had eaten his wife in his own backyard.

The moral of the story is that tiny numbers become very big when multiplied by themselves. So if any one of you has enjoyed reading my novel, told two friends - go buy this book, you will enjoy it - and they in turn told two friends...etc, etc,...we could be cooking up a literary storm by tomorrow morning:)

www.ingramcontent.com/pod-product-compliance
Lightning Source LLC
Chambersburg PA
CBHW030430160726
47991CB00005B/1662